# SNIPER

*A Reed Security Romance*

## GIULIA LAGOMARSINO

# CAST OF CHARACTERS

Sebastian "Cap" Reed- owner
    Maggie "Freckles" Reed
    Caitlin Reed
    Clara Reed
    Gunner Reed
    Tucker Reed

**Team 1:**

Derek "Irish" Cortell- team leader and part owner
    Claire Cortell

Hunter "Pappy" Papacosta
    Lucy Papacosta
    Rylee Papacosta

Rocco Turner
    Evelyn Rose Turner

**Team 2:**

Sam "Cazzo" Galmacci- team leader and part owner
    Vanessa Galmacci
    Sofia Galmacci
    Leo Galmacci

Mark "Sinner" Sinn
    Cara Sinn
    Violet Sinn
    Asher Sinn

Blake "Burg" Reasenburg
    Emma Reasenburg
    Ryker Reasenburg
    Beatrix (Bea)

**Team 3:**

John "Ice" Peters- team leader and part owner
    Lindsey Peters
    Zoe Peters
    Cade Peters
    Willow Peters

Julian "Jules" Siegrist
    Ivy Siegrist
    John Christopher Hudson Siegrist

Chris "Jack" McKay
    Alison (Ali) McKay
    Axel McKay
    Elizabeth (Lizzie) McKay

**Team 4:**

Chance "Sniper" Hendrix
    Morgan James (Shyla)

Payton James

Jackson Lewis
  Raegan Cartwright
  Parents: Susan and Robert Cartwright

Gabe Moore
  Isabella (Isa) Moore
  Vittoria
  Lorenzo (Enzo)
  Grayson Moore

**Team 5:**

Alec Wesley
  Florrie Younge

Craig Devereux
  Reese Pearson
  **Training:**

Hudson Knight- formerly known as Garrick Knight
  Kate Knight
  Raven Knight
  Griffin Knight

Lola "Brave" Pruitt
  Ryan Jackson
  James Jackson (Cassandra Jackson- mother)
  Piper Jackson
  Ryder Jackson

**Team 6:**

Storm Hart

Daniel "Coop" Cooper
    Kayla Cooper (daughter)

Tony "Tacos" Russo

**IT Department:**

Becky Harding

Robert "Rob" Markum

*Chapter One*

# SNIPER

Pulling into the lot, the sign that flashed a half naked woman in bright neon lights made me want to turn around immediately and head home. But I had promised Jeremy Wick, the Master Chief I served with in the Navy, that I would come check it out. The last thing I wanted to do with my night was hang out in a smoke-filled club where women took off their clothes.

That had never been my scene, and as I walked through the doors, I cringed at the smarmy feel that washed over me. Why any man would want to go to a club and watch naked women prance around on the stage when they could put in a little effort and find a willing woman to take to bed, was something I would never understand.

"Chief, how ya doing?" I pulled my old military buddy in for a hug. It had been years since I'd seen him. He'd asked me to go in with him opening this strip club, but I had politely declined. Besides, I didn't want to be sitting behind a desk or watching men get off in public. I wanted to do something purposeful with the rest of my life. I was used to the structure of the military and I had never wanted to leave in the first place, so finding a job at Reed Security had turned out to be a blessing.

"Sniper, it's good to see you, man," he grinned. Nobody had called me Sniper in years. To everyone at Reed Security, I was Chance and that was fine with me. I had given up being a sniper a long time ago. "Business is booming. I bet you're regretting not getting in when I started up."

"Are you doing that well?"

"Hell, I'm practically shoveling money into the bank. If I make any more money, I'm going to have to buy out the bank. How's the security job going?"

"It's my dream job. Money, guns, and as many pretty women as I can get."

A woman in a thong and see-through bra walked up to Chief and wrapped herself around him. "Anything I can do for you tonight, baby?"

"Take care of my friend here. Sniper, this is one of my best dancers, Shyla."

She was fucking gorgeous, but she looked nothing like a Shyla. Hell, I didn't even like the name, but as far as stripper names went, it fit the bill. She had blonde hair that brushed across her breasts that were coated in way too much of that shimmery shit. The blue of her eyes was sharp, but again, she was fucking covered in makeup that made her look all caked on. Women didn't need that shit and it was a major turnoff for me. Still, this woman was a knockout. With those long legs that were accentuated by her sky high heels, and curves that made my dick hard, she was the sexiest woman I'd ever laid eyes on. If only she didn't work at a strip club, she would be someone that I would take home and twist up the sheets with for one night.

She looked disappointed for just a second that Chief had asked her to take care of me, but then she put a sultry smile on her face and wrapped her arms around me. If it was any other stripper, I would probably shove her off me. I didn't do strip clubs and I had no desire to have any diseases come within ten feet of me. But the way this woman acted, she didn't seem like a career stripper to me. I didn't know what it was, but she looked classy. Maybe it was the way she carried herself, like she wasn't really used to walking around naked in front of people, or the way her eyes were a clear bright blue. Most strippers that I had come in contact with were high most of the time.

I glanced down at her arms and breathed a sigh of relief when I didn't see any track marks. Of course, now people were being more creative about how they injected their drugs. Still, she didn't show any signs of being an addict.

"What can I do for you, Sniper?" she purred.

"I'm just here to hang with Chief and watch the show."

"Lucky for you, I'm on in ten. I'll look for you in the front row."

"Sure, Shyla."

She strutted her fine ass away from me, glancing back for just a moment, but she wasn't looking at me. Her eyes were all for Chief. For some reason, that fucking irritated me. "Looks like one of your strippers wants a piece of the boss."

"I never sleep with my staff. The last thing I need is a cat fight around here." He glanced down at his watch and slapped me on the arm. "I have some business to take care of. Why don't you enjoy the show and I'll come find you when I'm done." He tapped the bar, getting the bartender's attention. "Drinks are on the house for this guy."

"Thanks, Chief."

He walked away, leaving me alone with the stench of sweaty sex and cigarettes. I was disgusted by being in this place, but I would never tell Chief that. He had been begging me to come check his place out for a while and I couldn't put him off any longer.

I took my drink and sat in the front row so I could see Shyla when she took the stage. I wished I hadn't come when I got to the front and realized that the place was packed and I didn't have anyone to watch my back. There were too many ways for someone to sneak up on me in here. I was just about to get up and head back to the bar where I could see the whole room when the music started.

Shyla came on stage, her hips swaying and tits jiggling. I could tell that they were real when she pushed up against me earlier and they looked even better up on stage. She danced around the pole, swinging her body and bending it in ways that had me thinking about taking her home at the end of the night and trying out all those positions with her. Her ass was spectacular, but what really caught my attention were her calves. They were well defined and sexy as hell.

I couldn't stop staring at her and when her eyes locked with mine, it was like everything started moving in slow motion. Her moves became more sensual, as if she was dancing just for me. I had never wanted a stripper before, but hell, this woman danced for me like we were already fucking in my bed. I could have thrown some money on the stage like the others, but I didn't want a strip tease from this woman. Even though I'd never brought a stripper home, I'd gladly pay to have her in my bed just so I could feel the sweat from her body sliding against mine. Something about her just snagged me and made me watch her. I couldn't figure out what the hell it was, but when she finished her dance, I did something I'd never done before and found my way to the hall that led to the stage.

"You can't be back here." I glared at the man that was standing in my way. Most definitely military. I could always tell a military man when I saw one. It was the way he stood, held himself like he knew who the biggest threat in the room was and how to take him out with as few casualties as possible. I got it. It was his job to take care of the dancers, but there was no way I was leaving without Shyla tonight.

"Storm, he's the boss's friend." Shyla had walked up behind him and placed her hand on his arm, trying to calm him down. I growled when I saw the touch. She was going to be mine tonight. Shyla smirked at me and batted her eyelashes.

"Something I can do for you?"

"What time do you get off?"

"Whatever time you take me home."

I grabbed her hand and pushed past the bouncer. I walked down the hall until I saw the dressing room and pushed the door open. "You have two minutes to grab your shit."

Ten minutes later, we were pulling up to her apartment. It was in a shitty part of town and the lock on her door barely worked. If I jiggled the handle enough, the door would slip right open. But I wasn't there to take care of her apartment or try and keep her safe. I was there for a quick fuck and that was it.

I dragged her back to the bedroom and pushed her down on the twin bed. She immediately shoved her ass up in the air. I pulled at the edges of her thong and ripped it in two. I probably shouldn't have, considering where she was living, but I was hard and needed to be inside her. I quickly undid my belt buckle and yanked my zipper down, doing my best not to catch it on my dick. Grabbing a condom, I tore open the packet and rolled it on.

"I'm clean," she said indignantly.

"You also work at a strip club, so I'm not taking your word for it."

"I'm not a prostitute!"

"You're acting like one right now," I said as I shoved myself inside her. I wasn't sure why I threw that little jab in there. It was probably because I was a little pissed at myself for wanting someone that stripped for a living. Her pussy was tight as fuck, so maybe she wasn't lying, but I still wasn't taking any chances. "Fuck, you're tight."

"It's been a while," she panted as I rammed into her a second time. She gripped the sheets and moaned as she rested her head on the bed. I ran my hand down her spine and then slipped my thumb into her ass. She jerked as her ass tightened around me. Holding onto her hip with my other hand, I pounded into her pussy as I pushed my thumb deeper into her ass. Soon, she was pushing back against me, fucking my dick and my thumb with desperate need.

As good as her pussy was, I wanted that ass. I pulled my dick out and pressed it lightly against her back hole. When I started to push in, she pushed off the bed. "Wait!"

I stopped pushing and fingered her clit as she adjusted.

"I don't...I've never done this. I don't want it."

"You sure about that? When I slipped my thumb in you, your body said otherwise. You were fucking me with that ass."

She was quiet for a moment and I took that as my cue. I shoved deep inside her, not allowing her any time to think twice about it. She let out a pained moan and I grinned. I didn't necessarily want to cause her pain, but the way her ass tightened around me made me hard. I liked that I was the first to take her ass and I would make it good for her. Slowly, I started fucking her and played with her pussy. I could hear her crying lightly, but then her ass started to relax, allowing me to move faster. Just as I thought, within a minute, she was shoving that ass back toward me and begging me for more.

"Goddamn," I breathed hard. "I love fucking your ass."

"Yes," she shouted. "Fuck it hard."

"Baby, there's no better way to get fucked in the ass."

"Oh, shit! I'm coming!"

I felt like I was going to black out from the pressure surrounding my dick, but I didn't let that stop me. If anything, it spurred me on faster. I slammed back into her a few more times, burying my cock deep inside her. I flopped down on top of her as my breathing slowed. When I felt like I could stand without collapsing, I pulled out and tied off my condom, tossing it in the trash can in the corner of the room.

"Thanks for the fuck," I said as I shoved myself back in my pants and zipped up. Suddenly, I was very aware of the fact that I had just fucked a stripper. I pulled out my wallet and tossed two fifty dollar bills on the bed.

"What the fuck is this?" She was holding up the money and glaring at me. "I'm not a fucking prostitute. I told you that."

"You really expect me to believe that you took me home just because you wanted to fuck me after meeting me for three minutes?" God, I was treating her like a whore now. I didn't know what the hell was wrong with me, but that didn't stop me from being an asshole.

"I needed to get laid."

"And you did."

I turned and walked out of her apartment without another word. No matter how much I just enjoyed fucking her, I wouldn't be making the hour trip back to see her again. I didn't date strippers and I didn't date women that threw themselves at me in just a matter of minutes. Well, that's what I was telling myself.

*Chapter Two*

# MORGAN

That asshole just threw money at me and walked out the door. I hadn't fucked him for money. I had fucked him because I was attracted to him. When I'd seen him in the front row while I was dancing, the only thing I could think about was forgetting about everything for just a little while. The way he watched me dance made me feel like I was the sexiest woman in the room, and I hadn't felt that way in years.

I told myself that I had taken him for information, which I didn't get, but that was a lie. I had been trying to get something out of my boss, Jeremy, for weeks now. He was the owner of the club. He had to know something.

My four year old daughter, Payton, had disappeared six months ago. Nobody could find anything on her disappearance and the police had said they hit a roadblock. She was still considered a missing person, but I couldn't stand for that. I would do whatever it took to get my daughter back.

About three months ago, I started asking around for someone who had information on unsavory things that went on in the city. A druggie gave me a name, which led me to another name, which led me to another name. Now here I was, working as a stripper to find out anything I could about a man named The Broker. My last source said to look for him, but didn't say if he was involved or someone that could help me get my daughter back.

When Jeremy first asked me to look after his friend, I was irritated. I was trying to cozy up to Jeremy and see if he knew anything about The Broker, but he was notorious for not getting involved with the girls. So, when I thought about his request, I realized that Sniper might be able to help me also, since he was friends with the boss. He was good looking too, so it wasn't like it was a hardship to cozy up to him. He was taller than anyone I'd ever dated and his features were sharp, but his expression lacked anything serious. He had black hair just a little longer than a crew cut and it gave him a bad boy look with the tattoos creeping up his neck.

Too bad he only saw me as a hole to fuck. He even insisted he use a condom because I was a stripper, like that automatically made me a whore. Not that I wasn't grateful that he was being that thoughtful, but it wasn't for my protection. He just thought I was diseased. That was another downside of where I was working. I missed feeling like a human being. I missed my normal life with my daughter. My life now consisted of practically selling myself for information.

I got dressed for work the next day, having hardly slept the night before. Sleep never came easy to me anymore. I slept just enough to keep going, but thoughts of my daughter always kept me awake. When I wasn't at the club, I was looking for information and updates on my daughter's case. If I had the chance, I went down to the local library and did some digging on their computers for anything that might help me. Sometimes that was reading about other cases of missing children and other times, it was corresponding with my FBI contact to see if they had come up with anything new, even though they told me they would call if they found anything new.

Storm greeted me at the door, practically blocking the whole thing with his large frame. He was tall with a fierce look that could scare the shit out of the toughest man. I assumed that he was former military because of the way he stood and his military haircut. I could be wrong, but the way he was constantly assessing the room and his stance was unlike anything I had ever seen before. The other bouncers were tough, but they had wandering eyes and didn't watch the room with the same intensity. I could always feel his dark brown eyes on me. And to top off the badass look, he had two full sleeves of tattoos that covered his bulging muscles.

He was always looking out for us, but especially me. I think he knew that this wasn't really my life, that I didn't belong here. I wasn't like the other girls. I didn't do drugs and I didn't take men in the back to screw. The first few times I spoke with him, I practically gave myself away with how I spoke. I had to learn to adapt quickly.

"How are you today, sweet pea?"

I smiled at his nickname for me. I got the feeling he didn't believe that my name was Shyla. That was the only name I ever gave. "I'm okay."

"You look like you still haven't gotten any sleep."

"Well, I was up all night screwing this new guy I met at a bar."

He rolled his eyes at me, knowing I was full of shit. "Sure you were. What time are you on tonight?"

"In an hour. I've got a special routine for tonight."

"Good luck. I hear we're going to have a special audience tonight."

"Really?" I said curiously. Maybe this was my chance. "Any idea who's coming?"

He shrugged his large shoulders. "Some friend of the boss."

The first thing I thought was that Sniper had returned. He wasn't going to be of any use to me. My shoulders sagged in disappointment. I was never going to get a break.

"You sure you're alright? You know I'll help you out if you need it."

I knew he would, but I also knew that his job would be on the line and I couldn't risk that. He was my one ally at the club. Everyone else was friendly, but they'd sell out their children if they thought it would get them ahead.

"Yeah, I'm good. I gotta get back there and get ready. I'll catch you later."

I smiled my most flirtatious smile and shook my ass as I walked away. I wasn't interested in doing anything with Storm. He was hot and a great guy, from what I could tell, but there was nothing more important at the moment than getting my daughter back.

I knew I wasn't as sexy as the other girls when I danced, but I had to be at my best tonight. I needed to draw the attention of whoever this special guest was. I figured that anyone that wasn't a regular was another opportunity for me to gain information.

When I took the stage, my eyes immediately looked for him. He was there, right in the front row. I could tell by his expensive suit and the cigar hanging out of his mouth that this was not a man that normally went to a strip club. I sauntered onstage, making sure to keep eye contact with him. I did my whole routine right in front of him, making sure to put extra sway in my hips and a good shot at what my thong was covering. I even grabbed my breasts and played with my nipples. And he watched the whole time.

When I finished my routine, he stood and walked over to the stage, tossing a few hundreds at me. The way he stared at my breasts gave me the creeps. It wasn't a look of desire, but something more sinister. He motioned me forward with his hand and I didn't feel like I could tell him no. I got to my knees, spreading them wide so my breasts were right in his face.

"Did you dance for me?" His voice sent chills down my spine, but I held it together, giving him a nod. His hand brushed across my breast and over my nipple. He pinched it and twisted until I almost screamed, but I kept my face as clear as possible. When his hand skimmed down my body and slipped inside my thong, I thought I might actually throw up. My body shook with fear, and the way he looked at me, I was pretty sure he got off on that. I couldn't stand his hands on me, but I needed information and he was my ticket. At least, I hoped so.

When he shoved his fingers inside me, my body reacted. I didn't want his fingers there, but my body flooded with desire anyway. He took that as a sign that I liked it. To my embarrassment, he started finger fucking me right on the stage. My eyes darted around to see if anyone was watching, and there were a few men that were staring at me.

"Don't look at them, sweetheart. When my fingers are in your pussy, you're all mine." I locked eyes with him as he continued thrusting his fingers in me. My heart was beating so fast I was sure it would burst out of my chest and my breathing was so ragged that he actually thought I was excited by this. I jerked my hips and tightened myself around him, hoping that he took it as a real orgasm and this could stop.

Those evil, black orbs mocked me as I kneeled on the stage before him. He made a show of pulling his fingers out and showing my cream all over them. When he stuck them in his mouth, I smirked, hoping it came off as sexy and not disgusted. He grabbed onto my arm suddenly and jerked me forward so he could whisper in my ear.

"I wish I could take you home and fuck you right now, but I'm going out of town for work. When I come back, you'll be in my bed while I fuck you hard." He licked my ear and then pulled back. "Be ready." He turned and walked away without a second glance.

"Wait!"

He turned back around, his face pinched in anger. I guess I wasn't supposed to talk, but I had to know his name before he left.

"What's your name?"

"Steven."

When he walked away, I stood on shaky legs and made my way off the stage. It seemed like that had lasted for hours, when in fact it was only about five minutes. The girl that was waiting to go on after me shot me an evil look, probably pissed that I had not only delayed her set, but also got so much money. But I didn't want it. I shoved the hundreds into her hands. Her face morphed in shock, but she seemed satisfied. I didn't care. I didn't want that creep's money.

I stepped into the hallway and almost collapsed against the wall, but strong arms caught me. I knew it was Storm by his scent. He held me up in his arms and started dragging me away from the stage. By the time we got to the dressing room, I had tears running down my face.

"Why did you let him do that to you?" he asked angrily.

"I had to."

"No, you didn't. All you had to do was move away and give me the signal. I would have been there and I would have beat his ass."

"He's a special friend of Jeremy's."

He shoved me gently onto a bench and then knelt in front of me, grabbing my chin and forcing me to look at him. "I don't give a fuck who he is. Nobody has the right to touch you when you don't want it."

"I need to know who he is," I said quietly. "I can't tell you why, but it's important."

He stared at me for a moment and then stood, pacing the dressing room. I knew he was angry and he wanted to help, but I just didn't know if I could fully trust him not to spill my secrets.

"What are you looking for from him?"

"Information."

"About what?" he bit out.

"I can't tell you. Just leave it alone."

"Sweet pea, I can help you. I'm not just some big muscled baboon. I was a Ranger in the Army. I know how to deal with men like him."

"I don't want you to," I said quickly. "Please, I think he has information I need and I won't stop until I get it."

"What makes you think this guy has the information you need?"

"I...I don't know," I said, shaking my head in defeat. I felt battered down from the months of searching with no results. Something had to give soon. "He looks powerful and powerful men have information."

"So, you allow men to touch you on the off chance that they might be able to help you?" he asked incredulously.

I cringed at his spot-on assessment of my behavior. Most women would never trade their bodies for what a man could give them. At least, not the women I knew. But I hadn't been around those people in months. My new life was in a world that would disgust most women.

"I'm desperate," I whimpered. "I'll do anything, give anything to find out what I need to. Even to a man like that. If there's even the slightest chance he can help, I'm going to take it."

He was pissed at me. I could tell by the way his jaw worked in anger and he ran his hand repeatedly over the back of his head. He was trying not to hit something, but I knew he would never hit me.

"I'm going to be watching you, and if I think for one minute you're in trouble, I won't hesitate to break his fucking neck."

"I swear, I'll tell you if I need help."

He nodded and walked out of the room. I cleaned myself up quickly, washing my ruined makeup from my face, and then headed to work the floor for the rest of the night. By the time I headed home, I was exhausted, but all I could think about was who Steven was and how I could find out more about him. He wouldn't be back for a month. Somehow, I had to find another way to get information. A month would be way too long to wait.

Turning the corner to my building, I was grabbed and shoved up against the wall. My head smacked lightly against the cold wall. Staring down at me were the most intense eyes I had ever seen. He was back, the man that had so callously fucked me and tossed money on the bed for me. I shouldn't want him, but something inside me yearned for his touch. Maybe it was that it had been too long since any man outside the club had touched me in any way other than to slip money in my thong. His strong, hard hands held me tightly in place and his knee shoved my legs apart, forcing his way closer to my body.

He looked at me like he didn't understand what he was doing here, like he didn't understand the attraction. He would be right. In no way should we be attracted to each other. I was posing as a stripper and he was some badass warrior. He deserved someone that would get down on her knees and praise the ground he walked on. That wasn't me. I might enjoy an hour with him, but I had more important things to worry about than some guy that would never think of me as more than an easy lay.

And he proved my point when he pulled my skirt up and ran his hand across my wetness. Without any hesitation, he had his pants down, his cock sheathed, and shoved himself inside me. I gripped his shoulders as he thrust up into me, shoving my back against the hard wall. I didn't care about anything else right now but forgetting about what had happened to my life. He was the perfect distraction, one that would make me come, but would leave in time for me to focus on what I needed to do.

It wasn't long before he was finished, thrusting himself inside me one last time as he breathed heavily against my neck. I felt his heart racing against mine as we both slowly came down from our high. When he pulled out, I could feel my own juices slickening the insides of my thighs. Thank God I was so close to home. I corrected my skirt and picked up my bag that I had dropped on the ground, throwing it over my shoulder as I headed for the mouth of the alley.

I was just a few steps down the sidewalk when I felt him come up behind me. He didn't say anything, but walked next to me all the way back to my apartment. He walked inside with me and up the stairs. I kept glancing back at him, wondering what he was doing. Was he thinking he was going to stay the night? I wasn't really okay with that.

My question was answered when I unlocked the door and he nodded to me, turned around, and headed back down the stairs. I shook my head, completely confused by the man. If I wasn't good enough for a bed, why bother walking me home? I shook off those thoughts, not really needing an answer. I needed sleep and I needed to do some searching online like I did every night in hopes that I would find something that would lead me to my daughter.

As usual, there was nothing new. I sank down on my uncomfortable bed and stared at the ceiling like I usually did, thinking about Payton and praying that she was okay.

*Chapter Three*

# SNIPER

"Come on," Cap grinned. "Time to pay up."

We were all in the conference room, waiting on our instructions for upcoming assignments. Last night had been poker night. We didn't actually play poker, but we continued to call it that. I had lost big time. I slapped down two fifty dollar bills and shoved them over to Cap. He had been the big winner last night, but luckily, I wasn't the one that lost the most money. That had been Cazzo, coming in at a loss of two hundred dollars.

"One of these days, I'm gonna win and take all of your money."

Cap laughed at me, like the thought of me winning was completely ridiculous. "Sure, I'll believe it when I see it. The day you walk away with even two dollars will be the day I let you make the assignments for the week."

"You have so little faith in me."

"Chance, you don't need someone to have faith in you," Gabe jabbed. "You need the hand of God on your side, and last I remember, you don't believe in God."

"Hey, I wasn't the biggest loser last night. Cazzo lost two hundred dollars."

"You what? Samuel Galmacci, please tell me that I just misheard what Chance said." We all spun around in surprise at the feminine shriek that emanated from the doorway. Vanessa, Cazzo's wife, was holding a long box and her face was beat red. "You blew two hundred dollars on poker last night?"

"Samuel? Somebody's in trouble," Sinner laughed. Cazzo punched him in the shoulder and took a tentative step toward Vanessa.

"I didn't blow it," Cazzo said placatingly. "I just had a run of bad luck."

"Yeah, and it wasn't poker," Sinner chimed in. "It was Go Fish."

Cazzo slapped him across the back of the head. "Thanks a lot, asshole."

"How the hell does someone lose that much money playing Go Fish?"

"I was barely down and every time I told myself I had to stop betting, someone was in my head telling me to keep playing, that I could win it all back. It's a sickness, sweetheart."

"Was that someone that was in your head the same someone that told you to buy this rifle?"

Cazzo's eyes went wide and he visibly swallowed. "Uh, that's not what it looks like."

"Really? Because it looks like it's a rifle that's so old it was used in World War I."

"It was actually the Civil War. It was the first sniper rifle ever made."

"Fuck, man. You got a Whitworth Rifle?" I stood up so fast, my chair flew backwards. I stalked over to Vanessa and tore the box from her hands. I laid the box on the table and took a deep breath before I opened the lid. It was the most beautiful thing I had ever seen. Holding the Holy Grail would have been nothing compared to this.

"Give me some gloves," I snapped. No one did anything for a minute, but when I glared around the room, Craig took off and was back just a minute later with a pair of gloves for me. I pulled them on and then ever so gently picked up the rifle.

"Vanessa, you don't know what you have here. This magnificent weapon was designed by Joseph Whitworth in 1854. There were only thirteen thousand four hundred built between 1857 and 1865. Do you know how many of these still exist? There probably aren't any left. This could be the very last original rifle in existence."

I ran my hand over the gun lovingly, murmuring to myself. "49 inches in length with a 33-inch barrel. Fires two to three rounds per minute with an effective firing range up to a thousand yards, with a classic iron sights scope. Fucking beautiful."

"Should we leave you two alone?" Jackson asked.

"You don't know how amazing this is."

"I do," Cazzo cut in. "That's why I bought it."

"Yet, somehow you forgot to mention it to your wife," Vanessa scolded.

"Now, sweetheart, this is a collectible. For how old it is and how rare, I got a great price."

"Really? How much was it?"

"Just a few thousand dollars."

"Oh," Vanessa sighed in relief. "That really had me worried for a minute."

"Baby, I would never go out and spend a ton of money without talking to you first."

Vanessa smiled at him. "I know, Sam." She walked forward, pulling out a piece of paper. "I was just really worried when I saw this bill for a Whitworth Rifle that was sold at auction for $161,000!" She slammed the paper against his chest and stormed out of the room. Cazzo gripped the paper before it fell to the floor and then turned to us all with an oops shrug.

"You seriously spent $161,000 on a gun?" Burg asked.

"Hey," I cut in, coming to Cazzo's defense. "It's totally worth it. If I had seen it up for auction, I would have bought it."

"You may have to buy it from me now. I have a feeling Vanessa's gonna bitch about this until I get the money back."

"And she's going to withhold sex," Sinner pointed out. "Been there, done that. Do yourself a favor and sell it."

"She won't withhold sex. She'll do something worse."

"What's worse?" Gabe asked.

"She's gonna call my mother."

"Amy Shultz. Age twenty-six." I was reading from the file Cap sent me. We would normally meet in the conference room, but she was insistent that we get to her as soon as possible. Jackson was driving so I could go over the file on the way. Gabe sat in the back and prepared weapons for us, making sure everything was loaded so we could get to work right away.

"She called us because her duplex was broken into two nights ago and she was raped. They didn't catch the perpetrator and she's scared to be alone now. From what she told police, her attacker threatened to slit her throat if she told anyone what happened. There's a police cruiser parked outside her house, but there are two entrances and she doesn't feel safe."

"Does the department know we're on our way?" Jackson asked. "I don't really want to get shot today. I've got a date Friday."

"Really? What happened with what's her face?" I asked curiously.

"Raegan? She's just staying with me until we can be sure that no one's looking for her."

Raegan Cartwright was the woman that we rescued from her abusive boyfriend when her parents called and begged us to get her out. Jackson had taken to her right away, so it was highly suspicious that he was dating.

"Don't give me that bullshit." Gabe leaned forward over the seat to join in the conversation. "I saw your face when you rescued her. She means something to you and I can fucking guarantee you would do anything to be with her. You were so protective of her that you invited her and her parents to stay with you."

"She needed a place to go," Jackson said defensively.

I grinned, knowing Gabe and I were thinking the same thing. "You could have stashed her in a safe house, but you invited her to stay with you. I would imagine that a woman that's been beat on like that wouldn't want to be around any men right now, but she went willingly with you."

"She didn't have a choice," he shot back. "Remember? She was unconscious when we took her to my house."

"That was over a year ago. After she got better, she could have gone to a safe house with her parents. You wanted her to stay. In fact, I believe you convinced her to stay with you."

Jackson wasn't fooling me. I saw the way he carried her into his house and sat by her side night and day. I had stayed with him for a few days to make sure that we were in the clear. The man never left her side. If she was really just someone to protect, he wouldn't have yelled at her dad when he insisted that Jackson let him take care of his daughter.

Jackson sighed heavily, but didn't look over at me. "She's not exactly in the right frame of mind to have anyone in her life like that. We mostly keep to our own sides of the house."

"So, you *do* like her." Gabe smacked Jackson on the shoulder, bouncing up and down in his seat like a little kid. "I fucking knew it."

"Look, it doesn't matter if I like her or not. She doesn't want any man near her. She practically runs in the other direction when I'm around. I'm not gonna sit around and wait for her."

"Sure," I grinned. "Anyway, back to the job, we're being assigned to protect her until this bastard is caught or until she wants us to leave."

"Sounds like this could be a long one."

I glanced at Gabe in confusion. He was newly married. He shouldn't sound quite so excited about this extended stay.

"What did you do?" I asked.

"Huh? Nothing, I'm just excited to have a more exciting job. It's been kind of dull lately."

"We just went out on a job two weeks ago. Remember? We were shot at? You got to kill someone. Ring any bells?"

"Yeah, and two weeks is a long time to go."

"Seriously, what did you do to piss off Isa?"

Running a hand over his face, he plopped back in his seat. "I fucked up the laundry."

"How?" Jackson peered in the rearview mirror at Gabe.

"Isa asked me to switch laundry loads when I got home last night. She had a basket of whites on top of the washer, so I put that in after I switched loads."

"Sounds like you're the perfectly whipped husband," I snorted.

"Yeah, well, I'm definitely gonna get whipped when I get home. She was washing these special microfiber rags. They're purple and they have to be washed separately. I missed one in the washer and now all her whites are lavender."

I busted into laughter at his predicament. He was so fucked. Women didn't like men helping out for a reason and Gabe was that reason. "See, there's a reason I'm not married anymore. If I turn all my clothes another color, I don't give a shit. I buy new stuff and move on, but women aren't like that. She's gonna hold this over your head for at least the next few months."

"That's why I figure this job should last at least a few weeks. It'll give her time to cool down."

"And if it doesn't?" Jackson asked.

"Then one of you are gonna have to shoot me. Nothing too life-threatening or anything that'll take me out of commission. Just some-thing that'll play on her sympathy."

"You want one of us to shoot you so that your wife won't be angry about her purple underwear?"

"Hey, you were married. You know how irrational women can be."

"Not just irrational, vindictive. Why do you think I haven't remarried?"

"Because you fuck strippers and now your dick could fall off at any time?" Jackson quirked an eyebrow at me with a faint smile on his face. I should have never said anything to them. They weren't going to let this go anytime soon.

"You guys are as bad as a woman. I tell you one fucking thing and I'm gonna get my balls busted for months to come."

"Look on the bright side," Jackson gave me a sidelong glance. "At least we won't have to shoot you at the end of this job."

---

Stepping out of the SUV, I checked my surroundings as I approached the duplex. We made quick work of checking out the whole property and then walked up the porch to her side of the house. I knocked on the door several times, but no one answered. I banged harder on the door and that's when I heard it. A piercing scream ripped through the quiet of the neighborhood.

I stepped aside just as Gabe put a boot through the door. The wood splintered as the door crashed against the wall. I stepped into the living room with Gabe and Jackson on my six. We cleared each room on the first floor and then I motioned for us to head upstairs.

Quietly, we crept up the stairs. The closer we got we could hear the whimpers of what I could only assume was our client. With Gabe on the top stair and Jackson to my right, I slowly turned the knob on the door. With a nod to Gabe, I threw the door open and stepped into the room with my gun drawn.

A woman was tied to the bed completely naked, spread eagle. I motioned for Jackson and Gabe to clear the rest of the floor and stepped over to the woman with a finger to my lips, signaling for her to be quiet. Her tear-stained cheeks ripped my heart wide open. She looked absolutely terrified. I grabbed a blanket and threw it over her naked body. Her eyes slipped closed and her body trembled. She was trying to get herself under control.

"All clear," Gabe said as he walked back into the room. Jackson stood guard outside the room, watching for anyone who might attempt to breach the house.

I had already started on untying her binds, but as soon as the rope started to loosen, she screamed. I stepped back and glanced over at Gabe. We'd have to tread carefully.

"Ma'am, we're from Reed Security. Are you Amy Shultz?"

She nodded quickly as more tears streamed down her cheeks.

"I'm going to untie you, okay?"

Again she nodded. Gabe and I both stepped forward carefully and reached for her binds again.

"No! Stop!" she screamed. We backed up instantly, not sure of how to handle this. If she wouldn't let us undo her binds, we couldn't get her to safety.

"Amy," I said gently. "Was this the same man that attacked you the other day?"

"Please don't hurt me," she pleaded.

"I'm not going to. We need to get you to safety. We need to untie you, okay? I promise we won't touch you."

She nodded again and closed her eyes tightly. Gabe and I approached again, both of us careful to not touch her as we worked the ropes. I had to pull the rope around her wrist tighter to get the knot undone.

"Oh," she moaned loudly, her hips bucking up in the air.

I glanced over at Gabe, wondering what the hell was going on. He had a similar look on his face. I continued with the rope and her moans got louder. At this point, she looked like she was humping the air.

"Uh, Amy? Is everything alright?"

"Stop! What are you doing? Don't do this!" She started writhing around on the bed and moaning like she was in pain. Tears started to drip down her face again.

*What the fuck?* Gabe mouthed to me.

I shrugged. I had no fucking clue what was going on. I tried again to untie her wrist, but she just kept screaming. I pointed down to her feet. Maybe she'd let us get her legs untied. We both moved to the other end of the bed and started to untie her.

"Yes, yes! Please, give me more."

I stood back and stared at her. This woman was all over the map. Maybe she had mixed feelings about the rape. I had heard about women that liked it against their will. Maybe that was what was happening.

"I think we need to call in a therapist to walk you through this, Amy. We're not prepared to handle the stress you're under."

Her eyes flew open and she stared at me in confusion. "What? I've never had to call in another person. Aren't the three of you enough?"

She was calm now, way too fucking calm. "Amy, what are you talking about?"

"Well, I called your company because I wanted the best."

"We are that, but we're trying to help you and one minute you want it and the next you're yelling at us. We're not used to dealing with rape, so you're going to have to tell us what you need."

She nodded excitedly. "Right. I can do that. Can you bring the other one in?"

"Jackson!" I called out. He walked in and stood beside me. "Okay, we're all here. What can we do to make this work?"

"I think it would be best if...if one of you got on top of me."

"What?" Gabe barked.

"You asked," she said as she hung her head in embarrassment.

I motioned for Jackson to climb on top of her. This was so fucked up, but I wasn't a woman. I didn't know what was running through her head right now. Jackson slowly got on top of her, his legs straddling each side of her stomach. He was careful to keep his weight off her.

"Does this help?"

"Yes. Now, can you hold my wrist?" she asked me. When I looked at her in alarm, she quickly explained. "I need to feel like I can fight."

I stepped forward and held on to one of her wrists, and motioned for Gabe to start with her feet. He got her right ankle untied and was just about to move when her foot shot up and kicked him in the face.

"Fuck!" he shouted as blood poured from his nose. She was thrashing around on the bed and Jackson finally took over, sitting down on her to keep her from moving around too much.

"Stop fighting me," he said loudly. I ran around to the foot of the bed and held her leg down as Jackson tried to calm her down. "I'm not trying to hurt you, Amy."

"Oh, yes!" She started bucking her hips up against Jackson, grinding against him.

"Shit," Jackson groaned as she continued to thrust up against his cock. "This isn't good."

"Hold her down," I said sharply. He put his hands down, but ended up grabbing her tits.

"Yes, pinch them!"

"Not her tits, you asshole!"

"There's no other place to put them. She keeps moving around."

"Hold her shoulders!"

He leaned forward and placed his hands on her shoulders, but she raised her head and licked him on the face.

"Yes! Hold me down. Fuck me hard. Stuff your cock in my mouth until I gag all over you."

Jackson reared back and jumped off the bed, getting his foot caught in the blanket and falling to the floor. "What the fuck is wrong with you?" Jackson shouted.

"Isn't this what you guys do?"

"What the hell are you talking about?" Gabe asked.

"I was told your company would send out three strong men to take care of me."

"Protect you," I clarified.

"Well, protect and serve," she said with a wink.

I shook my head as I realized where she was going with this. "We aren't that kind of place. We're an actual security company. We're not strippers."

"I didn't think you were. I paid for a certain kind of service, one that includes three strong men to take care of me in every way I need."

"Lady, you filed a police report for rape. There's a cop sitting outside your apartment." Gabe pointed to the window as he glared at her. "Were you actually raped?"

"Well, fantastically speaking, yes, I was."

"Shit," I mumbled. "Why do we always get the crazy ones? Jackson, go down and get that cop. Tell him we need to speak with him now."

Jackson practically ran out the door and down the steps.

"Do you think he'll use his cuffs on me?"

"That's a very great possibility."

"Will he be bringing a friend along? Do you think he'll use his nightstick on me?"

"I'm getting the fuck out of here," Gabe said, still holding his nose. I followed him out the door. I wasn't getting accused of rape as some part of her sexual fantasies. When I got downstairs, the cop walked through the front door with Jackson.

"What's going on here? Has her attacker come back?"

"There is no attacker. She made it up." I was beyond pissed right now. What a fucking waste of time, and with a crazy woman, nonetheless.

"Sir, we take every woman's claim seriously around here."

"Yeah? Well, I'd suggest you call in backup before you go up there. She tied herself to the bed and called us in to fulfill her rape fantasies."

"Her what?"

"You see my fucking face?" Gabe snapped. "This is from her kicking me when I was trying to untie her. Then she started humping Jackson and begging for more. The woman is a fucking lunatic."

"Why don't you come up with me?" the cop suggested.

"Sorry, I've had enough crazy for one day. This is in your hands now."

"Help!" the woman screamed from upstairs. The cop looked up there and then back to us.

"Don't do it, man. You'll have nightmares about that one," I said before I walked out the door.

"Looks like you're not out of the doghouse with Isa," Jackson said matter of factly to Gabe as we headed for the truck.

"Shut up, asshole."

*Chapter Four*

# MORGAN

I stared at the picture in my locket of Payton. Every day that passed that she was still gone was like shoving a knife in my gut. Every possible scenario ran through my mind. She could be locked up in a basement somewhere, starving and cold. What almost seemed like the better option was her assimilating to a new family. Maybe she didn't even remember me by now, but maybe she was safe. Then there was the possibility that she wasn't even in the country anymore. She could have been trafficked, taken for child pornography or sex trafficking. That was the hardest pill to swallow.

I snapped the locket shut, refusing to let those thoughts go through my mind right now. I wasn't going to help her by feeling sorry for myself. I needed something I could go on. I was getting desperate and before I could think too much about it, I walked down the hallway like I had a purpose in heading for the boss's office.

His door was open just a few inches, but it was enough to hear him on the phone with someone. I got as close as I dared and strained to listen to the conversation.

"I want that shipment here in two weeks. Anything more than that and I lose money."

That wasn't very helpful. A shipment in a strip club could be anything. He could be ordering liquor and he would lose money if he had to go to another vendor. That was most likely what he was talking about.

"Wes will be back in town by the end of the month and he'll expect to see what you have for him. Get your shit together before then or you won't like what happens. Don't fuck this up."

Wes. He had to be someone important if Jeremy was getting all worked up over him being in town. I heard the click of the phone being put back on the receiver. Damn, I didn't get the day Wes would be here, but that didn't matter. I would probably hear more about it over the next week or so. Everybody had eyes and ears around the club. It was all about what you could offer for the information that could be provided.

"Something you need, sweet cheeks?"

I spun around quickly and tried my best not to scream. The voice was one I recognized and dreaded at the same time. But that didn't stop me from letting my eyes wander over his body. Even though I hadn't gotten any information out of him, Sniper had a body that was definitely worth exploring.

"I was just waiting to talk with him."

"It looked like you were snooping."

"I wasn't. I heard him on the phone, so I waited out here until he was off, which he is. So, if you'll excuse me, I'm gonna go talk to him." I had let myself slip back into my stripper persona. If I wasn't careful, he would see right through me. So, I stepped toward him and gripped his cock through his jeans, leaning in to whisper in his ear. "After the show, come back to my place and I'll give you a private viewing."

When I stepped away, I was taken aback by the stern look on his face. I had been expecting that he would melt into my proposal, but he didn't.

"I fucked you two times, but that doesn't mean I want to again."

Shit. Talk about a slap in the face. He had taken me right outside my apartment, but was now as cold as ice. What the hell had happened between then and now? Not that it really mattered. I was using him just as much as he was using me, but the tone in his voice still hurt.

"Is there something you need, Shyla?" Jeremy's voice snapped me out of my thoughts. When I looked over at him, suspicion marred his features. I had to fix this fast. I couldn't afford to be on his bad side.

"I just needed to talk to you about something, if you have a minute."

"Sure. Come on in." He glanced over at Sniper before turning and walking back into his office. I followed him in and sat down across from his desk. "So, what do you need?"

"I was hoping I could pick up a few more hours."

"You're already working six nights a week. I pay you well and I know you bring in good tips. So, why do you need the money?"

For the first time since I started, Jeremy looked at me with suspicion. I watched his eyes flick to my arms and then look at my eyes. He thought I was into drugs. I had to come up with something to keep him off my back about this.

"I didn't take you for one to get caught up in drugs."

"It's not that-"

"Do you owe the wrong people money?"

"No. My niece is sick," I said quickly. "She doesn't have insurance and her treatments are expensive. I need to send my sister money so her daughter can get what she needs to get better."

"I'm sorry," he said sympathetically. "I can give you another shift, but you know that Wednesdays are our slow night."

"I realize that, but every little bit helps."

He nodded, leaning forward and resting his elbows on the desk. He didn't say anything as he stared down at his paperwork. I didn't really need the extra hours, but if I was here more, the chances of me learning something were better.

"I have some clients that are looking for something...particular. I really don't think it's something you would want to do. Honestly, I was going to ask one of the other girls to do this job."

"What do they want?"

"I've set up a poker game for some of my more lucrative clients. They would like some entertainment at the game, someone to look at. You would need to dress just as you do when you dance. You'd be serving drinks to them, dancing for them, whatever they require."

"That doesn't sound that different from what I do now."

He was stalling. He didn't want to tell me what the catch was, and there definitely was a catch. One that I probably wouldn't like.

"Some of them would want more than just entertainment. The poker game will be held upstairs. You may hear things that could get you in a lot of trouble if you were to repeat anything."

"So, keep my mouth shut and be the entertainment."

"Exactly. Do you think you can do that?"

One of the things I liked about Jeremy was that he seemed like a pretty upstanding guy. I knew he was former military and he ran his strip club with what I would imagine was the same intensity. He didn't treat us girls like we were cheap, trashy whores. He was strict with what he expected, but always fair. The club wasn't at all what I expected when I took this job. It was higher class clientele and he didn't tolerate men getting too handsy. If they stepped over the line, they were thrown out without any second chances.

That being said, what he was asking was basically for me to have sex with this particular group of men. I would be there to please them in whatever way they needed. I had only slept with one man in the last five years and my so called attempt at getting information from him didn't really work out. In fact, the information bit was only an excuse since I didn't actually try to get information from him. I wasn't so sure that trying to get information out of these men through sex was the way to go. What I really needed to know was if these men had any connections that could help me. I didn't want to sleep with these men, but for my daughter, I would do anything.

"What do these men do?"

"That's none of your business," he said harshly.

"I just want to know if mobsters are going to be coming after me. I don't want to get involved with anything that'll get me killed."

He seemed to relax slightly. "They're all businessmen of some sort. I'm not going to lie, some of them are shady, but as long as you keep your mouth shut, you'll be fine."

"Will you be in the room?"

"Yes, I'll make sure they stay in line."

"Okay. I'll do it."

"Good. We'll see how the first game goes. If everyone's satisfied, you'll get to continue with this weekly. I'll have to take you off the rotation one night, but you'll bring in ten times what you could if you were dancing."

I didn't give a shit about the money. If they were businessmen, they had connections that I could never fathom. Maybe even this Wes guy was part of the game. He did say that Wes would be here at the end of the month. That meant that in a few weeks, I could have the answers I was looking for. In the meantime, I couldn't just sit around and wait.

"Thank you, Jeremy. I won't let you down."

## Chapter Five

# SNIPER

I stood outside the office and felt like shit for the way I treated Shyla. She was doing this because she was trying to help her sick niece. I wondered what she would be doing if she didn't need all the extra money. Maybe she would have a normal job and she wouldn't have to take off her clothes for men.

"Some of them would want more than just entertainment," Chief said.

What the hell? He was actually going to let one of the women prostitute herself out for these men? I had never thought that he would do something like that. But then again, we weren't in the military anymore. He was just trying to run a business, and if the women chose to sell their bodies for money, that was on them.

There was no way Shyla would take the job though. She couldn't. As much as I implied that she slept with men that came into the club, I didn't actually believe that she did. She was different from the other girls. She had her shit together more than the other girls I had seen.

"Okay. I'll do it."

"Good. We'll see how the first game goes."

I didn't hear the rest because I was too pissed to stay and listen to whatever they had to talk about. She was actually going to do it. Even to save her niece, this was going too far. Men that would fuck a stripper at a poker game were not the kind of men that would be gentle with her. They would hurt her and do things that no woman ever wanted to go through. It made me sick to think of her at that poker game.

There was no way I was letting this happen. I'd just have to talk with Chief and make sure she wasn't allowed to work there. He could find some way to help her out without her fucking men. I stormed back down the hall to bust into his office and tell him just that when I ran into Shyla and lost all sense of reason.

"What the fuck are you thinking taking that job?" I shouted at her. "Are you really so desperate that you'd fuck a bunch of men that are gonna get off on hurting you? Because that's what they'll do. They're not gonna be gentle or make sure you come. They're gonna use you like a warm hole that they can get off in, and then they're gonna take out their fantasies on you. I can fucking guarantee that it'll break you long before you ever make enough money to help out your sister."

She just stared at me with her mouth slightly open. I waited for her to give me some excuse or tell me to fuck off, but she didn't do either. She held her head high as she walked past me and into the dressing room. Since she wasn't willing to acknowledge anything, I'd have to go talk to Chief. Storming into his office, I slammed the door behind me.

"Are you really going to let her do this?"

"I see you're still listening in on private conversations," he said drolly.

"She's not the kind of woman that should be doing something like this."

He leaned back in his chair, giving me the same stern stare I remembered from our military days. "And you came to this conclusion before or after you fucked her?"

"I never could keep anything from you," I grumbled.

"It's my club. Do you think I don't know what's going on around here? I know everything. Believe me, I don't think she's the right person for the job either, but she needs the money."

"So find her something else to do."

"Sniper, she agreed to it. I didn't lie to her about what went on at these games."

"Speaking of which, when did you start dealing with men that are so dirty?"

"It's the industry. I may do business with them, but it's all legit."

"Still, it's basically prostitution. You know Shyla isn't like that."

His eyes zeroed in on me, looking at me bafflement. "You don't even know her real name. It's obvious it isn't Shyla."

"And you do?"

He shook his head slightly. "No, I couldn't find out a single thing about her. I figured that she was running from someone because she was pretty secretive about who she was."

"That doesn't make sense. Why would she try to hide who she is if she's just trying to earn extra money to help her sister?"

"I'm guessing that she doesn't want her sister finding out how she's getting the money. Hell, who knows what her life was like before this. Maybe she's ashamed that she's coming here to strip."

That could be a possibility. She held herself with a lot more dignity than the other strippers, so it was very possible that she was trying to keep a piece of her old life. Either way, I didn't like it.

"Isn't there something else you can find for her?"

"I already had her scheduled for six nights a week. She stays as long as possible and always takes the extra jobs. It's almost like she doesn't want to go home."

"Because her place is a shithole," I grumbled.

"Look, I can't do anything else. She needs the money and I need a woman to work the room. You're not going to change her mind on this, so let it go."

I nodded, but didn't actually intend to. I'd have another talk with Shyla and do everything I could to change her mind. It just really rubbed me wrong to think of her fucking dirty, old men.

"Can we get to why I called you here today?"

"Yeah, man. What do you need?"

"I have a job for you."

"What kind of job?"

"KP duty. What the hell do you think? You're in security and I need someone to help me out with a situation. I have a special ship-ment coming in and I need a security detail to protect my investment."

This whole fucking thing sounded shady and I didn't want any part of that. "What kind of shipment?"

"That doesn't matter, but if you do a good job, it'll mean more jobs for you. And it's good money."

"You'll have to talk to my boss. He's the one that approves jobs."

"You mean you don't have any pull with him?" he smirked.

I didn't know how to respond. This was my Chief in the military, but now, he was into some shady shit. That wasn't something I wanted to drag my team into.

"He'll want to know what the shipment is before he agrees." His jaw clenched and his nostrils flared. He didn't like that answer, which confirmed my suspicions that he was doing something illegal.

"You can't just take my word for it? It's a sensitive matter."

"We can't protect your investment if we don't know what we're protecting."

"Give me the card."

I handed it over against my better judgement. I didn't want to insult the man. He had been my superior and a damn good man, but now I was starting to wonder if I really ever knew him. I was going to have to talk to Cap about this.

"You coming by this weekend?"

"I wasn't planning on it."

His lips twitched in amusement. "Not your scene?"

"Not at all."

"I'll tell you what, bring some of your friends by this weekend. Drinks are on the house."

I rolled my eyes at his blatant refusal to accept my dislike of his club. "I'll see what I can do."

Not that I wanted to come back, but some of the guys would like it. At least, the single ones would. It was doubtful any of the married guys would make an appearance, not if they wanted to keep their dicks in working order.

I was about to leave when I remembered my conversation with Shyla. I needed to talk with her again and try to get her to stop this insanity. There were already a few girls in the dressing room and Shyla was putting shit all over her face. I didn't like her looking like a whore. I wanted to see her without any makeup.

"Shyla, you got a minute?"

She looked at the other women and glared at me as she stood. She pulled me out of the room and down a dark hall. "What do you want?"

"You need to back out of the deal."

"Not a chance in hell."

"Why? You can get money a different way. You don't need to whore yourself out for that."

"You didn't seem to have a problem when it was you," she snapped.

"I wasn't-"

"Don't even go there. You fucked me from behind so you didn't have to see my face. There was nothing even remotely romantic about what we did. You didn't even wait two minutes after you finished to leave my apartment. And let's not forget the money you threw at me before you left."

This woman was infuriating, but the look of anger on her face had me backing down real fast.

"Look, I'm an asshole. I know that, but that doesn't change the fact that you don't have to do this."

"And why not?" I looked at her like she was crazy. "No, seriously. Why are you so concerned with whether or not I work that game? I'm a stripper. I take my clothes off for men all the time. I give lap dances and let men touch me. Why do you give a damn?"

"Because I have a feeling that this is not who you want to be. You don't talk like a stripper. You don't throw yourself at men for money the way all the others do. You let the men come to you, and yeah, you don't stop them from touching you, but you don't even look like you want it."

"Do you really think any stripper wants men to fondle them? It's our job. It pays the bills. That's why we're here. You barely know me, so what makes you think you know anything about me?"

She was right. Sleeping with her once didn't make me an expert on who she was. I had seen her dance at the club and interact with other men, but that could have been an off day for her. The truth was, I really didn't know this woman and hearing one sob story about her niece shouldn't change my opinion of her. Everyone had problems, but it was how they dealt with those problems that showed who they were.

"I don't know. Maybe I was just hoping you weren't the slut you appear to be."

I had to get out of here before I got wrapped up in anything else. This wasn't my life. I didn't need to be here or deal with other people's problems. I had a great job and a large family that would always be there for me. Hanging around here just made me depressed.

*Chapter Six*

# MORGAN

I was visibly shaking as I waited for the time to pass. Tonight was the night that I worked the poker game and I was nervous as hell. The thought of walking around naked in front of those men made my skin crawl. Sure, I was a stripper, but I was in a dark club and I could pretend I was someone else. Tonight, I would be in a room that would show off my body under bright lights.

The only article of clothing I could wear was a thong. I had to serve drinks like that while men stared at my breasts and my ass. Some of them would grab me and I had to pretend that it didn't bother me. There was a very good possibility that I would be fucked by a stranger tonight, a pervert that would take what he wanted from me. As much as I wanted to throw up and call Jeremy to tell him I couldn't do it, I needed information. I wouldn't have been led to this club unless someone had some piece of information that could help me.

I had to do this, but I couldn't do it if I was shaking. Nobody would want me there and I would probably end up throwing up on someone. I had been prescribed anxiety meds after Payton had disappeared. That was before I took control of the investigation since no one had any leads. Knowing that I had to go through with this, I took one before I headed to the club.

By the time I got there, I wasn't shaking quite as bad, but I was still nervous about all of this. I was supposed to serve drinks and I really hoped that all they wanted was straight up alcohol. I went through the motions of getting my makeup finished and adding some shimmer to my body. The other women were already there and giving me nasty looks. Apparently they heard about my new job.

I rolled my eyes at how petty women could be. It really was ridiculous that they were mad at me because I was going to walk around naked in front of men. I grabbed my robe, but then realized how silly that was. I worked in a strip club and I pretty much walked around naked wherever I went.

When I got upstairs, Jeremy was already there setting up for the game. There were six chairs around the table and a few bottles of alcohol sitting on a cart with clean glasses.

"Good, you're here. Are you ready for this?"

"As ready as I can be."

"You know, if you're not up to this, you can back out. I'm sure one of the other girls would step in for you."

"No, I can do this."

"Are you sure? You're shaking a little."

"Just first time jitters. Besides, I took some anxiety meds, so I should be good for the rest of the night."

He nodded, but didn't look convinced. "Don't ask about names tonight or any other night. To you, they're all just men that you're serving and entertaining. To them, you're just a sweet ass to look at. These men are not men you want to fuck with. Don't ask questions and don't offer anything unless they ask for it. Understood?"

I nodded and kept myself over by the serving cart. The men slowly started arriving and glanced at me from time to time, but mostly talked with each other. I ignored the fact that I was naked in front of these men and focused on what I could gain from being here. I didn't recognize any of the men, so I assumed that they didn't frequent the club. Then again, Jeremy had said that these were all businessmen, so it wasn't likely I would recognize any of them.

I waited for Jeremy to wave me over and then I plastered a smile on my face and wheeled the cart over. "What can I get you gentlemen?"

Jeremy raised an eyebrow at me as his jaw tensed. Maybe I wasn't supposed to speak at all. There was an older man at the table that looked like he was about sixty. He had the decency to not stare at me. Probably the only good man at the table.

"Whiskey," he said gruffly.

I poured whiskey for him and moved onto the next man. He had a sinister look to him. His hair was dark and slicked back with gel and he had a bushy mustache that matched his eyebrows. His dark eyes moved across my body like he was actually fucking me in that moment. I was disgusted, but I kept my grin in place.

"Vodka." As I poured it, his eyes never left my body and when I placed it on the table, he snatched my wrist and pulled me toward him. With two fingers he motioned me closer. He grabbed the back of my neck and squeezed painfully, bringing me right down to his face, so he could force me to look into his eyes.

"When the game is over, you *will* come with me to one of the rooms." His hand slid across the small of my back and pulled at the waistband of my thong. "I intend to use some of my toys on you."

His hand cupped my breast and then he pinched my nipple so hard that it brought tears to my eyes. His eyes darkened and a slow, evil grin spread across his face. When he released me, I took a step back and blinked to clear my eyes before everyone could see what he had done to me. No one dared look at me. Even Jeremy had his face buried in his cards. Whoever this man was, he wielded power like a king and feared no one.

I finished serving drinks and moved to the corner where I could hide myself slightly from everyone. I knew this was going to be bad, but I hadn't expected someone to outright command me to a room in front of everyone else. I shook off the promise of what would happen after the game and listened to the banter at the table. It was difficult to follow the conversation since I didn't know who any of these men were, their businesses, or how they knew one another.

I was beginning to regret offering myself up for this job when it seemed like the men weren't talking business at all. I had thought I might get something out of tonight, but if they were talking about anything that might help me, they were talking in code. I could have saved myself the embarrassment and the promise of what would happen later if I had known this was going to be a bust.

Hours passed and I only went over as I was beckoned. My feet were killing me from standing in one place for so long in these heels and my body started shivering from the chill of the room. When I was moving, it wasn't bad, but just standing here really let the cold seep into my bones.

The man with the evil eyes motioned me over, so I pushed the cart and stood next to him, waiting for him to tell me what he wanted. Instead, he slid his hand around my waist and yanked me onto his lap. His fingers dug into my side painfully, sending shivers down my spine. "What do you think, gentlemen? I think she'd make a fine example of our products."

His right hand skimmed up my chest again until his hand was wrapped around my throat. His nails dug into the sides of my neck, making it difficult to swallow, let alone breathe. I held my head high, trying to keep the pressure of his hand off my neck. My body shook in anticipation of what he was going to do. Would he fuck me in front of everyone at the table? I blinked back tears that tried to fill my eyes and tried not to make eye contact with anyone.

"Watch it," one man said, eyeing Evil Eyes.

The older man looked over at Jeremy as he puffed on his cigar. "This isn't how we do business."

"The way you do business is a thing of the past," Evil Eyes said harshly. "Your contribution to our little project is minuscule at best. I could have you replaced with the snap of my fingers. And I could make you disappear just as fast. No one would ever find your body."

My heart was thudding so loud in my ears that I barely registered the meaning of the conversation. I had been looking for answers and I had a feeling if I stuck around, I would get them.

The man shoved me off his lap so harshly that I stumbled and fell to the ground. Jeremy stood quickly, shoving back his chair in the process. "I think that's enough for tonight, gentlemen. I think we all got what we came for. We'll resume next week."

Jeremy walked over to me and hauled me up by my arms. "Go to the room across the hall and get something to cover yourself with."

I nodded and slipped out before he had a chance to change his mind. When I shut the door behind me, I sank down to the floor and took deep breaths, needing to wash the feeling of that man's hands off me. I stood quickly and went to the closet, flinging the door open and searching for something to wear. Everything in the closet was men's clothes. This must be Jeremy's personal closet for at the club. I grabbed a t-shirt off the top shelf and a pair of sweatpants. It was all way too big on me and my heels would look ridiculous with it, but I didn't care. I just needed to get out of the club.

I opened the door just a crack to make sure no one was in the hallway and slipped out the door. I ran through the back halls to the dressing room, ignoring anyone that was looking at me. I snatched my purse out of my locker and pushed out the back door of the club. I was shaking hard, finding it difficult to walk, but I pushed on, knowing that when I was in the safety of my apartment, I would calm down.

I hurried down the street and raced up the stairs to my apartment. I couldn't find my key in my purse, so I reached over the door where I left the spare. There was nothing there. I stood on my tiptoes and felt around, sure that I had just missed it, but the ledge was empty.

"Shit!" I pounded on the door, angry that I had locked myself out, but the force of my fist pushed the door in. I knew I wasn't that strong. Someone was in my apartment. I slowly pushed the door open and let the light of the hallway fill the apartment. There was a man sitting at my table, and only one man I knew that would break into my apartment. He was here to take me. I shouldn't have come back here.

I spun to run out the door, but my heel slipped, making me crash into the doorframe. I took one step out of the apartment before a hand clamped over my mouth and I was hauled back inside. I screamed behind his hand and struggled my hardest to get away, but he was stronger. There was no way I was going down without a fight. Using all my strength, I stomped my spiked heel down on his foot. His grip loosened and I spun out of his arms and threw my weight behind my fist, hitting him in the face.

"Fuck! Shyla, stop."

I had been just about to send my knee up into his stomach when I recognized the voice. I instantly flicked on the light switch to see Sniper leaning over slightly, favoring his right foot. I was still breathing heavily and now I was shaking even harder than I had been before. I pulled back and slammed my fist one more time into his face, making him stumble back a step as he gripped his nose.

"Fuck, why did you hit me? You already know it's me."

I shook out my hand, feeling the pain shoot through my knuckles. Maybe it hadn't been such a good idea to punch him again. "Because, asshole, you broke into my apartment and waited for me in the dark. Who does that?" I shrieked.

"Who leaves a fucking key above the door frame? Don't you have any sense of security? You're practically inviting people into your apartment!"

"I've never had any problems."

"Until tonight! Believe me, you wouldn't have made it five steps down the hall. An attacker would have dragged you back inside and no one in this shitty building would have helped you."

"Why are you even here? I've met you a few times and now you think you can come to my apartment and help yourself inside?"

"Fuck, I don't know. I guess I came to make sure that you were okay after the game tonight."

"How did you know it was tonight?"

He walked over to my fridge and pulled out ice, stuffing it into some paper towels. He snatched my right wrist, the hand I had been cradling against my stomach, and pulled it toward him. I hissed in pain when he set the cold ice on my knuckles.

"Where'd you learn to punch like that?"

"Would you believe me if I said Tae-bo?"

"The Billy Blanks videos?"

I laughed slightly. I knew it sounded ridiculous, but I loved those workouts. "Don't judge. He does an excellent job teaching self-defense moves."

"I wouldn't say excellent. That couldn't have taught you how to hit someone without practicing on an actual person."

I shrugged. "Maybe I go around punching assholes that break into my apartment."

"Just one problem, you don't even have a tv, so how are you doing those videos?"

HIs question immediately killed the banter we had going. I pushed away from him and went to sit on my couch. I was tired and starting to crash from everything that had happened. I couldn't take anything else tonight. Sniper sauntered over to me and stood with his arms crossed, his eyes boring into my mind. The man wasn't going to stop.

"Can we not do this right now? I just want to go to sleep."

"Why are you wearing Jeremy's clothes?"

"How do you know that I am?"

He jerked his head toward my shirt. I looked at it and saw some kind of insignia with SEAL Team written under it.

"So, what happened that you needed to wear another man's clothes home?"

"He was just being nice."

"You have your own clothes that you wear to the club. Which means that either something happened to your clothes or you were getting dressed and out of there in a hurry. So, what the fuck happened?"

I stood, anger washing over me as this man continued to throw his way too intuitive questions at me. I didn't need to tell him jack shit. "It's none of your goddamn business what happened. I didn't ask you to come here and check on me. I don't even know why you bothered. I'm just a stripper, so why drive over here to check and see what happened?"

He didn't say anything, so I walked toward my bedroom. "Lock the door on your way out."

I felt the air shift around me just before he spun me around and shoved me up against the wall outside my bedroom. His body was flush against mine and his lips were just inches from mine. "I don't fucking know why I'm here. You would think that I would just walk away, but for some reason I can't."

"Don't come here and try to be some good guy that's gonna save me," I breathed heavily. Tonight had fucked with me and I really shouldn't want him, but dammit, I wanted him to erase the touch of that prick.

"Did anyone fuck you?" His voice was low and deadly and his face showed murder.

"I told you it's none of your business," I snapped.

"Did anyone fuck you?" he shouted.

I tried to push him away, but the man was like a hulk. He didn't budge even an inch. "No, I didn't fuck anyone. I-"

His lips crashed against mine before I could finish my sentence. I gave a half-hearted attempt to shove him away, but quickly melted into his kiss, wrapping my arms around his neck and running my fingers through his hair. My body was on fire and every kiss seemed to wipe away another memory from tonight. He shoved my sweatpants down and I quickly stepped out of them. Just moments later, he hoisted me in the air with his hands on my ass and shoved my thong to the side right before he thrust up into me.

Wrapping my legs around his waist, I thudded my head back against the wall, enjoying every time he pushed himself further inside me. But it wasn't enough for me. I needed more. I pushed off the wall and dug my heels into his ass for support. I started bouncing on his dick, taking over and giving myself what I needed.

I stared at him unapologetically. I didn't want to be pushed around by another man. This was my decision and I was going to fuck the way I wanted. He groaned the harder I bounced and then tripped on his jeans that were still around his ankles. His arms wrapped around me as we crashed to the ground, but I didn't give him a chance to recover. I planted my feet on either side of him and rode him until I could feel myself tighten around him.

His hands slid under my shirt and cupped my breasts, tweaking my nipples until I was squeezing his dick hard. He lifted his hips and thrust up in me hard and fast just a few times before groaning and coming inside me. His fingers dug into my hips as he held me in place.

"Fuck, Shyla. You fuck like you dance."

And just like that, I felt like a bucket of ice water had been poured over my head, killing the heat between us. I stood and walked away, treating him just like he had treated me the last time he was in my apartment.

I couldn't tell what pissed me off more, the fact that I had been more concerned about fucking him than about my daughter, or that his comment reminded me that none of this was real. He was just someone that liked to watch me dance and fuck me. This would never be more and I couldn't trust him, so why was I wasting my time with a man when I should be writing down what I heard tonight and trying to figure out if anything could relate to my daughter?

"Lock the door on your way out."

I got into the shower and pushed Sniper from my mind. He was a good resource for getting information from my boss, but he was way too intuitive. He would figure things out sooner or later and there was no telling where his loyalties would fall.

*Chapter Seven*

# SNIPER

I knocked on Cap's office door. I had to get this shit with Chief straightened out fast. For all I knew, he had already talked to Cap and made a deal.

"Come in."

I walked in, giving Cap a chin lift as I walked over and sat down in the chair across from him. Cap eyed me speculatively. I had bruises all over my face and my nose looked like it had been busted up. It didn't take a genius to figure out that I had been in a fight, but I wasn't about to admit to Cap that I had been beat up by a girl.

"You want to talk about it?" he asked, jerking head toward my face.

"Not even a little."

"So, if you don't want to talk about why your face has been rearranged, why are you here?"

"I need to talk to you about something." Cap nodded and set down his pen, realizing that I had something important to say. "I went to see my old Master Chief from my Navy days. He owns a strip club in Pittsburgh now and he asked me to come by the other day. He wants to hire us for a security detail."

"That's fine. Have him give me a call."

I hesitated. I didn't want to be suspicious of a man that I had served with, but I had to think about the men I worked with now. I couldn't put them in danger for someone that was dirty.

"I don't think it's a good idea. He wants us to make sure a shipment arrives safely, but when I asked him what he was transporting, he wouldn't tell me."

"So, you're thinking he's doing something illegal."

"I don't want to, but it's pretty standard to know what exactly you're protecting. I just don't get a good feeling about this."

"What kind of man is he?"

"I haven't seen him in years, but I always thought highly of him when we served together."

Cap thought on it a moment. The thing was, we always took it seriously when one of us was uneasy about a job. We all had been in this field long enough to know when something wasn't right.

"If he calls, I'll ask him to come in and meet with me. But it's probably nothing as bad as you're thinking, but we'll err on the side of caution."

"I'd like to be in on that meeting."

"That's fine with me, but if he asks you to leave the room, I can't do anything about that."

I stood, knowing our conversation was over. There was nothing more I could do right now and I had a job to get back to.

"Chance, I need your team in the conference room in a half hour."

"Will do, Cap."

I called the guys and told them to meet me upstairs in fifteen minutes and headed for my locker to get some shit I needed. When I headed back upstairs, Jackson and Gabe were already waiting for me in the conference room.

"Holy fuck, what happened to your face?" Jackson asked when I walked into the conference room. He sat up and instantly looked like he was ready to go to war.

"I don't want to talk about it," I grumbled.

I was still pissed that Shyla wouldn't tell me what had happened last night, but I had to admit, she had a great swing.

"It was a woman," Gabe grinned. "What'd you do? I hope you didn't compare her to the stripper. Women don't really like that."

"I don't have to compare her. It was the stripper."

"What?" Jackson practically fell over in his chair. He had just put his feet on the table when I let that piece of information slip. "Did you learn nothing from your marriage?"

"Yes, I learned that I don't want to be married."

"So you fucked a stripper? Man, your dick is gonna fall off before you ever get the chance to find another girl to marry."

Leave it to Gabe to become the romancer in the bunch of us. Ever since he fell for Cazzo's sister, everything was about love and marriage. I'd already had that and it was not something I wanted to repeat.

"I'm not getting married," I said irritatedly. "Which is why a stripper is a great solution."

"Because you'll die of a deadly illness that you contracted before you ever find a girl that'll try to tie you down?" Jackson asked.

"Because she's hot as fuck and she knows how to move her body. We both know it'll never go anywhere. In fact, I should have been doing this all along. There have been way too many women that have tried to get my phone number after a quick fuck."

"Sure," Gabe snorted. "We'll just start going around to strip clubs and find loose women that don't have any STDs and don't mind being fucked as long as they don't expect anything in return."

"I'd get on board with that," Jackson admitted.

"I'm not going out looking for strippers. I already have one. There's a spark between us that makes the sex unbelievable and I already know when she gets off work, so dropping in is fairly easy. And, I can get up and leave right after sex. It's one of the things I love about her."

"Wait," Gabe said, shaking his head in confusion. "Let me get this straight. You have a regular woman that you go see. There's great chemistry, you know her work schedule, and you're finding things you love about her." He looked over at Jackson with a raised eyebrow. "Sounds to me like he's found himself a relationship."

"It's not a fucking relationship. We fuck and that's it."

"Hey, I'm not judging, man. When I fell for Isa, it happened so fast, I didn't know what hit me."

"I'm not falling for her. I went to see her because I knew that she had some shitty job last night."

"And you wanted to make sure she was okay," Jackson said sweetly as he batted his eyelashes and held his hands together under his chin. The bastard. I couldn't wait to give him shit over Raegan.

"Look, she got herself into some shitty job for extra money and I told her not to fucking do it. I was just checking on her!"

"That's so sweet," Gabe chuckled. "He doesn't even realize he likes her. He's checking up on her and making sure she's okay. Next thing you know, he's gonna be checking out her place to make sure it's safe."

I looked away, not wanting them to see the flush of heat crawling up my face. Too damn late. These guys were like attack dogs. They just wouldn't let shit go until they tore every last scrap of information from you.

"You already checked out her place?" Jackson laughed hysterically, but he was no better.

"At least I didn't move a woman home with me and keep her *and* her parents for the last two years."

Jackson's laughter immediately stopped and he glared at me. "I'm not keeping them," he growled. "I'm making sure they're safe."

"Which you could have done at a safe house," I shot back. "We've been through this before."

"So, what did she say when you started playing *The Stripper and The Security Stud*? Does she have a pole in her place? Does she dance for you? Maybe she makes you dance for her."

I glared at Gabe. Playacting was his thing. I didn't need something to entertain me to get off. "I was already there when she got home. That's how I got the black eye."

"She didn't like that, huh? Shocker," Gabe snorted.

"She didn't know it was me. I was sitting in the dark, waiting for her, and she thought I was someone else. The woman has some skills."

Gabe turned to Jackson, tapping his finger on his lip. "Jackson, what's that thing they call when you let yourself into someone else's place when they're not home?"

"Breaking and entering."

"I didn't break in. She had a fucking key on the top of her door frame."

Gabe groaned and plopped down in a chair. "Are you fucking serious? It's amazing that she hasn't been raped and murdered yet."

"That's what I was saying," I agreed. "Who puts a fucking key over a door? That's like setting a potted plant outside the door and hiding a key under it."

"I take it your lesson to her didn't go exactly as planned," Jackson smirked.

"After she stabbed her fucking heel into my foot, she punched me in the face. Then, when she realized it was me, she punched me again. And you know what really chaps my ass? She says she learned it all from Tae-Bo."

"I love that dude," Gabe said, wide-eyed and dreamy. "He has the most impressive muscles and his ass is really toned." Jackson and I stared at Gabe curiously. "What? You know I'm not gay, but I'm man enough to admit when another man has a great body."

"You've never said I have a great ass." Jackson crossed his arms over his chest, trying his best to appear insulted. Gabe carried on as if Jackson hadn't said anything.

"Look, all I'm saying is that you should be happy it's Billy Blanks and not Richard Simmons. Somehow, I don't think *Sweatin' To The Oldies* would have helped her in a situation like that."

"Dance fighting is becoming very popular," Jackson said.

"It's not the dance fighting you have to worry about. Those red and white short shorts and that curly hair that Richard always had are what would really scare people away."

"You seem to know a lot about him," I side-eyed Gabe. "Is there something you want to share with us?"

He shrugged lightly. "My mom might have done it when I was a kid."

"And did you dance with her?" I stifled my laughter, trying not to imagine Gabe as a kid, dancing along with Richard Simmons.

"Hey, don't judge. Those were some great songs and the dancing was really catchy."

"Hang on," Jackson said, fiddling with his phone. Suddenly, the screen on the wall showed a life-sized version of Richard Simmons. "Show us your moves, Gabe."

"Fine," he said, walking toward the center of the room, puffing out his chest as if to show us that he was completely comfortable and confident in doing this. "But you assholes have to do it with me. You're gonna like it."

"There's no fucking way I'm doing that." I crossed my arms and leaned back against the wall.

"I'm in!" Jackson jumped up and stood next to Gabe.

"Not all exercises are suitable for everyone and may result in injury," I read from the disclaimer on the tv. "What the fuck is he doing that could result in injury?"

"Damn, look at the way he moves. Take off that sweater!" Jackson yelled.

They were shaking from side to side and doing some crazy chopping thing with their arms. All these other women, and some men, were on the dance floor with him. It was so weird. Who would actually do this?

"What's with those socks?"

"You have to admit," Gabe said as he danced along. "He has great calves."

"He has his socks rolled like a little girl," I said in astonishment. "He looks like a fucking monkey, swinging his arms like that. Oh, fuck. Are they swimming?"

"This is just the warm-up. Just wait for the next song. You're gonna love it," Gabe grinned.

"He's snapping," I rolled my eyes. "I'm sure that would have helped Shyla last night. Someone attacks and she snaps at them. Any intruder would have backed down right away with that move."

Gabe and Jackson sizzled along with Richard and the gang, hissing through their teeth. This was embarrassing to watch.

"Did he just say rump bends? Please tell me I did not just see that!"

"Seriously, man. Just chill out and do it with us. I swear, you'll feel better than you ever have. It really loosens you up and the songs just make you feel so happy and light."

I couldn't believe how Gabe was talking about this video, but I had to admit, even Jackson looked like he was having a good time. I even found myself tapping my foot along to the music. I pushed off the wall and very discreetly started dancing behind Jackson and Gabe. I found myself shaking my shoulders and dancing along to *It's My Party and I'll Cry If I Want To*. I actually found that it did a great job stretching out my muscles and my heart rate was up. Maybe there was something to this.

"You know, we should really get some shorts to wear when we do this," Jackson suggested.

"I'm not wearing any short, striped shorts. I draw the line at that."

"Fuck, I think we should get them just for fun," Gabe grinned.

"Oh, and I want you Peggy Sue," Jackson sang.

"Hey, this is the best part," Gabe said, smacking Jackson on the arm. "It's time to check your heart rate."

They put their fingers to their necks and stomped in place along with Richard. When he asked if everyone was alright, they hollered along with the people on the tv.

"Goodness gracious, great balls of fire!"

Our arms were flailing in the air along with the music in a fast rhythm. I was even singing along to the music at this point. They had really chosen some good music to dance to. We were doing the twist and throwing our hands up in the air as we rocked our bodies.

Then we were doing *The Pony* along to *Wipeout,* but the best was when they played *He's a Rebel*. When we turned to the side and started stomping in place, I noticed Cap, Sinner, Cazzo, Lola, Chris, and Ice standing in the doorway watching us. I stopped for a minute, breathing hard from all the dancing, but then I figured I'd already made an ass of myself and I wanted to finish.

"Fuck it." I turned back with the guys and finished the dance and went into the last song with *Personality*.

"I'm not holding your fucking hand," Cap snapped at Sinner. I glanced over my shoulder and saw Sinner and Ice had joined us and Sinner was trying to pull Cap in also.

"But they're doing it on the tv," Sinner griped. "It's part of the exercise."

"I don't give a fuck," Cap said. "Hold Chris's hand if you need to hold onto someone."

Cazzo finally joined in after I waved him over a few times. There were a lot of eye rolls, but after a few minutes, he was awkwardly moving along with the rest of us. Chris was videotaping it all on his phone.

"Do you think we could get Knight to work this into our routine?" Ice asked.

"If not, I know a good strip club you could use," Lola smirked next to Cap.

"Maybe we could get matching outfits like Richard," Gabe grinned. "Man, I love this."

"Feel the burn," Jackson said as we stretched out on the floor. "Damn, I think this is the most flexible I've ever been."

"You know, I think this will be really good for my joints," Cazzo said. "I've been really stiff lately."

"Old age catching up?" Ice asked.

"Shut it. You're just as old, asshole."

When the music ended, we all grinned at each other. Sure, it was a little weird, but it had felt good.

"Uh, I know I'm the new guy, but is this something you normally do?" Rocco said from the doorway. "I feel like this is weirder than walking in on Gabe in a thong."

## Chapter Eight

# MORGAN

*She'd make a fine example of our product.*

Thinking of what Evil Eyes had said at the party made a shiver run down my spine. They were into sex trafficking. That had to be it. I couldn't wrap my head around how Jeremy could be involved in something like that. He had defended me in that room. It just didn't make any sense. I wanted to confront him about it, but what would happen to me? Would I end up being trafficked also? I couldn't let that happen. I had to get my little girl back, and as much as I wanted to help the women that were being sold, my daughter had to come first.

The next few nights in the club were a little more difficult for me. I tried to act like I normally did, but every time a man came close to me, I got all skittish, thinking that one of them was going to try to grope me. Sniper had done a great job of getting the memories of that poker game out of my head that night, but now that he wasn't here, I could still feel those harsh fingers against my breast and smell the alcohol that had wafted in front of my face. I wasn't sure that I could do that again and I had to decide what I was going to tell Jeremy. It wouldn't be too long before there was another poker night and if I decided not to do it, Jeremy would have to find a new girl.

I made my trip to the library to look into my daughter's case and check out the status of other missing children cases. There was nothing new to note, so I slung my bag over my shoulder and started the long trek home. As I walked down the sidewalk, past the alleys between the old buildings, I started to get the feeling that I was being followed. I tried to discreetely look over my shoulder, but I was afraid that I was going to give myself away. I started walking a little faster and when I saw the drugstore up ahead on the corner, I decided to slip inside and try to lose my tail, or at the very least, figure out who was following me.

I stepped inside the store and quickly moved behind a floor display. A man walked past the shop, glancing inside as he moved past the door. He didn't stop though, which made me wonder if I had made it all up in my head. I waited for a few minutes, but when I couldn't see him outside, I left the shop and looked both ways as I stepped back onto the sidewalk. No one was around.

I hadn't made it two steps past the alley when a hand shot out and grabbed me by the hair, dragging me into the alley as a hand clamped over my mouth. I tried to scream, but it didn't do any good. It had to be a man, based on his scent and his strength. My first thought was that it was Evil Eyes from the poker game, but this was a different scent. It was more like smoke and sex than cigars and brandy.

I was shoved up against the wall, my back to my attacker, when his hoarse voice whispered in my ear.

"You need to stop digging. Unless you want to end up like everyone else, you'll walk away."

I couldn't say anything or even nod. The hand was wrapped so tight around my mouth that I actually thought I would lose oxygen and pass out if he didn't back up soon. I was starting to hyperventilate and knew it wouldn't be long before I completely lost it.

"Do you fucking understand me?"

I jerked my head as best I could, trying to signal that I understood. Then next instant, the wall was coming toward my face and then I felt the brick crush my skull. Everything blurred as I fell to the ground in a heap. I could feel the trickle of blood down my face and I vaguely heard running before I passed out.

I wasn't sure how long I had been out, but the light wasn't as bright any more. I lifted my hand and looked at the watch on my wrist. I was going to be late for work if I didn't get my ass off the ground. I realized belatedly that I was laying in some kind of puddle and would have to take a shower so that I didn't smell for work.

I got to my feet, a little irritated that I wasn't that far inside the alley and no one had stopped to check on me. We weren't in an isolated part of town, but I had noticed over the past few months that people over here didn't really get involved in other people's business. A woman lying on the ground was just that and really none of their business.

I swiped at my face, feeling the dried blood, and headed home. I kept checking over my shoulder as I practically ran back to my apartment. I kept getting dizzy, but pushed on, not wanting to be outside any longer than I had to after what happened. I had only a few minutes to take a shower and get ready for work before I had to leave. Washing my hair was out of the question since I didn't have time to dry it.

The lump on my head was easily covered by my hair and the gash wasn't nearly as bad as I first thought it was. I could cover it up without anyone noticing in the dark of the club. Luckily, when I got to work, most of the girls were already out on the floor or on stage, so I had the dressing room to myself to pull my shit together before I went on. I couldn't afford to lose this job, but I also had to be careful now. Someone knew that I was digging and it was only a matter of time before I ended up dead.

*Chapter Nine*

# SNIPER

I headed up to Cap's office for our meeting with Chief. He had called Cap the other day and had reluctantly agreed to a meeting. That only confirmed my suspicions. Still, we had to hear him out first. I saw him waiting in the lobby and put on a smile so that he didn't realize I was wary of working with him.

"Sniper, my man." Chief held out his hand and slapped me on the back as he shook my hand. "It's good to see you again."

"And without the naked women walking around."

"I don't think I ever heard you complain about naked women when we were overseas."

"I was young and stupid. Now I just want someone that's not going to send me to the doctor for medication for my dick. Come on, let's go see my boss."

He nodded and followed me to Cap's office. After knocking, Cap waved us in and walked around his desk to meet Chief.

"Sebastian Reed. Chance told me he used to serve with you."

Cap was direct and to the point. No fucking around with him. He didn't waste time shaking hands and getting to know someone. This was business and that left no room for error.

"Jeremy Wick. I was Master Chief in the Navy, serving with the same SEAL team as Sniper."

Cap nodded, his eyes reading every line of Chief's face. "He said that you need some help on a job. Why don't we get right down to it."

Cap walked back around his desk and sat down. Chief and I sat down across from Cap and my stomach turned as I thought about what it would implicate if Chief still wouldn't talk to us.

"So, what's the job?"

"I have some merchandise coming in that I need guarded during transport and handoff. It's a very sensitive situation and I need the best."

"What's the merchandise?"

Chief chuckled. "Sniper told me that you would want to know that little detail."

"I don't do business unless I know exactly what I'm dealing with. It's all access or nothing."

"Yeah, I figured you'd say that." He shifted uncomfortably, like what he was about to say was something he couldn't even fathom saying out loud, which fucking scared me. "Can we close the door?"

Cap hit the button for the door to close and the locks to engage. "The room is secure now. The cameras are off and there's no audio."

That wasn't entirely true. Whenever the locks were engaged for a meeting, there was always someone on the other end of the feed watching just in case. Especially when someone outside of Reed Security was in the room. So, even though the cameras weren't recording, there was still someone aware of what was going on.

"I started a strip club after I got out of the military. I actually asked Sniper to go in on it with me, but he wanted more action. A few years ago, one of the alphabet agencies approached me. They wanted me to help them out with a case they'd been working on. After going over all the information with them, I agreed to help in any way I could."

"Why did they go to you? Surely there are more strip clubs in Pittsburgh."

"It was because of my Navy record. They did a hell of an investigation into me before they ever approached me. I was given a handler and together, we've been working this case and trying to gather enough evidence on the big players."

"That's all very vague and still doesn't tell me what I need to know," Cap said.

"It's a sex trafficking ring. From the research I've done, your company has been involved in a couple takedowns. That's why I contacted Sniper. I need men that are familiar with this type of situation and can stay calm under pressure. I can't go to just anyone for this. There's a lot of shit that's pretty ugly, stuff that I don't want to do, but I have to in order to gain intel. My job is to get to the men that are running this, and I'm close to getting the evidence I need, but things are starting to get dicey and I need someone to have my back."

"You want us to help you traffic women so that you can get the big fish," Cap said in disgust.

"I know, it's a sick part of the job. Every time it happens, I'm so close to saying 'screw it' and killing all the assholes that are there. But I have to remember the bigger picture. If I were to start taking out those men, they'd ghost and all the hard work we've put in would be for nothing. This is the biggest ring in the country and if we don't take them down, soon we won't be able to. These men have connections that are almost impossible to ever come in contact with, but *I have*. I've been acting as the middle man. The club is one of the places we get our women from, and I know that sucks, but most of those women are drug addicts or whores."

"Are you fucking kidding me?" I said angrily, shoving my chair back as I stood. "You're selling women and it's okay because they've made bad life choices? What about Shyla? Is that why you had her in that room? You wanted to show off your merchandise to those sick fucks? Were you just planning on letting her get carted off to be some sex slave all in the name of justice?"

"I never had any intention of letting her get wrapped up in this. Remember, she asked for more money. I didn't recruit her to do this."

"You also didn't tell her what she was getting involved in, asshole."

"Let's calm down."

Cap directed that at me, but I could read on his face that he wasn't through with this yet. Cap was always strategizing, always trying to find the benefit for him and his company. Right now, he was trying to figure out how to help take down this ring and keep Shyla safe. I didn't have to tell him about her. He could tell by my outburst that she wasn't just some random woman to me. Even if I wasn't sure exactly what that was yet.

"What exactly are you looking for from us?"

Chief directed his gaze back at Cap and got back to business. "I have a guy coming to the club in a couple of weeks. He's one of the higher ups in this ring. From what I gather, he checks out the merchandise and contacts buyers when he's found women that meet their specific needs. Blonde, brunette, curvy, skinny, long hair, pouty lips, innocent or sex kitten; the list goes on and on. When he's found someone that meets the criteria for a buyer, if that woman comes from my club, he has a pickup scheduled. This time is different though. He's not looking for specific women. He's after one large shipment of women."

"Do you know why?" Cap asked. "What's changed that he's not cherry picking women anymore?"

"I'm not one hundred percent sure, but I get the feeling that he's moving locations. I don't know if he suspects that the government is onto him or if he just doesn't stay in one place too long. Either way, he's never taken this many women at once."

"Do you have files on the previous women?" I asked.

"No, I have a list of who they are, but these are just strippers. There's nothing special about these women. He doesn't ever ask about their personal lives or worry about who would come after him. It's all about tits and ass with him."

"So, he's taking a large shipment of women this time. Is he coming to check out the women beforehand?" Cap asked.

Chief shook his head. "I think that's why he's coming in two weeks. He hasn't said specifically, but he's told me he needs all the women at the club that night. I'm guessing he's going to pick out the women he thinks will bring him the most money. None of them are going to specific buyers this time. I have no idea where they'll be going, actually."

"So, you're going to allow him to walk into your club and take his pick of the women he wants?" I asked incredulously. "Don't you care about your employees at all?"

"I get it," he said angrily. "I don't like this either, but if he's really moving out, it'll take a long time for someone to track down the next location he moves on to. Once he's gone, my part in this is over. I can't follow wherever he goes because it would tip him off. We can't afford for this guy to go underground."

"We have access to some of the best technology," Cap said. "I have a great team that could gather intel on him when he comes. Why not try to take him out when this guy comes and use him to get information on the guy running all this?"

"It won't matter. My handler said that they've already tried that. The guy was taken out before they could get anything out of him. He was replaced within a day. Whoever's running this doesn't have any loyalty to his employees. All the guys that were at my poker game have an important role in this operation, but they're just a group in a long list I've dealt with over the past three years."

Cap looked to me and I shook my head slightly. I couldn't go along with this. To let him sell women off was insane.

"Jeremy, step outside while I discuss this with Chance."

Chief looked mad that he was being kicked out, but stood anyway and left when Cap unlocked the door.

"Cap, I know what they're trying to do here, but there's no fucking way I can help him sell off women to be sex slaves."

"I agree. I don't believe in sacrificing for the bigger picture either. Those women are innocent, but now we know what's going on and we can't just walk away."

"What are you suggesting?"

"I think we should tell Chief we'll help him out, but have our own plans in place. If he can't get the information he needs by the time they come back to do the pickup, we snatch this middle man and save the girls. Fuck Chief and his operation. If this guy really is moving on, we don't need to give him any more women to sell."

I nodded in approval. It was the best we could do at the moment. Cap hit the button for his receptionist.

"Colleen, please send Mr. Wick back in."

"Right away, sir."

The door opened and Chief walked back in, taking his seat beside me.

"Alright, we're on board. I'll need to know the minute you do about when the girls will be taken. I'd also like to set up a crew the night he comes in to check out the girls. Any information we can gather on him beforehand will help us the night of the sale. I won't take any risks with my men because we aren't fully prepared."

"Fine." He stood and held out his hand to Cap. "I'll be in touch."

Cap shook his head and Chief gave me a nod before walking out the door.

*Chapter Ten*

# MORGAN

I stepped into the dressing room and was a little surprised at how many girls were working tonight. There had to be at least five girls more than needed. I shoved my stuff in my locker and ignored the other girls. I didn't really get along with any of them, not that I had tried much. When I first started here, I had started asking around about the club and things that happened here. The girls seemed nice enough, but the minute I mentioned Wes, they all clammed up and refused to speak to me anymore.

"Shyla."

I turned to see Jeremy standing in the doorway of the club. It was odd for him to come down to the dressing room. He normally called us to the office if he needed something. I glanced around, wondering if the other girls knew something I didn't, as I made my way over to him.

"Hey," I said uncertainly when I got to the door.

"I have some special guests today. That's why so many people are here today. I'm going to have some of the ladies in the private rooms and then I have a few extra girls on the floor tonight."

"Okay, where do you want me?"

He looked uncomfortable, which made me nervous. "I've had a special request for you."

My stomach churned. The only person I could think of that would request me and made him nervous was that asshole from the poker game. There was no way I could be alone with him again.

"It's a man that met you at the club one night a few weeks ago. He wants a private dance."

"Is it the guy-"

"No," he said quickly. "His name is Wes."

I didn't hear the rest of what he said. So many things were rushing through my head that I completely spaced out. Wes was the man that was coming into town that Jeremy had been so worked up over. Maybe he was just an important client, but I had to look into anyone that garnered that much attention around here. I took a deep breath and steeled myself, tuning back into Jeremy.

"So, are you okay with this?"

"Of course," I said quickly, completely ignoring the fact that I hadn't heard all he said. I would do whatever this guy wanted if it could get me even a scrap of information.

"Good. He's waiting for you in room three. He's paid for the whole night with you."

I nodded quickly, but Jeremy still seemed a little hesitant to have me do this.

"What? Is something wrong?"

"This guy seems a little infatuated with you. Are you sure you want to do this? I can't put anyone outside your room with this special group coming in."

"I'm sure. Don't worry about me. I can handle this."

"Okay. Finish getting ready and head over there."

He left and I hurried along getting ready. I made myself look like a bombshell tonight. If I wanted to secure my chances of him helping me, I needed to look my best. Men didn't come here for innocent women. They came here to have their fantasies fulfilled.

A hand grabbed me right when I was about to enter the room. It was Storm. He dragged me down the hallway and shoved me into a small room.

"What the fuck do you think you're doing?" he spat.

"There's a client that's paying for my entertainment."

"Yeah, for the fucking night. What the hell are you thinking agreeing to that?"

"This is my job. What do you expect me to do?"

"This isn't like you. You don't like to go in those rooms. You never have, so why are you doing it now?"

"Because he might be able to help me."

"With what? If you're horny, find someone else. This guy is bad news. Whenever he comes to the club, someone always ends up leaving here in tears."

"I have to do this. I have to take that risk."

"Why? Just tell me. You know I'll do anything to help you."

I knew I could trust Storm and it wouldn't be a bad idea to let someone else know in case something happened to me. If this went bad, maybe he would take over the search for my daughter. I decided to trust him.

"This isn't my normal job."

"No shit," he said irritatedly.

"I came to work here because my daughter went missing a little over six months ago. The investigation pretty much stopped after three months when the trail went dead. I took things into my own hands and it led me here, to a man named The Broker. I haven't even come close to finding him, but Jeremy made it sound like the guy in room three is a powerful man. He might be able to help me."

Storm had a look of pity on his face, but still didn't look convinced that I should do this.

"Don't try and stop me. I need to do this."

He let out a harsh breath and clenched his jaw. "What are you going to do if he rapes you or worse, you end up dead? Who's going to help your daughter then?"

He had a point. I took a deep breath and did something I hadn't done in three months. I said her name out loud. "Her name is Payton. Payton James. My name is Morgan."

He shook his head and his eyes went wild. "No. Hell fucking no. I am not getting involved in this shit. I did my time and-"

"Please," I begged with tears in my eyes. "Please, I have to get my daughter back. I can't let her down. If something happens to me, you have to continue looking for her. There was a guy in here a few times. He's friends with Jeremy. He works for a security company." I searched my memory for the name of the company. He had only said it in passing. "It's something with an R. I looked it up once and it's located about an hour west of here. Reed, that's it! Reed Security. The guy that was here had the name Sniper. I never caught his real name, but you can go to him and see if he'll help you."

"Sweet pea, this is bullshit. Don't do this."

"I have to. If it was your daughter, would you walk away because it was dangerous?"

His shoulders sagged and he nodded slightly. "Fine, but if you think things are going south, get out of there. Scream and fight until someone hears you. Understand?"

"Yes. Thank you."

I went back to the room and took a deep breath before I entered. There he was, sitting in a chair, lounging with a bottle of scotch. He was just as handsome and evil looking as I remembered. But his name wasn't Wes. This was Steven.

"Do I have the wrong room? I'm looking for Wes."

"That's me."

"But...you told me your name was Steven."

An evil smirk spread across his face. "Glad you remembered me, sweetheart."

The endearment was anything but sweet. The way he said it make me shiver uncontrollably. His dark hair fell in a slight wave over his forehead and those dark eyes trailed over my body in appreciation. When he stood, I could see the muscles under his dress shirt rippling, stretching the fabric on his upper arms. He walked toward me like a lion stalking his prey. For a moment, my heart stuttered to a stop, but then I remembered my objective for tonight.

"I'm sorry, but I'm supposed to meet Wes. I'm sure one of the other girls will be in to see you."

"I am Wes." One side of his mouth quirked up.

"Then why did you tell me your name was Steven?"

"My name is Wes, but I don't like to hand it out. Too many people hear my name and assume that I have something they want. They assume they can swindle me, but they don't realize that I know every-thing and everyone. If anyone fucks with me, I fuck them back twice as hard until there's no one left in their family. There aren't many people that fuck with me and live to tell about it. If you want to be one of those people, I suggest you don't piss me off."

I gulped and jerked my head up and down. "Of course."

He grabbed me by the elbow and pulled me over to the chair. He pulled me onto his lap as he sat down and rested his hands on my hips. "Dance for me." I tried to stand, but he gripped me tighter. "Right where you are."

I did my best to move my body as I straddled his lap. There wasn't much room for movement and I had never actually given a lap dance before. I was pretty sure that staying like this wasn't all I was supposed to do though. I swirled my hips and ran my hands under my hair, lifting it off my neck, shoving my breasts in his face.

I shivered in revulsion when I felt his tongue lick my nipple. It didn't matter how handsome he was. Everything about this man made me feel sick to my stomach, but I had to remember that this man might be able to help me.

"So, why did you come looking for me?"

I stopped moving and he glared at me. I continued moving, but he held my hips down right against him. His dick grew against my body.

"I don't know what you're talking about."

"I could see it in your eyes the minute you walked through the door. There's something you need and you think I can give it to you."

I couldn't lie to him. If he had seen my intentions as soon as I walked into the room, I wouldn't be able to fib my way through this.

"I'm looking for my daughter. She disappeared six months ago."

His mouth moved down the center of my chest and back up, licking and nipping at my flesh. "And you thought I could find her?"

"I thought you might have information. I heard that you're a powerful man and powerful men have a lot of resources at their disposal."

"And what are you going to give me in return?"

His fingers moved down to my thong, slipping inside. I forced myself to stay relaxed, even though I hated the feel of his fingers on me again.

"Whatever you want."

"Anything?" I nodded. There was no question that I would do anything to get my little girl back. "I want you to come home with me."

He studied my face, trying to see if I was serious. I kissed him hard, slipping my tongue inside his mouth, kissing him with the desperation I felt. When I pulled back, I slipped off his lap.

"Let me grab my stuff."

He smirked at me as he adjusted himself. I slipped out the door and shuddered, thinking about what I would have to do to get information from him. I reminded myself the entire walk to the dressing room that this was for Payton, and again on the way back to the room.

"Ready?"

He walked with a certain air that made him both sexy and dangerous. For me, it was more dangerous. He took my hand and lead me to the front door. Storm glared at Wes and grabbed my arm as I passed. I shook my head slightly at him, but those damn brown eyes of his pleaded with me not to go. When Wes came back to my side and raised an eyebrow at Storm, he finally released me. I could feel Storm's eyes on me the whole way to the vehicle that was waiting for Wes.

I sank into the backseat of the black Audi and felt ridiculously out of place. The leather against my skin felt completely wrong since I had just been in a thong and grinding against Wes in the back room of a strip club. Wes climbed in the other side and gave the driver an address that I didn't recognize. Pittsburgh was big so that wasn't unusual.

"Where are we going?"

Wes smiled as he stared at me. He hit a button and the privacy window went up, blocking the driver from us. "I'm taking you to find your daughter. But in order to do that, I need you to do something."

"Anything," I said eagerly.

He took something out of his pocket and then opened his hand. Laying in his palm was a pill of some kind. "What is that?"

"The price for finding your daughter."

My heart thudded in my chest. It was one thing to go with him and sleep with him, knowing exactly what I was doing, but to take a pill that I knew nothing about was completely different. Anything could happen and I'd heard enough stories about women being drugged to know that this wasn't a good idea.

"I guess you don't want to get your daughter back."

He closed his palm and started to put it away. "I'll take it!"

His head slowly turned to mine as he held his hand back out in front of me. I slowly took the pill, swallowing the thick coat of saliva in my throat. He handed me a bottle of water and I uncapped it and swallowed the pill. I had done it and there was no turning back now. I just had to hope that I got what I needed out of this.

We drove in silence for a while and slowly, the scenery outside my window started to swirl and blur as we drove. My head felt heavy and I was no longer able to hold my eyes open. I felt my head flop back against the seat and then Wes unbuckle me and lay me down on the seat. His fingers brushed across my face, but I was too out of it to protest. This was my choice and I had to live with it now.

## Chapter Eleven

# SNIPER

"What's up, Cap?" I asked as I walked into his office just minutes after he called me upstairs.

He waved me over and set the phone back on the base after he hit the speakerphone button. "I've got Chance here. Go ahead."

"Are you Sniper?"

My eyes flashed up to Cap's. The only person that ever called me Sniper was Chief. Was he in trouble? Had something happened already? "Yeah, this is Sniper, but I don't go by that anymore. My name is Chance."

"My name is Storm. I work at the strip club that Shyla works for. I'm one of the bouncers."

"Okay," I said hesitantly. That made sense. She had only ever heard me referred to as Sniper.

"She told me to call you if something happened to her."

My heart rate sped up as I prepared for whatever he had to say. It wasn't like we were a couple or anything, but I had this strange need to keep her safe after hearing why she was working in that strip club to begin with.

"What happened?"

"Nothing yet. But she was supposed to be in one of the back rooms with a man named Wes tonight. He's what everyone calls The Broker. Not many people know him by the name Wes because not many people actually meet him. He deals in information all over the city. If you need to know anything about weapons, drugs, trafficking, basically any illegal activity you can think of, he's your man."

"What does this have to do with Shyla?"

"Right before she went in the room, she told me that her daughter had disappeared six months ago and she was told to get in contact with The Broker. He was in the club a little over a month ago, but Shyla didn't know who he was. He showed up again tonight and she just left with him. She's trying to get information and I have a feeling she'll stop at nothing to get what she needs. This man is dangerous. He's not someone that she should be taking on by herself."

"Do you know where they were going? What vehicle they got in? Anything like that?"

"I saw them get in a black Audi, but I couldn't get the plates." He sighed into the phone. "She said you could help her and I'm really hoping that's true because I have a feeling she won't be coming back after tonight."

"I can head to the club now."

"I'm sure you can access the cameras, but there won't be much else."

"I'm about an hour away. I'll get there as soon as I can."

"One more thing, her name is Morgan James and her daughter is Payton. You might want to have someone look into the police reports and see if you can get anything from there."

"Thanks. I'll see you soon."

Cap hit the end button and flopped back in his seat. "This bullshit never ends. Grab your team and I'll have Alec's team join you. Becky can get started on the police files and we'll let you know more when we've gone over everything."

I nodded and rushed out the door, telling the teams what was going on. We were on our way fifteen minutes later and I prayed that didn't make us fifteen minutes too late.

"What's the deal with this woman?" Jackson asked. "One minute, she's a stripper and the next she's got a missing kid?"

"Fuck if I know," I grumbled. I was staring out the window, my elbow resting on the door. We were headed to Pittsburgh to try and find Shyla, or Morgan, before she became a missing person. I was still trying to piece everything together myself. "I didn't know much about her in the first place. I'm not sure what's real and what's not."

"Who was the guy that called?" Gabe asked.

"A bouncer at the club. I think I met him before. If it's the same guy, he seemed to really look after the girls. My guess is he's ex-military."

"So, all we have to go on are security cameras outside the club?" Jackson asked. "Do we at least know who this Wes guy is?"

"He's called The Broker. He's who you go to when you want information. The problem is, nobody really knows him as Wes. He doesn't let anyone know him and if they do, they don't live very long."

"So how did this bouncer know who he was?" Gabe asked.

"I'm guessing that working in a club like that, people don't really see him. He probably knows more about what goes on in that city than people would think."

When my phone vibrated in my pocket, I pulled it out to see Cap calling.

"Yeah," I said, putting it on speakerphone for Gabe and Jackson to hear.

"We've got the police report for the abduction of Payton James. We don't have a lot to go on yet. We're still researching, but here are the basics of the case. Payton was with a babysitter at the park when she was snatched from the playground by two men in a white van."

"How cliche," Jackson said.

"The babysitter was there with six other kids and she couldn't do anything without leaving the other kids at risk. She called 911 immediately, but she didn't get any plates. That was the last lead they really had. The police had offered a reward for any information, but nothing panned out. After three months, the police basically told Morgan that they would keep looking, but there was nothing more they could do without any leads."

"That's it? There's nothing more to the file?"

"That's pretty much all there was."

"How did Morgan get as far as she did if the police said there was nothing to go on?"

"She must have asked the right people. What we need is to talk to Morgan and find out who pointed her in the direction of The Broker."

"We're almost to the club. I'll talk with Chief and see if he can shed any light on Morgan before we head out to look for her. If this guy was in his club, maybe he knew him or where he might hang out."

"Keep me updated."

Cap hung up and I tossed my phone on the dash. That was absolutely no help whatsoever.

"How much do you trust Chief?" Gabe asked.

"In the Navy? He was a great man. I would have followed him into any battle. I don't know him anymore. People change over time. I would hope that he's still the same man, but I can't say that for sure. When I found out that he was basically letting women get sold off so he could gain intel, that was really fucking hard to hear. I never thought Chief would do something like that."

"Just remember that he was trying to bring down some serious players."

I glanced at Jackson and wondered if he would be willing to sacrifice Raegan if it meant bringing down weapons dealers. He seemed to understand what I was thinking.

"I'm not saying it's right or it's what I would do. But he thought he was doing the right thing. He thought the end would justify the means. That doesn't mean he's not the same man you knew."

We pulled into the club at a little past eleven. The place was packed and if not for the call I got from Storm, I never would have thought anything shady was going down. He must have looked up my profile on the Reed Security website because he approached me immediately.

"Chance, I'm Storm."

I shook his hand with a nod. "This is Gabe and that's Jackson. I have another team parked out front waiting for instructions. Where's Chief?"

"In his office."

"Does he know about Morgan leaving?"

"I told him that she left, but he didn't seem to think it was a big deal. The last time Wes was in, Morgan let him do some shit to her. I guess the boss thinks that they have something going on."

I stiffened at his comment. "What do you mean s*he let him do shit to her?*"

"It was pretty fucked up. She was on stage dancing and he walked right up to the stage and started touching her. Finger fucked her right in front of everyone."

"And she let him?" I exploded.

"I don't think she wanted to. When I asked her why she didn't stop him, she said she needed him or something. Now I know why."

"So she left here thinking he was going to lead her to her daughter."

I scoffed, irritated that there wasn't a whole lot I could do right now. I had nothing to go on and she fucking voluntarily went with him.

"I need to see Chief. He has to know something that can help me find her."

"I'll take you back there."

He signaled someone over and then led us down a few dimly lit hallways until we reached a closed door. He knocked twice and then opened the door to Chief's office. I probably could have found it on my own, but the last time I was here, the lights were on and there wasn't all this smoky shit in the air.

"Sniper, glad you could bring some friends for the show. I've been waiting for-"

"I'm not here for the show," I cut in. "I'm here to find Morgan."

He stuffed his hands in his pockets, shooting me a confused look. "Morgan? I don't have anyone named Morgan working for me."

"Shyla?"

He laughed lightly, but sobered when he saw I was serious. "Shyla's name is Morgan? Why are you looking for her?"

"I think she's in danger. You said yourself that you thought she was running from something."

He sank down in his chair, shaking his head slightly. "Yeah, but I don't understand why she would be in danger now. I mean, I figured she was hiding from an ex or something. Storm's always looking out for her, so I let it slide. She's never brought any trouble here." He shook his head and looked back up at me. "Why do you think she's in danger?"

"She left tonight with a man named Wes."

"Yeah. I know him. He comes into the club at least once a month. He does business with a lot of people in Pittsburgh."

"He's The Broker." I watched his reaction, waiting to see if he was hiding shit from me. But the shock on his face couldn't be faked.

"Wes is The Broker? Weston Hughes? No. No fucking way. That guy is-" He shook his head as he stared off in the distance, like he was going over things in his head. He dropped his head in his hands, swearing loudly. "I've been so focused on dealing with the players in the trafficking ring that I let him walk right through the fucking door!" He slammed his hand down on his desk and got up, stalking around the room in anger. "No wonder we couldn't get to the guy in charge. The Broker is said to be a fucking expert at gaining intel. He fucking played me."

"Did he ever sit in on any meetings with you?"

"No, but he wouldn't have to. All he needed were the guys behind the scenes. The Broker knows everyone and everything, which means he knew all along that I was working to bring down that ring. He's probably been using it against me."

"Didn't you suspect him?" Gabe asked.

"He checks out. Wes runs one of the biggest corporations in the city. He has offices all over the country. I figured he came in here to blow off some steam when he was in town."

Okay, I did not know that. I must have been living under a tree for the last ten years because I had no fucking idea who Weston Hughes was. But as I looked at Gabe and Jackson, it seemed I wasn't alone.

"Storm told me that no one knows the two identities are the same person."

"Nobody actually sees The Broker. If they do, it's because they're looking down the barrel of a gun. He keeps his identity a secret. If Storm knows and he's not dead, it's because he's smart enough to not let on that he knows they're the same man."

"So, we go after Wes. We take him out and make him talk."

"You don't get it," Chief laughed. "The guy has an army of men around him at all times. Even when he comes in here, there are men hidden discreetly around the club, inside and out. You wouldn't even be able to take him out with a sniper rifle. Doesn't matter that you're the best shot I've ever seen, his security team is the best."

"Then we spread the word who he really is. There's gotta be somebody that he's pissed off enough to want revenge. If enough people are after him-"

"It won't make a fucking difference. When I say this guy has the best security, it's because he can buy anyone. He's one of the wealthiest men in the country, and that's only what shows on his fucking taxes. As The Broker, when he gets paid, there's no wire transfer. The guy doesn't let anything get tracked. His guys scan every fucking bill before a transaction is complete. He trusts no one. And if you can't pay the fee, you pay in favors. He has so many people in his back pocket that you couldn't go to anyone without suspecting they would turn on you."

This was giving me a fucking migraine. "Fine, fuck Wes. I don't give a shit about him right now. I need to find Morgan. Obviously she's gotten herself into deep shit and she doesn't even know it."

"I don't know what I can do for you. He could literally take her anywhere. The sky's the limit with this guy. I can give you video feed, but that's not gonna get you very far."

"We'll take it. I'll send the feed to Reed Security. Maybe they can give me something."

An hour later, I was on the phone with Becky as she told us our starting point. She didn't have anything definitive yet, but we had to get moving if we had any hopes of finding her.

"Take Storm with you. The man is ex-military and Shyla trusts him," Chief told me as he walked us out. Storm nodded his agreement and followed Gabe out to the SUV. Normally, I wouldn't take along someone I didn't know, but the man had called us and warned us about Morgan.

"Thanks for your help."

"I'll call you if I hear anything. Good luck finding her."

I shook his hand and headed for the SUV, calling Becky back to see what she had.

"Okay, I'm tracking him by the cameras around the city and Rob is looking into any properties he owns nearby or has any association with."

Jackson followed her directions, zigzagging around the city and heading out of Pittsburgh.

"Becky, what the fuck is going on? That was one long ass way to get from point A to point B."

"I'm looking into it. I don't have any camera feed from here, so just stay on that route for now."

"Chance, it's Rob." His voice boomed over the speakerphone. Rob was another tech specialist, but we normally went right through Becky. He was more of a field techie as of late. He went along on jobs that required a bit more skill. "Wes has a property outside the city. The road you're on leads right to it, but it's fucking huge. There are outbuildings and homes. It's like the place is its own little city."

"Why would he drive all around the city like that when we could have gotten on 376 and headed right to the same fucking road?"

"He was going where the cameras were," Becky's voice cut in. "I'm looking at the traffic cams and the city is currently installing new systems around the city. There are a few lines that aren't up and running yet. He specifically took you on a route that we could follow."

"He wants us to know where he's taking her. But why?"

"A trap?" Gabe suggested. "Maybe he wants something on Reed Security."

"How would he even know we would come after her?" I asked.

"A distraction," Storm said. "He wants us away from the club."

"If he knows that Chief's working to take down the ring, then he probably knows that we were planning to be here for the next pickup." I pulled out my phone to call Chief. "He's gonna take the girls tonight while we're distracted."

I pressed the phone to my ear, waiting for Chief to pick up. "Did you find Morgan?" he asked almost frantically.

"We might have a location, but Chief, we think the girls are gonna be taken tonight. He must know we're involved and he's leading us away from you."

"Shit. I sent Storm with you. I'm shorthanded tonight as it is."

"Send all the girls home," I said urgently.

"I think it's too late for that," he said grimly. "I gotta go."

"Chief!" But he didn't answer. "Fuck!" I dialed Cap and didn't even give him a chance to say anything before I was relaying what had just happened at the club.

"We can't get there in time," Cap said. "They'll be long gone before we can get anyone over there. I'll call the police, but if Wes has planned it this well, he'll be gone within five minutes of being at the club. I'll see if Becky can hack into the feed at the club."

"We'll let you know when we find something." Hanging up, I tossed my phone onto the dash. "This is fucked up. Storm, how did you know Wes was The Broker?"

"A friend crossed paths with The Broker a few months back. He found out The Broker's identity and knew he was gonna get killed. He told me if he disappeared that he had his family hidden and asked me to take care of them."

"Was he killed?" Jackson asked.

"The very same night," he said quietly as he gazed out the window.

## Chapter Twelve

# MORGAN

The pounding in my head made it nearly impossible to open my eyes. I felt dizzy and nauseous, but worse than that, every single part of my body hurt. I slowly blinked my eyes open, trying to figure out where I was. It was completely black with only a small hoop of light creeping in from above me. It seemed so far away. I blinked several times, trying to figure out where I could be.

I took stock of my body, trying to figure out why I felt so horrible. My stomach was cramping and combined with my headache, it was making me nauseous. I gripped my stomach, feeling flesh under my fingers. Oh, God. I was naked. Slowly, I began to feel the dirt digging into my butt and my back scraping against something rough. I tried to remember if I had been naked before I got here, but my brain was so muddled that trying to think just made my head hurt more. I was leaning against some kind of cold wall. I pressed my hand to it, trying to push myself up, but stumbled back to my knees when my legs gave out. If I couldn't stand, I could at least try and crawl around to see if I could find some clues.

My fingers ran over the cool wall, feeling grooves that seemed to be in a rectangular pattern. They felt like bricks. There was something slimy on the wall and felt like algae between my fingers. I followed the wall, crawling on my knees and realized that I was going in a circle. It didn't take long to circle back to where I thought I had started. I could have been wrong because I felt so disoriented, but it felt like I was in a small space.

The ground was moist beneath me and as I ran my hands over it, I felt puddles. That reminded me of how thirsty I was, but I didn't want to try and drink anything in here, not knowing exactly where I was. I sat down on my butt and stretched my legs, trying to judge exactly how big the space was. I was able to stretch them all the way, but there were only a few more inches before my feet hit the other side. So, the space was probably a little over three feet wide.

I leaned back against the wall, exhausted from just that little bit of movement. I closed my eyes and tried to remember anything from what happened. I remembered being in the room with Wes and he had said something about helping me. But what happened after that? My mind was too fuzzy right now to keep thinking.

I desperately wanted to go back to sleep and let my head rest against the wall, but it kept lulling to one side, giving me a crick in my neck. Against my better judgement, I laid down on the ground, hiking my knees up to my chest so I would fit in the small space and rested my head on my arm. I stared up at the light up above and wondered if I would ever be in the light again.

Slowly, the light started growing brighter. It must be morning. I blinked lazily up above, trying to count the minutes as they went by, but kept dozing off. My muscles were cramping from laying in the fetal position, so I sat up again and stretched my legs out. My stomach growled in hunger and my throat was so dry that I felt like I was choking.

Getting to my knees, I felt around the ground for the puddles I had felt earlier. When I came to one, I bent down and started slurping what water I could. It was disgusting, tasting like dirt and something else that had me gagging. But once I felt the liquid in my throat, I pushed past the disgust and got every last drop I could out of the puddle. As it was, I knew that wasn't nearly enough. It had been not even one gulp from a glass of water.

"Help." My pathetic attempt to call out for someone was barely audible to my own ears. I didn't even have any saliva in my mouth to try and swallow. The little bit that I had drunk wasn't enough to give me the strength in my voice that I needed.

Feeling around on the ground, I found two more puddles. I would have to save them for later. I had no idea how long I would be down here or if I would ever get out. I looked up at the bright light above and got to my feet again, feeling along the wall. There were small notches between the bricks, but I wasn't sure if it was enough for me to grip onto.

I slipped off my heels and pressed the back of my right foot against the wall and then fell forward, catching myself on the other side of the wall with my hands. Holding myself as straight as I could, I slowly placed the back of my left foot a little higher on the wall. One hand at a time, I moved a little higher and then started to move my right foot. My arms shook from the strain and my stomach was aching from trying to hold myself up. I moved myself slowly, but by the time I was about five feet off the ground, my arms gave out and I fell back to the ground.

Pain shot through my side and arm because of how I landed and my already cold body felt scraped and bruised. I laid on the ground, panting and staring up at the hole that was just too far out of reach. Feeling around the ground again, I found another puddle and drank up what I could. I rested for a little while, regaining what little strength I had. Who was I kidding? I had nothing left and if I laid here too long, there was no way I was getting up again. I placed my right foot awkwardly against the wall, along with my right hand. This time, I was going to try and move straight up. I didn't even make it as high as the time before, and when I fell this time, I cut the bottom of my foot on a sharp piece of brick.

I couldn't see how bad it was, but I could feel the blood trickling out of the bottom of my foot. I winced as I ran a finger over the cut, feeling how long it was. It was a pretty decent sized gash and unfortunately, I didn't have anything to clean it with.

I started crying, but there were only faint tears leaking from my eyes. There was no way I was getting out of here on my own. Even if I had an endless supply of water, I just wasn't strong enough to do this on my own. Forgetting the fact that I was probably laying in mud, I sank down on my back and stared up at the light above. It was sunny out and probably a lot warmer up there than it was down here.

My mind drifted to Payton and all the wonderful memories of her. I remembered the day I found out I was pregnant. It had been the best and most depressing day of my life.


*I walked into my apartment that I shared with Matt. I hadn't been feeling well the last week, but I chalked it up to the flu. But when I was only getting sick in the morning, I knew it wasn't the flu and bought a pregnancy test. Now I just had to tell Matt and hope that he was okay with this.*

*We had been together for nearly five years, so I couldn't see him being too upset over this. We hadn't really talked about kids, but marriage had come up several times over the years. I found Matt in the bedroom, drying off after just getting out of the shower. He turned and smiled at me, his wet hair flopping slightly over his forehead and giving him a devil may care look.*

*"Hey, I got us reservations at that new restaurant you wanted to try. We have to leave in an hour."*

*"Sure," I said half-heartedly. "Um, can I talk to you about something first?"*

*"Yeah, babe."*

*"You know I haven't been feeling well this week."*

*"Yeah. Are you still feeling sick? Should I cancel?"*

*"No, it's not that. Um..." I fidgeted as I tried to gain the nerve to say this. I was worried, but I wasn't sure why. Maybe deep down I thought he wouldn't want us anymore, which was ridiculous. We loved each other. "I picked up a pregnancy test. I realized today that I've only felt sick in the morning."*

*He just stared at me, his face unreadable and completely devoid of emotion. "Well, we have reservations, so like I said, you should get ready."*

*I jerked back in shock. I didn't understand why he wanted to avoid this. Wasn't it better to find out and figure out what we were going to do? "Matt, I just told you I might be pregnant and you want me to go get ready for dinner?"*

*"What does it matter? Is it really that big of a deal if we wait until we've had a nice night?"*

*"I don't think I can sit through dinner knowing that I might be pregnant and a test is waiting at home for me."*

*"Fine," he huffed. "If you want to take the test, take the fucking test."*

*I backed away, shocked at his harsh tone. This didn't seem at all like the Matt I knew. He was always lighthearted and funny, but this man in front of me was cold and unfeeling. He wasn't even considering what this was doing to me. I turned and walked into the bathroom, slamming the door behind me. With shaky hands, I tore open the package and squatted on the toilet. The wait was excruciatingly slow. It didn't even take the full three minutes for the lines to show that I was pregnant.*

*Opening the door, I walked over to where Matt was sitting on the bed and sat down next to him. "It's positive."*

*He scoffed and rested his elbows on his knees. "This is fucking perfect. All I wanted was a nice night out with you and now I have to think about you having a fucking baby."*

*How had I never seen this side of him before? Had I been totally blinded by love? "Do you not want this baby?"*

*"We never fucking talked about it. We're not even engaged. Did you forget your pills or did you do this on purpose to try and get me to marry you?"*

*"Excuse me? Do you really think I'm the type of person that would do something like that?"*

*"I don't know, Morgan. You've always gone on and on about needing a family of your own and how your parents never gave you what you really needed. Now you're pregnant."*

*"Wait, so you think that because I want a family, I tried to trap you with a baby? Why the hell would I do that? We've talked about marriage before. It's not like I didn't think we would get married one day."*

*"No, Morgan. You talked about getting married. I listened to what you had to say, but I never actually fucking asked you about marrying me one day."*

*My brain was struggling to understand what was happening. I thought back over our conversations and remembered him saying, 'if we were ever married...' or something similar. It hadn't just been wishful thinking on my part.*

*"Whether you want to marry me or not, we still have a baby on the way. If you don't want to marry me, fine. We can stay together like we are now. We'd have to eventually get a bigger apartment, but we can make this work."*

*"I don't want to stick around and live with a baby day in and day out. I never fucking wanted this life."*

*"You...you don't want the baby?"*

*"I'll tell you what I want. I want a woman that doesn't expect me to change my life for her. I want a woman that I can just enjoy life with. I want to be able to go out on a Friday night and not worry about whether or not you're going to nag me about going out with friends instead of hanging out like an old man with a kid that I never wanted."*

*I stared at the ground, tears pricking my eyes. In a matter of five minutes, my life with Matt had gone from perfectly wonderful to complete shit. He didn't want the baby and in turn, didn't want me. This was the end of the road for us. I would never forgive myself if I didn't keep this baby and he wouldn't stick around just to be with us, to be a good guy.*

*"I need a little time to find a new place," I said quietly.*

*"Don't worry. I'll find someplace else to stay. I never wanted to live here to begin with, but you insisted we didn't waste money on a nicer place." He scoffed at me. "Now you can keep the shit hole and raise your kid here."*

*He walked out the door, not even sparing me a backwards glance. I slumped down on the bed and ran my hand across my flat tummy. I couldn't be upset about him walking out. If he didn't want this baby, life with him would be miserable. But life with this baby would be the best thing that ever happened to me and I wasn't going to let his lack of responsibility ruin this wonderful thing for me. It was going to be me and the baby for the rest of our lives and that was something to be happy about.*

I drifted off to sleep at some point. My mind wasn't really able to focus on time anymore. I couldn't remember the last time I had eaten or drank anything. It had to be going on twenty-four hours now.

Desperate for something to eat and drink, I got to my knees and felt around for my heels. If there was water sitting in puddles, maybe it was coming up from below. I dug with the heel of my shoe, but soon realized that with the ground so soft, it was better if I used my hands. I dug until my arms were sore and I couldn't feel my fingers anymore. There was no water, but I did feel bugs crawling around me.

Leaning back against the wall, I tried to work up the courage to do what I needed to do to survive. I wasn't sure that I would be able to stomach it, but I was running out of options. Maybe if I was able to do it this one time, the next time wouldn't be so bad.

Finally, after much debating, I scrambled back to the hole I dug and felt around until something wiggled over my hand. I snatched the worm in my hand and brought it to my mouth before I could think twice about it. I shoved the worm in my mouth and swallowed, but when it started wiggling in my throat, I gagged and threw up what little I had in my stomach. I couldn't do it.

With the stench of vomit in the hole with me now, I shoved the dirt back in the hole to cover it up and patted the dirt down until it was firmly in place. There was no more water. Unless it rained, I was going to die of dehydration.

When the light started to dim, I realized that an entire day had gone by. As night crept in, the chill of the bricks started to seep into my bones, or maybe it had already been there and I just hadn't realized it before. I snuggled into myself as best I could, but the ground below me was too cold to really get warm. Once it was completely dark and I couldn't see any light from above, I started to wonder if I would ever see my daughter again. Obviously, Wes hadn't held true to his promise and I had been played. What I couldn't figure out was why. He hadn't tried to sleep with me as far as I knew, and that could only mean that I had been onto something and he wanted to get rid of me.

I stared up through the dark hole and swore I saw a few stars sparkling in the sky above. A single tear slipped down my cheek as I realized that I had failed. I would never see my little girl again because no one was coming for me. Nobody knew where I was. Hell, I didn't even have a fucking clue, but I knew that I was in some kind of hole and there was no way out. It was so dark down here that no one would be able to see me even in the light of day.

Still, I had told Storm about my daughter. I had to hope that he would go after her. He was such a good guy and I knew he didn't really belong at that strip club. He was wasting time, trying to get over his demons. But he was a warrior, a savior. He could do what I couldn't for my little girl.

"Mommy." Payton's sweet voice echoed around me. I opened my eyes and saw her staring down at me, giggling like she always did when she woke me up in the morning. "Mommy, don't go to sleep. You have to stay awake."

"I'm so tired," I said weakly.

"Mommy, I need you." Her little face was scrunched up, her lips quivering. She kept looking behind her like she was watching for someone. I wanted to reach out and take her hand and tell her everything would be okay, but I just couldn't.

"I love you, baby. Someone will find you."

It was just barely a croak, not even audible to my own ears.

"Stay awake, Mommy. Come on, don't give up."

"I don't want to. I'm just so tired."

The whole world was spinning around me. There was light above me again and it rippled like I was looking through water. The light was coming closer and closer. This was my time. I was fading faster now and I knew it wouldn't be long. My eyelids were heavy and I could barely force them open.

The next time I did, I was surrounded by bright light. There were fields of green grass all around me and trees that were swaying in the breeze. The sun was hot on my face and the smell of flowers drifted past me. Heaven was a beautiful place. There were people all around me, welcoming me with open arms.

My face stung as something hit me and then my mouth was forced open and cool liquid was rushing down my throat. I choked, spitting up the water that I so desperately craved. It didn't make sense. If I was in heaven, why did I still feel so worn out? Why was my throat so dry and my eyes so heavy?

My mouth was opened again and this time, the water trickled down my throat slowly and I swallowed greedily. It stung when I swallowed and I could feel the liquid sloshing around in my stomach. As good as it felt going down my throat, it made me feel sick to my stomach. Something cool was brushed over my face and I sighed in contentment.

"Come on, Morgan. Open your eyes."

The voice was familiar, but it wasn't my daughter. Where was she?

She had just been here. I forced my eyes open and glanced around for her, but she wasn't there. Men stood around me and one knelt beside me with a bottle of water. I felt him shift under me, like he was cradling my head in his lap. The concern on his face was frightening. He looked at me like I was about to die. But wasn't I already dead?

I couldn't place him through the fog in my brain. I stared at him for a moment, but I was just too tired. I let my eyes slip closed and ignored the nagging shake from the man next to me. I felt my body being jostled and my head dropped back, dangling like it wasn't really attached to my body.

I was dizzy and the movement was making me feel sick. Opening my eyes made it worse. The sky seemed to be bouncing up and down and I wanted to shout at the men to stop jumping around me. My eyes fell on my hand that hung limply in the air, almost like it was floating next to me. A giggle bubbled up in my throat as I thought about saying hi to my hand as it floated along beside me.

Doors slammed around me and then the man was leaning over me again. I could see his lips moving, but it sounded like his voice was slowed down, like on an old tape. I frowned and tried to read his lips, but then he turned away from me, facing what I now saw was the front seat of a vehicle. There was a prick of something in my arm and then I went to sleep.

*Chapter Thirteen*

# SNIPER

I laid Morgan down on the bed in the master suite of the safe house. We had gone to the safe house just outside of Pittsburgh because it was closest and we had to get Morgan some treatment. Storm had started an IV line in the SUV and Rocco was on his way with Derek and Hunter. I wasn't a medic and only knew basic things to keep people alive until help arrived. We were doing that, but she needed Rocco's help.

We decided against going to the hospital on the off chance that Wes didn't know that we had found her. We had searched all over that property, but it took all day and all night to cover all the ground. We almost gave up and decided to look elsewhere when Alec found the old stone well buried in the tall grass. Shining a flashlight down didn't show much, but I had a nagging feeling that she was down there. The guys lowered me down with a pulley system we rigged and there she was, lying at the bottom of the well. She looked like she was already dead, but then she started mumbling about Payton.

I'd never been so scared in all my life. It wasn't like Morgan and I were an item, but I had fucked this woman. She was basically naked and helpless when we found her and she was so filthy that it would probably take a good hour of scrubbing in the shower to get her clean.

Even now, she laid in the bed, still dirty because we needed to get her hydrated first. The shower would come when Rocco had a chance to look her over.

While I waited for him to show, I took a warm rag and started washing her face. Dirt was caked everywhere, including inside her ears. If I didn't know better, I would think that she had been down in that well for weeks instead of two days. Her lips were cracked and bleeding and her cheeks looked sunken in. I supposed that could have been from exhaustion or even the dirt playing tricks on my mind.

"Hey," Rocco said from the doorway. "How's she doing?"

"She hasn't woken up since we put her in the SUV."

"That's pretty normal. She's gonna be out of it for a while. Why don't you give me some space and I'll check her over."

I didn't like the idea of leaving her alone, but Rocco was a good guy and he would take care of her. I decided that I would make a trip over to the club and let Chief know what had happened. But when I pulled into the club's parking lot, there didn't seem to be anyone there. The door was open, so I walked in and headed for his office. He appeared to be packing up.

"Chief, what's going on?"

He looked up at me and then looked around the office. "I'm packing up."

"I see that, but why?"

"They moved in last night," he said, staring down at his desk. "The operation is over. I failed."

"You weren't able to get them out?"

"They took all the girls. I didn't stand a chance. One minute, they were dancing on the stage and working the crowd, and the next, they were being hustled out the back door. I couldn't do shit. I had no backup."

He scoffed as he plopped down in his chair, pulling a bottle out of his desk drawer along with two shot glasses. Pouring himself a shot, he tossed it back and then offered some to me.

"When you called, I didn't want to believe you, that this could be a setup. I was so fucking close to getting the guy in charge. I could feel it and it just slipped through my fingers."

"So, what now?"

"They shut me down, pending an investigation."

"Are you fucking serious? They asked you for help, and now they're going to investigate you?"

"Sniper, you know as well as I do that anyone can be turned for the right price. I get why they're doing it."

"What are you gonna do now?"

"I don't know. Travel? Take a fucking vacation?" As if just remembering why I had been in town in the first place, he looked up at me. "Did you get her back?"

"Yeah. I'm not sure how she's doing yet. We have one of the team medics looking her over."

"Not that it's okay what she went through, but she's probably luckier than the girls that were here last night. Unless by some miracle the ring is tracked, those girls won't ever see home again."

I had been pissed before at him for allowing those women to be taken at all, but I could see now how badly he had wanted to stop the trafficking ring. He was doing everything he could and that was more than most people could say.

"Chief, don't blame yourself. You were trying. You know that assignments go sideways all the time. It sucks, but you did more for those women than most have. I'm sure the intel you gathered helped a lot."

"But it wasn't enough, was it? You know, in my entire military career, I never questioned a single assignment. Everything was for the greater good, to protect those that couldn't protect themselves. I thought that's what I was doing here. I really thought we would come out on top. You would think I would know better by now that good people die and you can't save everyone. I just didn't think it would happen here at home."

I didn't know what to say. There were no comforting words when you realized that an assignment you were a part of hurt other people. The guilt tore you to pieces until there was nothing left to feel. I had never seen Chief so broken. Not even in our military days when we lost brothers in battle. That was a different situation though. They signed up for the danger. They knew there was a possibility they would be going home in a wooden box. These women were just trying to make a living for themselves. They hadn't asked to be sold into sex trafficking and have their bodies used as sick men's playthings. Being part of that was something you could never get over.

———————

I sat by her bed, cursing myself for being such an asshole. Every fucking word I said to her floated through my mind on replay. Why had I treated her so badly, like she was beneath me? We were all just trying to survive in this world and I didn't know jack shit about her, but I threw money at her like she was just a quick fuck that wasn't worth anything more than a hundred dollars. I had fucked her against a wall outside her apartment. In fact, the only time I had actually treated her like a person was when I thought she was working to help her niece get the treatments she needed, which had been a total lie.

If only I had asked more questions or tried to be a decent person to her. But I let my baggage from my ex-wife get in the way. I saw women as liars and manipulators. I knew that there were good women out there, I just didn't want to take the risk that I would run into someone that would use me the way she had.

To everyone else, I said that she hadn't been able to deal with my life. That being a military wife was just too much. I told them that if I had gotten out sooner, I might have been able to save my marriage. But deep down, I knew that she had been using me. She had already found someone new by the time I got home. Now she had two kids and was married to a man that gave her more than I ever could.

Morgan looked like a ghost with the deep purple circles under her eyes on a face that was way too pale. She looked so tiny lying in this huge bed, like she hadn't eaten in a month. It had really been about two days, but the elements had been cruel to her. Cuts and scrapes on her hands and feet showed her fight to get out of that well. Her fingers were stained with dirt and her nails were cracked so far down that it had to be painful. And then there were those lips. I hadn't realized how much I liked kissing her until I pulled her out of that well and saw them cracked and bleeding.

I couldn't imagine what she had gone through, all in the hopes of finding some piece of information that would help her find her daughter. I didn't want to think about her sitting at the bottom of the well, thinking she would die down there and no one would be able to save her daughter. I knew deep down that was her only thought. She had been dreaming or hallucinating when I got to her. She had been talking to her daughter, telling her she was too tired to fight.

She had to be the strongest woman I'd ever come across. To lose her daughter and fight so hard to get her back, taking on the scum of the earth to get to her. That was a woman that never gave up. I admired her, but more than that, I felt ashamed that I hadn't seen it in her from the start.

When she finally stirred, I jumped to my feet and gripped her hand tight, letting her know she wasn't alone. Her eyes slowly opened and she looked around in confusion, almost like she had been expecting to still be in that well. When her eyes found mine, confusion and skepticism lit her face.

"Where am I?" Her voice was scratchy, so I grabbed a bottle of water and held it to her lips. She drank greedily, but I pulled the bottle away so she didn't get sick.

"You're at a safe house. We found you at the bottom of a well a day ago."

Her eyes opened and closed sluggishly as she tried to come out of her sleepy state. "How did you know to look for me?"

"Storm called us as soon as you left with Wes."

She nodded slightly, her eyes still drooping in exhaustion.

"Are you hungry?"

"A little. I really have to pee."

"Uh," I rubbed my neck uncomfortably. "I'll need to get Rocco to help you out. We've had an IV in your arm and..." She stared at me, expecting me to continue my thought when I hoped that she would understand without me explaining. "He had to put in a catheter."

Her face turned bright red, so I excused myself to go find Rocco. The woman had been through enough. She didn't need embarrassment to add on top of all the other shit.

"Rocco, she's awake," I said as I approached him on the stairs. He must have been coming up to check on her anyway.

"How does she seem?"

"So far, okay. We didn't really talk a whole lot. She has to go to the bathroom."

"Right. I'll go take care of that. You might want to come with me so she feels more comfortable."

"I don't want to see you remove that." I looked at him like he was crazy. There was a reason I wasn't a medic and that was mostly because I didn't do well with bodily fluids and IVs. I wasn't even the one to give her the IV in the SUV. Everyone knew that I didn't do needles or anything to do with medical equipment. It just wasn't my thing. I didn't even want to see it.

"Chance, you've seen her naked multiple times. What's the big deal?"

"It's different. She has a tube where I most definitely don't want to see a tube. It's weird and gross."

"You served in the military," he said in astonishment. "You've seen men with limbs blown off and blood spurting from necks. Eyeballs hanging from their sockets and guts spilled across the desert, but you can't handle a fucking catheter?"

"Look, that's all very clinical. It's normal."

"No, it isn't, you fuckhead. A catheter in a body is normal. Seeing eyeballs hanging from someone's face is not."

"In my world, that's normal. I can deal with that shit, but this is all very medical and..." I sighed and my shoulders dropped. "I've seen her down there. Seeing a tube coming out of her is kind of like seeing her pussy being spread and a head coming out. It's not right. There's just some shit you can't unsee."

"So, if she was bleeding out, you would do everything you could to save her."

"I'd slap some gauze on her and hold it down, sure."

"But you can't stand in a room to make her feel better while I remove a catheter from her most intimate parts so that she doesn't freak the fuck out?"

I shrugged. It made sense to me, even if it didn't to him. He stared at me a moment and then smacked me upside the head.

"Get the fuck in that room and shut up. You don't have to fucking look."

I glared at him, but he just glared back and I knew I had lost that battle.

## Chapter Fourteen

# MORGAN

When Sniper came back in the room, he was joined by another man who looked like he snapped necks for a living. His arms were thick and his forearms veiny. He had broad shoulders that made him look like a football player and his pants did nothing to hide his tree trunk thighs. I wanted to back away just so that I didn't have to be near him.

Sniper came to stand by me, his eyes anywhere but on me. It made me nervous that he was acting so distant, like maybe he had bad news or something.

"Is everything okay?" I asked hesitantly, my eyes shooting between the new man and Sniper. The new guy grinned, his face taking on a playful look.

"Everything's fine. Your boy is just a little squeamish around medical equipment."

"Shut up, fucker," Sniper growled from my other side. I had the feeling that I was missing out on something, but I didn't really have the energy to think about it right now.

"I'm Rocco. I'm the team medic. We didn't want to take you to the hospital after we found you because of the circumstances. You're at a safe house and I've treated you for dehydration and I've cleaned up your cuts. You've got a pretty nasty gash on your foot, but that's about the worst of your injuries."

"Why do I feel so beat up?"

"That's just exhaustion. Your body basically went into survival mode and was sort of feeding on itself to provide you with nutrients. You just need some more rest and a few good meals."

"And a shower," I added. "I feel disgusting."

"You might want to wait on the shower just a little bit. I can guarantee when you stand up, your body isn't going to have the energy to keep you upright very long."

"I'll sit on the floor of the shower if it means I can get the stench off me."

He smiled and pulled out some gloves, snapping them into place. "Let's go ahead and remove the catheter so you can use the bathroom."

Glancing at Sniper, I could tell he was really uncomfortable, and despite my need to pee, I couldn't help but mess with him a little. I gave him my most earnest look and held out my hand. "Would you please watch him."

"Watch him what?"

I glanced at Rocco like I was nervous, my throat cracking as I spoke, which only helped my ruse. "You know. You've seen me down there. I would feel better knowing that you were watching what he was doing."

Sniper's eyes grew wide and his body tilted just the smallest bit. "Uh..." He looked to Rocco for support, but Rocco just raised an eyebrow at him, as if to ask if he was going to man up.

Sniper cleared his throat with a tight nod and walked toward the end of the bed. "Alright, let's..." He gestured toward my core as his eyes danced around the room. "You know. Let's do it."

"You need to hold her labia open while I remove the catheter," Rocco said to Sniper. He tossed a pair of gloves at him and watched as Sniper fumbled with pulling them on. He kept clearing his throat, like a nervous tick and then cracked his neck from side to side. I should have stopped him, but it was just too funny to watch. And I needed a good laugh after what I had just been through.

"Alright, Morgan. I want you to let your legs fall open and put your feet together." I did as he asked and then he lifted the sheet. I watched Sniper's face go pale as he took a hesitant step forward.

"So...I just..." He swallowed hard and swayed slightly. He gestured toward my core with a gloved finger. "You just want me to..." He gestured with both hands like he was parting the Red Sea.

"Jesus, would you just put your fucking hands on her. It's not that hard."

I bit back my laughter as he slowly approached and assessed the area up close. Licking his lips, he took a few deep, huffing breaths and leaned forward. His eyes rolled back in his head and Rocco pushed him to the side just before he would have collapsed on top of me. He flopped on the bed to the side of me and then rolled off the bed and hit the floor with a thunk.

I peered over the side of the bed at his prone figure on the floor. "Is he gonna be okay?"

"I don't see any blood. He'll be fine."

"I didn't realize he was that squeamish or I wouldn't have pushed him to do it."

"Are you really uncomfortable with me doing this?" Rocco asked in concern.

"Nope. I just wanted to see how he would react."

"You're kind of evil. I like it."

I smiled and relaxed as he pulled the catheter from my body. "Alright, you're good to go. Do you want some help getting to the bathroom?"

"No, I think I can make it." I stood slowly and glanced back at Sniper. "Should we move him or something?"

"Nah. He'll wake up. Eventually."

---

Rocco was right about the whole shower thing. I was standing for just two minutes when my legs shook so hard that I couldn't hold myself up anymore. I sank down to the floor of the shower and let the warm water soothe my tired legs. I was starving, but being clean was more important at the moment. I lifted my head to wash my face, but the water stung my cracked lips. I jerked away, covering my mouth as I groaned.

"Problems?" Sniper asked from outside the shower.

"I just got water on my lips. It stung."

"Do you need some help?"

"I should be asking you that. You're the one that passed out."

He leaned against the counter and crossed his arms over his chest. "Hey, I don't do needles or tubes or anything that even remotely looks like something medical."

"Somehow I don't buy that. I think if you had to you would."

I grabbed the washcloth that was hanging on the bar, but then realized that all the soap was higher up, as was the shampoo and conditioner. I sighed, resigned to the fact that I was going to have to stand. I started to push myself up, but the sheer curtain slid open.

"Just stay where you are. I'll help you out."

"I can do it. I just need you to grab the stuff and hand it down to me."

Did he listen? No. He stripped his clothes off and stepped into the tub with me. I swallowed and licked my lips when I saw his semi-hard cock jutting out. No matter how tired I was, the sight of his magnificent body in front of me was enough to make me want things that I shouldn't even be thinking about right now.

He smirked as he knelt down in front of me with the body wash and bottles of shampoo and conditioner. "Get a good look?"

I rolled my eyes. I knew I had been caught, but what did it matter? We'd already slept together. We both knew how good his body was. "Please, it's right in front of me and we both know that I liked it. There's no point in pretending I wasn't staring."

His smirk grew bigger as he took the washcloth from me and lathered it up with soap. He took my hand and gently started washing my fingers. I was a little taken aback by him washing me. I hadn't expected that level of caring. I stared at him like he was an enigma.

His eyes flicked up to mine and he shook his head slightly. "What? I can be a nice guy."

"But you're washing me," I said stupidly, as if he didn't realize what he was doing. "I can do it myself."

"I know you can," he said quietly. He continued to wash the same hand. My fingers were so caked in dirt that he had to really scrub to get it off. "I'm sorry I was such a jackass to you. I shouldn't have judged you so harshly."

"No, you shouldn't have. You know, those women are just trying to survive. They're not all saints or anything, but they all have their reasons for stripping."

He nodded and stopped washing my hand, his eyes locking on mine. "I realized that when Chief came to Reed Security and talked with my boss and me. There was a trafficking ring being run in the area. Chief was trying to help take them down."

I jerked back in surprise. "Wait, there were women being taken? For sex trafficking?"

"Yeah."

Something niggled in the back of my brain, but my brain was still sluggish from everything that had happened recently. I closed my eyes, trying to remember why that sounded familiar.

"That's what he meant," I said to myself when it finally dawned on me. "There was this guy at the poker game. He had really evil eyes and he was very...anyway, he pulled me into his lap and said something about me being a good example of the merchandise. I kind of figured that it was something along those lines, but hearing it confirmed is just disgusting."

Sniper was quiet, not saying or looking at me as he moved on to my other hand. I watched him, waiting for some reaction, but it was like he didn't want to look at me. "What is it?"

He didn't answer. He just kept rinsing the washcloth, pouring on more soap, and continued washing me. I wanted to ask him again, but I figured that he would either tell me when he was ready or I would pry it out of him later. He cleaned my foot up and inspected the cut on the bottom.

"It looks pretty good. Rocco did a good job cleaning it up."

"I would hope so. He's your medic."

He gave me a wry look and patted my foot. I pulled it back and slid my other foot over to him. After cleaning that foot, he rinsed the washcloth again and worked on my legs and then up my stomach. The rag slid over my skin, the soap bubbling up in a thick lather. I watched as his eyes heated as he moved up to my breasts and gently cleaned my nipples. The roughness of the rag against them had me moaning slightly under my breath. I did my best to keep him from hearing it, but the way his eyes darkened told me that I hadn't hidden it as well as I had hoped.

He stood and moved behind me, putting his legs on either side of my body. It was a tight fit, but he managed, snuggling his hard cock against my ass. He massaged the cloth into my neck and into my shoulders as he cleaned me. As he wiped the rag down my arms, he leaned in and kissed my neck. I tilted my head, allowing him better access. The rag was still running up and down my arm, but I wasn't sure at this point if he was even paying attention to what he was doing.

He switched arms and ran his tongue along the back of my neck, sending shivers down my spine. His tongue swiped at my ear, licking the inside of the shell and trailing behind my ear and back down the side of my neck. All I could do was feel. Every touch from him was like fire licking at my skin. His hands slid around to my breasts, slowly letting his fingers trail down the sides and underneath. He was teasing me, torturing me until my hands were gripping onto his legs and I was pushing back against him.

My body clenched when his hand slipped between my legs and he washed my most intimate area. Soon the cloth disappeared and his fingers were all that were on me, rubbing and then pushing inside me. His magnetic touch erased all thoughts of the disgusting men that had touched me there before. This was passionate, whereas the others had just seen me as a warm and wet fuck hole. Someone to use and easily discard.

In all honesty, I hadn't been with anyone since Matt. I had my daughter and until Sniper came along, no one else had even made me think about sex. I was instantly attracted to Sniper, but that was something I would never tell him.

He moved suddenly, his cock brushing against my back as he stood. He pulled me up from underneath my arms and spun me around, slamming his lips against mine. It hurt and when I tasted blood, I whimpered from the pain, but then he was licking and sucking away the pain and blood. It wasn't my lack of energy that had my knees wobbling. He pushed me back slightly, his arm waving around behind my back as he shut the water off. Then I was up and wrapped around his body as he carried me into the bedroom. I fisted his hair as I pulled him in closer to me. All I could think about was how he made me feel, and hell, I wanted to feel something other than despair over my missing daughter.

When he laid me down on the bed and slid between my legs, something more intimate, more electric flowed through our joined bodies. It was like we were finally coming together as more than just what we could provide each other. This was the connection I had been craving for years, for someone to hold and dream of the possibilities of more.

There were no barriers between us this time. I had a birth control shot and he finally trusted me at least a little. He didn't look away from my eyes once as he continued to pump inside me. Even when he lowered himself so our bodies were gliding against each other and he kissed me like I was the most precious thing in the world, his eyes were still laser focused on mine. When I shattered, he followed, pulling me to my side with his cock still resting inside me. I felt him soften and slowly slip out of me.

His fingers lightly traced my arm and his soft kisses to my forehead made me feel cherished. But then he tensed, almost like he had caught himself doing something he shouldn't have. I had to remind myself that we didn't really know each other. Everything we knew about each other was based on sex and lies. We probably should have cleared some of that up before jumping back into bed together.

I pushed up on my elbow and smiled at him to lighten the mood. "I'm Morgan James."

He stared at me in confusion and then grinned back. "Chance Hendrix. Nice to meet you."

I laughed lightly. "Chance is so much better than Sniper."

"No one really calls me that anymore. Just Chief. And I like Morgan a lot better than Shyla."

I grimaced at the name. "I never liked it either. That's why I chose it. I didn't want a name I liked to be associated with my profession."

His eyes sobered and his fingers pushed my wet hair back from my face. "My boss is looking into your daughter's disappearance. We'll do everything we can to find her."

"I was beginning to think that I would never find her," I said quietly, trying my best not to cry. I was tired of crying. If I let myself feel too much or think too much, I slipped into a depression that took days to pull myself out of.

"We will find her," Chance promised. "We will get your little girl back."

"Where do we even start though?"

"We'll go to Reed Security. Becky, our IT specialist, has been going over your daughter's case. She can look for anything that might have been happening around that time, anything suspicious. Cap will be going over the details to see if there's anything the police missed."

"Who's Cap?"

"He's my boss."

"I don't understand. Why would you all want to help me? You don't even know me."

"We became involved the minute Chief came to us about the trafficking ring."

"But those are two separate issues. I was only there because I was looking for my daughter and someone pointed me in that direction."

"And you don't think that's a little suspicious? That the same men that could know about your daughter or have some insight into the men that took her are also involved with abducting women?"

"I guess I hadn't thought about it that way. I mean, I knew it was a possibility that something similar had happened to her, but I hadn't considered that they could be the same people."

"We'll find out more later today. For now, you need to eat and drink more water. I'll go get you a tray."

He slid from the bed and I sat up also. I didn't want someone waiting on me hand and foot.

"Where do you think you're going?"

"I can go and-"

"No, you're not. You were extremely dehydrated and you need to take some time to rest until you have more energy. And you're not going to have more energy if you start walking around the house before you've even eaten."

"So, I'm just supposed to sit here?" I asked incredulously.

"Yeah, it's called relaxing."

"But I-"

"No," he said, holding up his hand. "If I catch you even trying to sneak around the house, I'll chain your ass to the bed."

I glared at him, but he just winked at me like he wanted me to try it. He didn't really seem like the kinky kind, but I supposed everyone had fantasies. He bent down and kissed me and then he was gone. I sank back down into the bed and closed my eyes. I might as well do as he said and relax.

*Chapter Fifteen*

# SNIPER

"How's she doing?" Gabe asked as I walked into the kitchen.

"Better. I need to get her some food."

"You haven't fed her yet?" he asked incredulously. "Rocco went up there hours ago. She's gotta be starving."

"I had to help her shower."

"For three hours?"

"She was dirty," I said, trying to make it sound believable.

"He was fucking her," Jackson said as he walked into the room eating an apple. "I went upstairs to get some shuteye and I heard moans and all kinds of shit coming from the room. I'm gonna need noise cancelling headphones so I can sleep at night."

"She's that loud, huh?" Gabe grinned.

"No," Jackson shook his head. "It wasn't her. It was him. I wouldn't have minded hearing her, but damn, I don't want to hear the shit that I heard coming from a dude. It felt like I was participating or something." He shivered in revulsion. He was being such a baby. It was just sex.

"What kind of stuff are we talking?" Gabe asked.

"Why? Should I make a video for you to watch?" I shot back.

He shrugged nonchalantly. "Put a bag over your face and I won't have to think about it being you. I wouldn't mind seeing your woman naked. If she's got the body to be a stripper-"

I heard the word stripper and lost it. Without thinking, I slammed my fist into his face, partly to shut him up, but mostly because nobody called Morgan a stripper. "You fucking know that she isn't actually a stripper."

He massaged his jaw and glared at me. "I didn't mean anything by it. Fuck, I was just pointing out that she had a good enough body to dance on the stage naked."

I reared back and threw another punch. His head snapped back and he just barely stayed on his feet. "Fuck, man. What the hell? Can't stand to hear the truth?"

"She's not a fucking stripper. She was trying to get her kid back."

"Yeah, by being a stripper."

I slammed my fist twice into his ribs. He doubled over in pain, gasping for air as he cradled his now bruised ribs. If he kept talking, I was gonna hit him in the kidneys and he could piss blood for a week. "Fuck, if you don't want me on your team, just say so."

"I don't want you on my team," I deadpanned.

He wheezed through the pain, shaking his head. "Just be glad you didn't see her strip more than once. You can't even stand to hear me talk about her *profession*. Could you imagine seeing all those men stuffing bills down her thong?"

"That's it." I walked over to the counter and grabbed a knife from the butcher block and stalked back toward him. Jackson shook his head, eyes wide as he stood in front of me.

"Think about this, man. He's your teammate and you..." He glanced over his shoulder at Gabe. "You don't normally want to kill him."

"He needs to learn when to shut the fuck up."

"Who needs to learn to shut up?" Alec asked as he walked into the kitchen, eyeing the knife in my hand.

"Gabe's running his mouth about Morgan posing as a stripper," Jackson said carefully.

Alec stretched out his fingers and cracked his knuckles. "Cool, so, we're like, teaching him a lesson on how to speak nicely about a stripper?"

"She's not a fucking stripper," I yelled.

"Well, technically-"

I threw the knife down, intending to go shut Alec up, but Jackson yelled, grimacing in pain.

"What the fuck! You just threw a fucking knife in my foot."

I looked down and sure enough, the knife was protruding from the top of his boot.

"Oops. I did not mean to do that," I said, holding my hands up in a placating gesture.

"I don't give a fuck if you meant to or not, asshole." He swung and I didn't move. I had it coming after all. The force of his punch was more than I thought it would be and I flew backwards into Gabe.

"Fuck!" he yelled. "You just hit my ribs."

Gabe shoved me back to Jackson and he shoved me away just enough that I slammed against the front of Alec.

"Let's all just calm down," Alec said, right as a fist was flying at my face. I ducked and Jackson nailed Alec right in the nose.

"You fucker! Why the fuck did you punch me?"

"I was meaning to punch him. He stabbed me in the fucking foot!" Jackson yelled at Alec.

"Then warn a guy next time. I would have fucking moved," Alec yelled back.

"Oh yeah, that would have worked out real well," Jackson said sarcastically. "Hey, Chance, I'm gonna punch you in the face. Watch out, Alec. Don't put your face in front of my fist."

"You don't have to fucking say it. Wink at me or jerk your head."

"Wink at you? You want me to fucking wink at you?"

"Yeah, I'd probably back away because I'd think you were hitting on me," Alec snapped back.

"Fine," Jackson shouted, then turned to me. "Hey, Chance," and then he winked at me right before turning and slugging Alec in the face again.

"Son of a bitch! What the fuck! That's twice you've hit me when you were supposed to hit him," Alec pointed at me, holding his cheek with the other hand.

"What? I winked first. Didn't you see it?"

Alec picked up the chair by the table so fast that no one saw it coming. Not even Craig, who had walked up behind him. The chair slammed into Craig's head and then Jackson's when Alec threw the chair at him. Craig momentarily stumbled, dazed from the hit to the head, but then ran forward, slamming into Alec like a freight train. I leapt out of the way, slamming into Gabe as Alec and Craig slid across the table.

Gabe shoved me off him and then Alec rolled off the table, landing on top of me when Craig gave him a hard shove. The breath whooshed out of my lungs and Alec's knee dug into my back as he tried to scramble away from Craig. I struggled to my feet just as Gabe tackled me from behind at the same time Jackson ran at me. The force of Gabe's attack made me slam heads with Jackson and then everything went fuzzy.

*Chapter Sixteen*

# MORGAN

I was starving and I couldn't wait for Chance to get back up here. I was about to chew off my arm, so I decided to just head downstairs and get some food myself. I was a little wobbly on my feet, but a good meal would fix that. I slowly made my way down the stairs and heard yelling when I reached the kitchen. A woman was sitting on a bar stool by the island just a few steps from me. She was eating and watching something with a grin on her face. I followed the direction of her gaze and saw Chance yelling at one of the men.

Walking over to her, I tapped her on the shoulder. "Uh, what's going on?"

The woman turned to me and I got a good look at her face. She had a slender face with high cheekbones and blue eyes. Her blonde hair was pulled back into a messy bun and the crows feet on the sides of her eyes made me think she laughed a lot.

She stood up and I stepped back to look at her. She was tall and skinny, like really skinny. But she was muscular, so she didn't seem like a waif. She pushed a stool over to me and pointed to it.

"I'm Florrie. You should sit down. The boys will be awhile."

I took the seat she offered and looked over at the guys yelling at each other. "I'm Morgan. So, what's going on?"

She popped some cheese in her mouth and then slid the tray over for me to take some. I gladly pulled off several slices and grabbed some crackers out of the packaging.

"It seems that Gabe insulted you, called you a stripper, which Chance took offense to. He punched him when he continued to clarify that you had actually been stripping. So, Chance kept punching him. At some point, Chance grabbed a knife."

"Seriously? Was he going to use it?"

She shrugged. "I don't think so, but it wouldn't be the first time someone was stabbed by another teammate."

"And you guys are all friends?" I said hesitantly.

"Yep," she said cheerfully.

I looked back at the guys, trying to see what she did. "Is that a knife sticking out of that guy's boot?"

"Yeah," she snorted. "Chance 'accidentally' threw the knife into Jackson's foot."

"How do you accidentally throw a knife into someone's foot?"

"Right? There are no accidents with these guys."

I watched as one of the guys picked up a chair and hit the guy that came up behind him and then smashed it into Jackson.

"Okay, so what's going on now? Who are we rooting for?"

She picked up another piece of cheese and held it between two fingers as she tilted her head, like she was thinking about how she wanted to answer. "Well, it's hard to say. I don't know that anyone's actually on anyone's side right now. They all just seem to be hitting each other."

"Does this happen a lot?"

"Not really. Usually they're checking out each others' waxing jobs."

I choked on my cheese, hitting my chest to help it down. Florrie shoved a bottle of water over to me and I quickly drank it down. "Like, they wax for the job or something?"

"No," she said nonchalantly. "It's usually to please a woman. Although Chris and Ice did it to Jules as a joke because he couldn't remember anything." I looked at her in confusion, but she just waved me off. "It's a long story."

"It sounds like there are a lot of those," I muttered. Just then,

Chance and Jackson ran head first into each other and both dropped to the floor. Everyone else continued to fight as the two of them just laid there. "Should we do something about that?"

"Nah. That's what Rocco's for."

I watched the floor, waiting for either Jackson or Chance to get up, but they both just laid there. I was getting a little worried. It was concerning that no one else seemed to think that a man passed out on the floor was something to check on.

"So, what kind of things do you worry about?"

"What? You mean with injuries?" I nodded. "Bullet wounds. Mostly to the torso. Arms don't count because it's usually a graze. In that case, you just suck it up and move on. I mean, you saw how Jackson was still walking around and fighting and he had a knife in his foot. And the leg you only worry about if it hits your femoral artery, and that's on the inner side of your leg. Anything else just means you walk it off."

"Are you serious?" She looked at me questioningly. "I mean, I kind of feel like a wuss now for being out of it because I was dehydrated."

"Well, that's different. Chance was all goo goo for you, and you should have seen him snapping at everyone when we found you. Family is off limits. Nobody fucks with our family and friends. If we hurt each other, it's no big deal."

"But Chance and I aren't together. I didn't even know his name until an hour ago." God, that made me sound like a slut.

"Well, obviously he cares about you more than he says because he was acting like someone had taken his wife. And I don't think he ever acted that way with his wife."

"He has a wife?" I said in shock.

"Divorced. I never knew her. It happened a long time ago, but from what I understand, she walked out the door and he didn't try to stop her. I'm pretty sure when you love someone, you fight for them."

That had me thinking about Matt. Did he ever really love me? Was I just someone to warm his bed and pass the day with? Florrie was right though. I loved Payton with all my heart and I would fight until the day I died to get her back.

Chance slowly sat up, holding his head as he groaned. He saw

Jackson laying on the floor also and kicked him in the side. I gasped in shock, but Jackson sat up, rubbing his head.

"Thanks a lot, fucker," Jackson growled.

"I didn't tell you to smash your head into mine," Chance bit back.

"You know, none of this would have happened if Alec hadn't smashed a chair in my face," Jackson sneered at Alec, who was leaning over and breathing heavily.

"Me? It wouldn't have happened if you hadn't punched me."

Jackson pointed at Gabe in accusation. "You were the one that shoved Chance into me in the first place."

"He threw a fucking knife in your foot and you're blaming me because I shoved him?" Gabe's shocked face made me laugh. These guys were kind of crazy. They reminded me of five year olds fighting over a toy. Only they were adult-sized.

"I wouldn't have thrown a knife in your foot if Gabe hadn't kept referring to Morgan as a stripper."

"She is!" Gabe shouted. Chance took a step forward and I figured this was a good time for me to step in. But Florrie had different ideas. She put her hand on my arm, stopping me from moving.

"Just wait."

"Would you stop fucking saying that," Chance yelled. "She did what she had to do for her kid. I know Isa would do the exact same thing if it was Enzo or Vittoria."

"Dude, you need to fucking relax," Gabe said. "I never said there was anything wrong with her stripping. I pointed out the fact that she was stripping when you got so defensive. I'm not the one that seems to have a problem with it. Maybe you need to ask yourself why it bothers you so much that someone would call her that."

Chance didn't have anything to say to that and I wondered if Gabe was right. Did Chance just hate the connotation or was he actually offended that I had been stripping? As if Chance finally sensed that I was in the room, he turned and locked eyes with me. I didn't really have anything to say. Nothing Gabe said was offensive and I really didn't care if any of Chance's friends thought badly of me. I knew my reasons for doing what I did, and that was all that mattered.

"Can someone go get Rocco so I can get this knife out of my foot?" Jackson asked, breaking the tension in the room.

---

"Would you stop holding me up? I'm not going to fall over walking into a building." Chance had been treating me like a fragile flower since the safe house. Sure, I had been dehydrated and I still felt pretty awful because I didn't have any energy, but I would get that back in a day or two. Besides lack of energy, the thing that was bothering me the most was my cracked lips. Every once in a while, one of the cracks would start to bleed if I wasn't careful. It was painful, but would heal in time.

"We should have stayed at the safe house longer. You needed to rest more."

I stopped in my tracks and stared at him pointedly.

"What?"

"This coming from a man who has a goose egg on his forehead. I'm thinking maybe it's you that should have taken more time to rest. You could have a concussion."

He shrugged like it was no big deal. "I've had 'em before. I'll have 'em again."

I repeated it, silently mocking him behind his back as we stepped onto the elevator. Men were such idiots. He was passed out on the floor after slamming his head into Jackson's, but he was worried about me because I wasn't back to the same energy level I had before. He went through a series of scans that had me rolling my eyes. I felt like I was entering the CIA.

When the elevator doors opened and we stepped off, I eyed the chairs longingly. I would never admit that I was tired from the trip from the parking garage to here. The last thing I needed was Chance deciding to take me for tests or something, which he probably would with the way he was acting. And it was strange to me. How could he go from so unfeeling to this? What exactly had changed to cause this one-eighty?

"Come on. Let's get you to a chair. You look like you're going to pass out if you don't sit down in the next five seconds." Chance gripped onto my elbow and I was thankful for the assistance. I did feel like I was about five seconds from just plopping down and planting my ass wherever my body landed. We walked into a conference room and Chance pushed me gently down in a chair, kneeling in front of me with concern all over his face.

"Are you feeling okay? You look a little green."

"I'm fine. I think the better question is what the hell is wrong with you?"

His eyebrows quirked in confusion. "What do you mean?"

"I mean that all the sudden you're worried about every move I make. Why? What's changed that now you feel the need to watch over me like a hawk?"

"I was looking out for you back at the club too. Remember? I warned you not to go to that poker game?"

"I remember, but I also remember you throwing money at me like a whore after you fucked me."

He hung his head in shame and then looked back up at me, his features unreadable. "I can be an asshole, but I'm man enough to admit when I'm wrong, and I was wrong about you. What you were doing in the club to get your daughter back was fucking amazing. You were risking everything for her and that just blows me away. You're an incredibly strong woman and I'm a fucking idiot for not having seen that sooner."

I eyed him skeptically. "Does this mean you like me?" I teased.

He rolled his eyes at me and stood. "Yes, I like you, alright?"

"So, are we like boyfriend and girlfriend now? Are you going to get me a promise ring?" I needled him a little more.

But instead of him joking back with me, his face turned serious. He ran his hand across the back of his neck and sighed. "I don't want you to get the wrong idea. I like you, a lot, but I can't offer you anything. Ever. I don't want to ever be married again or even make some kind of commitment to a woman again. That's not for me anymore."

Okay, that was interesting to know and way more than I had intended to get into so early in the morning, but I appreciated his honesty. Though, part of me was disappointed that he seemed to care about my well-being so much, but then told me that he didn't ever want any kind of commitment again. It killed things before they even had a chance to be anything.

"Relax, Chance. I'm not going to get stars in my eyes and start seeing you as some knight in shining armor that's come to sweep me off my feet. I was teasing you."

He eyed me skeptically before giving me a curt nod and turning away. "I'm gonna let Cap know we're here."

When he left the room, I looked around at the impressive equipment. Several large screens were on the walls. There was some kind of tablet on the long table and I wondered if it was a regular tablet or some super spy gadget that set off bombs with just the touch of a button.

"Morgan," I jerked my head to the door when the deep voice said my name. "It's nice to meet you. I'm Sebastian and I own Reed Security."

I stood and held out my hand to the handsome man who stood in front of me with all the airs of the man in charge, but his large hands and his muscular arms told me he was still deadly. I flicked my eyes to Chance, well aware that I had just been checking out his boss. I hadn't meant to, but every man I came across that Chance knew was freaking hot and had enough muscles to bench press the conference room table.

"Thank you for seeing me today."

"It's no problem." Sebastian walked around the table and grabbed the tablet off the table and turned on one of the screens. So, not a super spy tablet. "We've been going through your daughter's file and we're not finding anything new in there. I'd like you to tell me what you remember happening."

"It's all in the report," I said in confusion.

"I know, but sometimes we remember small details when we recount a story."

I nodded and glanced at Chance who had taken a seat next to me. Sebastian handed Chance a device and he set it in front of me, pressing a button.

"We're going to record it so we can go back through it if we need to."

"Okay, um..." I took a deep breath and pushed all emotional

thoughts aside. Falling into a pit of heartache wouldn't help right now. "It was a Thursday. I was rushing to get ready for work because I woke up late. The power had flickered sometime during the night and my alarm didn't go off. I was just about to leave and take Payton to daycare when I got a phone call from Carrie's husband. Carrie is my daycare provider. She was really sick, throwing up all night, I think. He gave me the number of another woman who would possibly have some openings for the day."

"And her name was?" Sebastian asked.

"Denise Sanders."

Sebastian nodded, his eyes intent on me as I told the story. "I called her and she told me she had room for one more child Payton's age. She gave me a price, which was way higher than I normally paid, but I didn't have many options. When I hesitated, she told me that she had another call coming in. I told her I would take the spot and she texted me the address. Her home was big, nice, clean. It was in a good neighborhood and the other kids seemed happy. The woman was even pretty nice, so I wasn't nervous when I left Payton there. Besides, Carrie had recommended her, so I figured she was good."

"What time was that?"

"Um...just after eight a.m. I went to work and I received a call at 10:20 from Denise. She said that they were at the playground down the road and Payton was snatched by two men in a white van. I told my boss what happened and left immediately, heading right for the police department. Denise had already talked to an officer after she got the other children back to her house. After that, it was just a long line of people that wanted to talk to me. Nothing happened after that. I didn't receive a ransom note or a phone call. She was just gone. The police searched for the white van, but the plates were tracked to a rental company and the name on the rental was fake. Whoever it was had already wiped down the van. There were no prints.

"The police put out an amber alert immediately after she was taken, but all they got were false leads. The police had searched through our house, talked to the neighbors, talked to all my family, friends, and colleagues. Nobody knew anything. The FBI came within two days and had set up phone taps and did their own investigations, but they couldn't find anything more than the police had. Eventually, the tips stopped coming in and there was nothing more to investigate. The FBI stayed in contact, but every update was the same. *We're sorry, Ms. James, but we don't have any new information on your child."*

I laughed, though it wasn't funny. "Every phone call killed me. Whenever I saw my contact on the caller I.D., I prayed they had something new to tell me and every time I was disappointed. After three months, the police told me they would stay in contact and they wouldn't stop looking, but they never had any new leads either."

"And that's when you started looking on your own."

"Yes."

"Who did you talk to?" Chance asked.

"I found druggies and asked who their dealers were. When I found one of the dealers, I asked for a meet with their supplier. I never got names, just dates and times to meet."

"Do you know how dangerous that was?" Chance said angrily.

"It was for my child," I said calmly. "I wasn't going to just give up."

"How did you end up with the name *The Broker?"* Sebastian asked.

"When I met with the supplier, he was a little upset when he found out what I wanted. I think he was actually going to kill me, but when I told him I was searching for my child, everything changed. He told me to go to a bar, The Saw House. He said that if I talked to George, the bartender, he could put me in contact with someone that might be able to help. I found the bartender and he told me I needed to meet with The Broker. He didn't say who he was or what he did, just that if I went to the strip club, he would find me. I was never told a real name or given a description."

"Why did you assume Chief knew something?" Chance asked.

"He was always on these phone calls that sounded so mysterious. I heard names, dates, locations…I guess I figured that maybe he knew who The Broker was, that I might be able to get information from him."

Something passed between Chance and Sebastian, a look that had me wondering what I was missing.

"Did you know that several girls went missing from the strip club over the past year?" Sebastian asked.

"No, but Chance told me there were men involved in a sex trafficking ring. I just assumed that the women went on to work somewhere else. I never would have imagined that they were disappearing from the club. Wouldn't Jeremy have done something about it?"

"He couldn't," Chance said. "Not without blowing the whole investigation."

I stared at him in shock. I couldn't believe that Jeremy wouldn't have done anything. "But Jeremy always seemed like such a good guy. I can't believe..."

"He didn't have a choice. They were close to getting the guy running the whole thing. If he gave away that he was working with the FBI or DOJ, whoever they were, the ring would have split up and disappeared. More women would get taken, just from another location."

"The night you went missing," Sebastian leaned forward, resting his arms on the table, "the ring moved out."

"Was Jeremy able to get the leader?"

"No," he said gravely. "All the women from the strip club were taken."

"What?" I stared at them both in shock. All those women were gone? I shook my head, unable to believe what I was hearing. "But... that's insane. That many people disappearing all at once would raise suspicion. Someone must have some information to go on."

"It happened so fast that Jeremy wasn't able to call for backup. There was nothing he could do to stop them. He said they were in and out in five minutes."

"I would have been there," I said quietly. "If I hadn't left with Wes, I would be God knows where now."

"Wes didn't exactly do you any favors. He left you in the bottom of a well," Chance said sharply. "You would have died if we hadn't found you."

"How am I going to find this guy now? I missed my chance."

"Morgan, Wes *is* The Broker."

My head whipped in Chance's direction again. "What?"

"He's The Broker. Storm knew that, but he never said anything because nobody ever lives when they figure that out."

"But he didn't kill me. He just—"

"He just made it so you would die a slow death," Chance cut in. "He's not going to help you and chances are, he has something to do with your daughter's disappearance."

"You don't know that for sure."

"No, I don't, but I do know that he left you for dead. If you go see him again, he's gonna put a bullet in your skull."

"He can't just do that. He's not invincible." I turned to Sebastian with pleading eyes. "Tell him. Tell him that we still have a chance. He didn't kill me."

"He was playing with us," Chance bit out. "He led us right to your location, but he didn't let us in on where you were."

"See?" I was desperate at this point. I would do or say anything to talk with him. "If he led you to me then he didn't actually want me dead. He probably just wanted me away from the club."

"There was no guarantee we would find you. He wasn't sparing your life. You have to stop thinking of him as the good guy that's going to save your daughter. He had no reason to save you or get you away from the club. He was trying to rid himself of someone he considered a nuisance. He was never going to help you find Payton!"

I slumped in my chair feeling defeated. I didn't have any arguments left. I knew that Chance was right, but he was the only person left that might have information on my daughter. It wasn't fair. She was only four. She didn't deserve whatever was happening to her.

Sebastian stood and walked out of the room as the reality of my situation sank in. My daughter was gone and I most likely would never see her again. My last hope had been extinguished.

My vision blurred as my eyes filled with tears. My heart felt like it was actually breaking inside me, like a knife had just pierced my chest and was being yanked around. I could hardly breathe through the overwhelming feeling of loss.

I could still see her beautiful face with those big, blue eyes and that huge smile when she laughed. I would never feel those little arms wrap around my neck again or be able to give her Eskimo kisses. She would never come climb into my arms after nap time or snuggle me in the middle of the night when she woke up. I would never hear her call me 'momma' again. Without her, my world didn't exist.

I doubled over, falling to the ground as sobs wracked my body, each one tearing through me and ripping my soul in tiny pieces. Chance's arms wrapped around me and I clawed at the fabric of his shirt, practically climbing up his body to get closer to him. He held me tightly, his hand running up and down my back soothingly. I wanted it to be comforting, but I was beyond being able to be comforted. I was on my way to just feeling dead inside.

I had never thought about losing Payton before. I don't think any parent ever really considers what it would be like to lose a child because the thought would be devastating. Now that she was gone, I wished that I could have had one last smile from her. Or maybe I could have held her a little tighter when she snuggled me at night instead of pushing her away when I got too warm. And I would have never yelled at her to be quiet when she got too loud when I had a headache. There were so many things I would have done differently if I had only realized how precious her little life was.

"Hey," Chance whispered in my ear. "This isn't the end. We'll keep looking. We'll never give up."

"You can't promise me that. You know as well as I do that the chances of me ever seeing her again aren't good." I wiped the snot that was leaking out of my nose and dried my face as my chest hitched with each strangled breath.

He held my face in his hands, forcing me to look into his eyes. They were so sincere and strong that I wanted to listen. I wanted to believe that he could actually find her. He couldn't promise me anything, but the sincerity in his expression had me crumbling.

"We won't. Give. Up. Do you understand me? I'll never stop looking for her. I promise you that. I don't make a lot of promises, but when I do, I keep them. So trust me. Put your faith in me to help you in any way I can."

I nodded, not because I believed that he would find her, but because I needed something to hold onto. And I would grab the chance with both hands and hold on until there was nothing left of me.

*Chapter Seventeen*

# SNIPER

Fuck, it killed me to be holding her and not being able to do anything but comfort her. My promises were sincere, but she was right, the chances of seeing her daughter again weren't very good.

"Hey, let me take you back to my place. We'll get some rest and then come back in the morning and start again."

She nodded against my chest, but didn't move, so I just held her a little longer. A few of the guys peeked their heads in the door, silently asking me if everything was okay. Nothing was okay right now. Not while a little girl was missing, but that wasn't something any of them could magically fix.

She pushed back from me after a while and wiped her face. Her cheeks were bright red and her eyes were puffy from crying, but she still looked beautiful. I pulled her to her feet and took her to my house. She didn't say anything the whole way. She was quiet and stared out the window the entire ride. There were no questions or even curiosity about where we were headed. She knew I was taking her back to my place and that seemed good enough for her.

Walking into my house, I had to practically hold my hand to her back the whole way to guide her inside. It was like she was a zombie. I guided her to my bedroom and pulled out a t-shirt for her to wear and showed her the bathroom, but still she said nothing. I watched as she just stared around the room, looking lost and alone.

I wanted to comfort her, but when I had been holding her in my arms earlier, it felt too good, too intimate with the way she gripped onto me like I was the only person that could save her. I could help her find her daughter, but I had to keep myself separated from all this. The problem with close protection or situations like this, where emotions ran high, was that you started to develop an attachment to who you were protecting. Suddenly, their problems became yours and all you wanted was to make sure that person would never have to be afraid again. I could see it now, working with her was going to be difficult because I had already slept with her, but also because I felt a connection to her. Now, I had promised to do everything I could to find her daughter and I had invited her back to my place.

Those eyes looked at me like I was her savior, and I certainly wasn't anyone's savior. I did my job and I did it well, but I was a killer at heart. That had been my job when I was a SEAL. I was a sniper and I was damn good at it. But the thrill I got when I took out some evil asshole made me enjoy my job just a little too much. That was why I had chosen to go into security when I left the service. I would be protecting people instead of taking them out. However, the last few years had proven to be much different from what I had expected. We had taken on more jobs that required me to use my sniper skills than I would have thought. I could feel that old urge seeping back into my bones, and now that I was dealing with the scum of the earth, people that would take women and children and sell their bodies to sexual deviants, I wanted more than ever to take out my rifle and put it to good use.

When it was clear that I wasn't going to get any words out of her, I closed the door and headed for the living room. My couch wasn't particularly comfortable, but I wasn't going to take advantage of her fragile state and sleep in the same bed with her. And I sure as hell wasn't going to put myself in the position to have her snuggling up to me at night. I knew her warm body would feel too damn good against mine.

Before I laid down for the night, I had to call Chief back and give him an update. He had been worried about Morgan since we got her back. She was the one girl that was left after all the chaos and knowing she was still safe was the one thing he was holding onto right now.

"Sniper, how's Shyla doing?"

"She's fine. She's sleeping now. I brought her back with me and we'll keep her safe until we can figure out who's behind this."

"Yeah," he sighed. "Whatever you do, don't underestimate The Broker. The rumors about him aren't misleading. He really is as ruthless as everyone says."

"I won't. Will you be around?"

"I think I'm heading out. After all the shit that I just dealt with, I need to get away from this."

"You could stay and help us wrap this up," I said hopefully.

"I can't," he said, just a touch of agony in his voice. "You know how it is when you're too deep into something. I just need some space."

"I get it. Let me know when you're back in town."

"I will. Let me know if you get her daughter back."

"Sure, Chief," I said as I hung up.

I stretched out on the couch, my feet hanging uncomfortably over the arm of the couch. While the couch being too small was a problem, the bigger issue was that there was no way I could sleep in my jeans. When I was on a job, that was a different story, but here in my house, I needed some goddamn sleep so I could focus on finding her daughter in the morning. I stood and tore off my clothes, flinging them to the chair across the room. I was naked, but I was an early riser and could get dressed again before she woke up.

Sleep didn't come easily after that. I would have tossed and turned if there was room to, but there wasn't. I shoved the coffee table to the wall and spread out on the floor. I had slept in worse conditions in the military. Sleeping on the floor would be fine for the night. I pulled one of those tiny throw pillows off the couch that I never thought had any purpose and used it as my pillow for the night.

It was sometime in the early morning hours when I was jolted awake. A dark figured moved toward me and it took me a few seconds to remember that Morgan was staying with me. I was just about to let her know that I was on the ground when her foot hit my leg and she went flying. I caught her around the waist and rolled, trapping her body gently under mine. Her eyes were bright and wide in the moonlight that was streaming in through the windows. Her chest was heaving and her warm breath fanned out across my face.

She wiggled under me, moving her legs slightly, allowing my body to drop down between her bare legs. She hadn't intended for that to happen, I realized, when her eyes went wide. She licked her lips quickly, her eyes dropping to mine, and then she slid her hands around my back, pulling me closer to her.

I shouldn't do it. She wasn't in the right frame of mind. She was upset over her daughter and she wasn't thinking clearly. But when she lifted her hips to meet mine, I couldn't deny her. Or I just didn't want to. I wanted her just as much and the small part of me that was worried about her state of mind was smothered by the larger part of me that wanted to sink inside her.

I smashed my lips to hers, hearing her groan slightly, reminding me that her lips were still cracked and sore from her days trapped in that well. I had kissed her roughly last time and drew blood. I didn't need to do that again. When she wrapped her legs around me, I forgot about being a gentleman or being gentle at all. I tore her panties from her body and thrust inside her so hard, that it was almost painful on my cock. But she pulled me tighter to her body, and wrapped her arms around my neck.

I kept myself distanced from her mentally. I always did when I was fucking. Sex led to feelings, no matter if you were a man or woman. Especially if you were attracted to who you were fucking. And I was definitely attracted to this woman. I had made the mistake several times of getting lost in the moment, of letting the situation allow me relax to the point of forgetting about keeping my distance. I wasn't ready to go there with her or with anyone else. So, no matter how those eyes looked at me, appearing to see right through me, or how good it felt to have her hands sliding over my back, I ignored the surge of what felt like feelings rising in my chest and pushed it aside for the feelings in my dick.

When I felt close to coming, I ground my hips against hers, pushing against her clit with each thrust. I wanted her to come. I may stay distant, but the woman in my bed always came. I shoved her shirt up and bit down on her nipple, sending a shock through her system that had her falling apart under me. It didn't take much to push me over the edge after that. My breathing was hard as I came down from my high and I was aware of my weight smothering her. Rolling off her, I stared up in the dark, pulling the blanket up to my hips to cover myself up.

I belatedly realized that I should have done the same for her, but she had already done it by the time I thought of it. That was part of distancing myself though. If I started doing shit like that, taking care of her afterwards, it was too easy to sink back into something that felt way too natural with this woman. She made everything seem so easy, so right. But I had already told her that I couldn't offer her anything and I hadn't been lying. I still felt that way and that wasn't going to change, no matter how right she felt in my arms.

"I just came out for a glass of water," she said after a few minutes.

"I'll get you one," I said, standing and letting the blanket slip from my body. Shit, I was already going against my own rules and taking care of her. Fuck it, I was just being nice. It wasn't the end of the world to get the woman a damn glass of water. When I got back to her, I handed it off and sat awkwardly on the couch, waiting for her to get up and go back to bed, but she didn't. She laid on the ground, taking sips every now and again until the cup started to tip in her hand as she started to drift off.

Sighing, I snatched the glass out of her hand before it could fall and set it on the table. I knelt down and covered her with the blanket and sat back on my ass, wondering what the hell I was supposed to do now. If I left her to go sleep in my bed, I would look like an asshole and while I didn't mind keeping my distance, I didn't want to purposely be an asshole. I could carry her to the bed, but fuck, I just wanted to go to sleep now.

I laid down and pulled another blanket from the couch, draping it over my body. I glanced over at her again, sleeping peacefully and tried not to think about what it would be like if we did this more often. Or if she were here in the winter and we had the fireplace going and fucked right here on the floor. I rolled to my side so I couldn't see her and wiped the images from my mind.

When I woke in the morning, Morgan was draped over my body. Her hand rested on my chest and her leg was slung over mine. Soft puffs of air fluttered across my chest, reminding me of a time when I had actually looked forward to mornings like this. It was too easy to get lost in the feeling, but as long as she was asleep, I'd let it slide. It was okay to admit every once in a while that I actually liked waking up next to a woman.

I must have fallen back asleep because the next time I opened my eyes, I was alone. There was a really good smell coming from the kitchen, but what I really needed was coffee. My back was a little stiff from laying on the ground, so I did some stretching and reached for my pants. But they weren't there. I looked around the room, wondering if I had accidentally put them someplace else and didn't realize it, but they were nowhere to be seen.

I wrapped the blanket around my waist and went into my bedroom. The floor was clean of all dirty laundry and the hamper was empty. What the hell? I didn't have any clean pants in my drawer, so I pulled on some sweats and headed for the kitchen. Morgan was at the stove cooking up a breakfast that no way could have come from the ingredients in my fridge.

"What are you doing?"

"Making breakfast," she said with a smile. "I wanted to make you something nice."

"But where did you get this stuff from? I know I didn't have any eggs."

She tilted her head as she looked at me. "Well, I saw that, so I went to your neighbor and asked for some eggs. They went out to their chicken coop and gave me some."

"My neighbors have chickens?"

She rolled her eyes at me and turned back to the stove. "I went to the store. You didn't have any food in the house and I wanted to make you something nice as a thank you. You were still sleeping, so I slipped out earlier and grabbed some stuff."

"With my truck," I said slowly.

"Yeah. Why? Is that a problem?"

I stared at her, wondering where on earth this woman came from. She took my truck. Aside from my hypoallergenic pillows and my extremely expensive bed, my truck was the only other thing in my life that I cherished. It was my baby and no one drove her but me.

"Don't touch my truck, okay?"

She frowned, but didn't argue. "Sure."

She turned back to the concoction she had on the stove and finished up, placing it on two plates. She slid one across the counter to me, eyeing me warily as I stared at the food. Then, after a minute, she poured me a cup of coffee and slid that to me also. It was so... domestic.

The food smelled good and there really wasn't any point in wasting good food. After the first bite, I knew I was fucked. It was the best thing I had ever tasted and if I got this every morning, I would never be able to let her go. I would have to take her as a maid and force her to make me breakfast every morning. The coffee was even better than the sludge I made. This was the perfect flavor and wasn't the bland shit that I normally got.

"So? Is it okay?"

I shoveled the last bite into my mouth and chewed quickly. Then I guzzled my coffee, trying not to choke when it was just a little too hot going down. I slid my stool back from the counter and walked over to the counter, slamming the plate into the sink. "Fucking fantastic," I muttered before walking away.

It was bullshit. Complete and utter bullshit. I would not be swayed by delicious food and I would not allow this woman to come into my home and drive my truck and tempt me with her cooking. I stormed back to my room, only to remember that I didn't have any fucking clothes. Stomping back out into the living room, I yelled to her in the kitchen.

"Did you take my clothes?"

"Yeah," she said brightly. "You had a lot laying on the ground and since I was up so early, I put a load in for you. It should be almost-" The buzzer sounded, signaling that the dryer was done. "I'll go grab your clothes now."

I stared at her retreating form in confusion. What the hell was going on? Doing my laundry? Going grocery shopping and making breakfast? Had I woken up in an alternate universe where a quick fuck became a girlfriend the next morning?

She brought out a laundry basket with still warm laundry and stopped in front of me. I side-eyed her for a moment, not sure what to do or say to this woman. Fuck, I didn't want to make her cry if I yelled at her for becoming some domesticated multi-night stand, but I also didn't want her to think this shit was okay. "Do you want me to fold it for you?"

"No," I said quickly, snatching the basket out of her hands. "I'll do it." I eyed her warily again, stepping backward but not turning my back to her as I headed for my room. She looked at me strangely. Me. Like I was the one that was batshit crazy. When I got to my room, I quickly dressed and headed back to the living room. Morgan was standing in the kitchen, wiping down the counters.

"Ready?"

"Yeah." She grabbed her purse and we were out the door, headed for Reed Security. I didn't say a thing to her as we made the short drive, but I kept my eye on her. It was so weird. One minute, she was a crying mess and now she was acting like a domesticated cat taking over my house.

I didn't wait for her as I got out of my truck. I just headed for the elevator and hoped she followed. When we got to the lobby, I stepped out and cleared my throat. "Um...You can go sit in the conference room. I'll be in after I talk to the guys."

"Sure." She turned and walked away and I bolted. Down in the training area, I found some of the guys working out. I walked right up to Gabe, tapping him on the shoulder. He turned to me with his beat up face and scowled.

"What do you want, fucker?"

"I've got a problem."

"Yeah? So do I. Do you see my face? I didn't get laid last night because of you. Isa didn't want 'to hurt me'."

"I've got bigger issues than your dick."

"Like what?"

"My dick. It ended up in Morgan last night and now she's acting all weird."

Gabe sighed, his shoulders sinking like he was carrying the weight of the world on them. "You already slept with her, so what's the problem?"

"Fuck if I know. We were here last night and talking about her daughter. She finally realized that she wasn't going to be able to find her daughter through Wes and she broke down. Being the nice guy that I am, I comforted her. I brought her home with me-"

"Whoa. You brought her home? Why would you do that?"

"Because, it's not like she had anywhere else to go."

"Bullshit, you could have sent her to a hotel or a safe house."

"I could have, but she was upset and I didn't want to be an asshole."

"When has that stopped you before?" he asked with a smirk.

"Look, I'm serious. You have to help me. I don't know what the fuck to do."

"Why don't you talk to someone else about this? In case you forgot, I actually had to convince Isa to give me a chance and then to move in with me. You need to talk to someone with the fear."

"The fear?"

"Yeah, someone who had the fear." He looked around the room, assessing who was around. "You need Hunter or Ice." He whistled loudly and then called for both of them. Of course, everyone and their mother followed because they were curious. This was fucking ridiculous.

"Thanks. Now everyone's gonna give their input."

"Hey, you need it. I can't help you on this one."

Hunter walked up and gave Gabe a chin lift, but kept his distance. Ever since he thought Gabe was hitting on him, he still couldn't be that close to him without getting skeeved out.

"Chance is having woman problems." Hunter nodded and all the guys gathered around closer to hear what the situation was. Thank God not everyone was here. I didn't need that many people up my ass.

"Hit me," Hunter said.

"Okay, so I slept with Morgan, that stripper that was actually not a stripper, but posing as a stripper to find her daughter."

"Yeah?"

I cleared my throat, uncomfortable having to say anything. "So, last night she freaked out about her daughter and I comforted her."

I got smacked on the back of the head and turned to see who it was. "What the fuck was that for, asshole?" Chris was glaring at me with those dark eyes that always freaked me the fuck out. If I was scared of anyone around here, besides Knight, it was Chris. The man just looked like he was always ready to murder someone. Unless he was around Ali and his kids. Then he was all rainbows and kittens.

"We respect women. You don't try and comfort a woman that lost her daughter with your dick."

"I didn't. I was giving her a hug while she cried. I *comforted* her. Anyway, she didn't have anywhere to go so I took her home and set her up in my bedroom. I slept in the living room and she came out in the middle of the night and tripped over my feet and the way we landed-"

"Nope," Ice said, shaking his head. "Don't even try it. Accidental fucking is mine and you can't steal it."

"I didn't accidentally fuck her. That's not even a real thing," I snapped. "We did fuck though and in the morning, she was all draped over me and shit."

"Yeah, I get it. She stifled you," Hunter said, nodding, but not really understanding.

"That wasn't all. I fell back asleep and when I woke up...she was doing stuff."

"Like, what kind of stuff?" Alec asked. "Kinky stuff?"

"No, like...domestic stuff." The guys all stared at me. Not one of them understood what I was saying. "She did my laundry. She went grocery shopping and made breakfast. She asked me if she should fold my clothes!"

Eyebrows went up all around me and suddenly, I wasn't quite the asshole they all thought I was.

*Chapter Eighteen*

# MORGAN

I sat in the conference room waiting for Chance. It had been ten minutes and I wondered if he was ever coming back. Based on the way he acted this morning, I was guessing that he was running for the hills. I'd never seen a man act so strange.

I sat there, drumming my fingers on the table as I waited and got more irritated by the minute. It wasn't until a woman with two kids and a swollen belly walked past the door and eyed me that I felt someone actually noticed I was here waiting. A minute later, she was back, sans kids, and sat down by me at the table.

"I'm Maggie," she smiled, waiting for me to introduce myself. She had shrewd eyes, like she was assessing me and trying to figure me out. Was this some sort of test to see if I was trustworthy?

"Morgan."

Her eyes lit up and she shoved her hand in front of me. "I'm Sebastian's wife. It's nice to meet you."

"You too."

"So, are you waiting for someone to meet with you?"

"Yeah. Chance plopped me down in here, saying he had to go talk with the guys. Whatever that means."

Her brows furrowed and she cocked her head to the side. "Are you with Chance?"

I blushed and ducked my head. Did sleeping with someone count as being with someone? Not really. "I wouldn't say that. We've..." I struggled to find an appropriate way to say 'we fuck'. Turns out, there really isn't a good way to say that.

"So, how often does this happen?"

"The fucking?" I slapped a hand over my mouth as her head bent back and she roared with laughter.

"Oh my gosh. Yeah, I think you're right for Chance."

"Um...right for Chance? I'm not interested in anything with Chance. I'm just trying to find my daughter and he was there," I shrugged.

"See? That right there proves that you're the one for Chance. Mr. 'I don't do relationships'."

"Neither do I. At least not until I find my daughter."

"Sebastian told me about that. Is there anything I can do to help? I used to be a reporter. I have lots of contacts." My ears perked up at that and she noticed. "So, what were you supposed to meet about today?"

"Well, I was looking for The Broker for information, but I ended up in a well for it. Now I'm just trying to find some scrap of information that can help me. I had this huge breakdown last night about it, but that's not going to help me get her back. Chance has been so good to me, so, well that's kind of why I was so confused this morning."

"What happened this morning?" she asked eagerly. I could see why she was a reporter. I had known her all of five minutes and I wanted to spill all my secrets to her. She was just so easy to talk to. And that pregnant belly really tricked me into thinking she was just a sweet housewife, but I had a feeling she was anything but.

"Well, after he took me home, he was so nice. He gave up his room and let me sleep in his bed. Then when I got up in the middle of the night, I tripped over him and we ended up having sex. It just really helped me take my mind off Payton and kind of reset my mind. So, I wanted to thank him. I went to make breakfast, but there was literally nothing in the fridge. And then I noticed that he had clothes everywhere, so I threw them in the laundry. I mean, I couldn't just stand around waiting for him to wake up, so I made myself useful. After I had the laundry in, I went to the store and picked up some groceries to make him a nice breakfast, but apparently that was the wrong thing to do because I took his truck and that's like some kind of offense punishable by death. You should have seen his face."

"Oh, I bet. These men are very sensitive about their trucks. Just do yourself a favor and don't bring it up in front of anyone, especially Sinner. His poor truck got wrecked right after he got it."

"It's a vehicle. How can men be so attached to it?"

"Because, the size of the truck equates to the size of the dick."

"Really?" She nodded like she couldn't believe it either. "Well, he was weird about breakfast and then when I took his laundry out of the dryer and held it out to him, he just looked at me like I was insane. So, I figured he wanted me to fold his laundry too. So, I asked him and he snapped at me and then did this weird walk where he wouldn't turn his back to me. It's like he thought I was going to attack him. And then he was quiet the whole way here and acted like he didn't know me."

She started laughing, but I didn't understand it.

"What? What's so funny?"

She started laughing harder, unable to stop as tears ran down her face. I wished she would stop laughing and clue me the fuck in. I slammed my hand down on the table and she finally reined in the laughter.

"I'm sorry, it's just so funny. He's gonna get so much shit from the guys."

"For what? I don't understand any of it."

She leaned forward, patting my hand with hers. "He thinks you're trying to basically wife him."

"Wife him? What does that even mean?"

"Like, move in. Take over the role of the wife in the house. You cooked breakfast. You did laundry. You offered to fold it," she laughed.

My eyes went wide as it dawned on me how he took my thank you. I burst out laughing along with Maggie and couldn't stop. "Why would he assume that I was trying to get together with him? I've never given him any ideas that was what I was looking for."

"It doesn't matter. Men are so suspicious. You can't do anything without one of them thinking you're trying to get something out of them."

"So, what? He's with the guys trying to figure out how to deal with me?"

"Basically. I swear, these men don't have a brain between them when it comes to women."

"Why wouldn't he just talk to me about it?"

"Why don't men stop and ask for directions?" she shot back. It was so very true.

"If he had asked, I would have just explained that I was trying to thank him. In fact, I think I did say that."

"It doesn't matter. They see our mouths moving and they just tune everything out. It's not about what you say, it's about what you do."

"No, that can't be it. Every time I tried to show my ex how I was feeling, he said that I had to be more specific; that he wasn't a mind reader."

"Well, that's because they can't make up their minds about what they actually think. Men always think that we're complicated, but really, they're the ones that are so damn confusing. They have basically three needs, right?"

"Food, sex, work."

"Right. So, everything is supposed to fit into one of those categories. Everything else doesn't mean jack shit to them, or so they say. However, if you ask a man if he can fix the steps on the porch, he'll say that he'll get to it later. Then, when it doesn't get fixed and you hire someone to do it, he complains that he could have done it if you had just told him you needed it done right away."

"But you shouldn't have to clarify that broken steps need to be fixed," I agreed.

"Exactly, but men say they can't read minds and you should have been more specific."

"Okay, well that fits into the work category. Simple. It's one of their basic needs."

"Ah, but it's not. See, there are many more needs that they have, but refuse to acknowledge or they're actually subcategories of the main categories. It's a very complicated system. I'd have to draw you a diagram."

"Okay, so if it's a subcategory, why wouldn't it get done?"

"Because it falls into that protective category, which every man here has in spades. Now, if you had fallen down the stairs and broken your arm, that step would have been fixed in five minutes. If you were pregnant, you wouldn't be able to walk down the stairs by yourself. But, if you are perfectly healthy, that protective category has a little leeway."

"Um...so I get what you're saying, but I'm confused about how it fits into my situations with Chance."

"To put it simply, last night, you were distraught and it kicked in his protective instincts. Then, this morning, you were this regular woman that was in his house and you didn't fall into any of his categories."

"But I made him breakfast," I said stupidly.

"Yes, but it was after sex and that went into another subcategory."

"Which one is that?"

"The morning after category. Every man has a way to deal with the morning after. Obviously, Chance has a specific way to deal with women he sleeps with and you threw him off. He didn't know how to deal with you, let alone open his mouth and talk to you about it."

"So, what do I do now?"

"Well, you can either ignore it and let it blow over or you can fuck with him."

"While fucking with him would be fun, I have bigger things to worry about than his after morning freak-out."

"Great!" She slapped her hands on the table energetically. "Are you ready to go find out some information?"

"About what?"

"Your daughter. I still have contacts and Pittsburgh is only an hour away. Come on, we're burning daylight!"

She practically jumped out of her chair, which was amazing to me considering she looked like she was at least six months pregnant. I got up quickly and followed her out. If no one else was going to come in here and get to work with me, I would go with the one person that really seemed excited to help at the moment.

I followed her into the elevator and watched as she gave the same hand print, eye sensor crap that Chance had. When we got to the garage and stepped out, she grabbed my hand and immediately started pulling me to the left like her pants were on fire.

"Hey, why are we practically running?"

"Freckles! Stop right there!"

I turned to see a man running after us. Maggie looked behind us and started waddling faster toward a truck that was still quite a good distance away. The man caught up to us in no time, running ahead until he was stopped right in front of us. He was such a handsome man, hot actually. Handsome was such an understatement for this man. His eyes were so amazing that I actually thought I might get lost in them. But he most definitely wasn't her husband.

"Where are you going?"

"I'm just taking Morgan for a drive."

"No, you're not. Morgan is supposed to be meeting with Cap this morning. In fact, she's supposed to be in there in just a few minutes."

I watched the two of them bicker back and forth like a married couple. It was really strange. Maggie got right in his face, pushing her belly into him. "Sinner, don't make me do it."

"Don't you dare," he warned. "Cara stays out of this."

I watched as her eyes misted over and she cradled one hand in the other. "Sinner, please. You know how difficult it's been for me since that night. I have this reminder every day that seeps into my dreams at night. I just need to feel alive, like myself again."

His face softened and he pulled her into his embrace, running his hand up and down her back as he rested his chin on top of her head. "I wish I could have stopped those assholes. I would have done anything to keep you from having to go through that."

"I know," she sniffled.

He sighed and pulled back, wiping the tears from her face. "Come on, I'll drive you wherever you need to go."

He took her hand and turned for the truck. She looked over her shoulder and winked at me and motioned for me to follow. I had no idea what that was all about, but I definitely needed lessons from her in whatever manipulation tactics she used.

## Chapter Nineteen

# SNIPER

"Wait, so she just started cleaning your house, like some psycho?" Hunter asked in confusion.

"Yeah." My eyes were practically bulging from my head as I talked to the guys about this. It was just insane and made me feel like I was losing my mind. "Do you know how fucking disturbing it is to wake up to a woman doing your laundry and cooking you breakfast?"

"It's called a wife," Chris shot back.

"To you it is, but I don't have a fucking wife."

"Maybe she's applying for the job," Gabe laughed.

"This is serious," I said as I got in his face. "She's upstairs right now and we're gonna spend all day together trying to find her kid. Then she's gonna come home with me and sleep in my bed and use my fucking hypoallergenic pillow. What the hell am I supposed to do while she takes over my house?"

"Buy another pillow?" Chris suggested.

I took a deep breath, trying not to unleash my anger. These guys thought everything was so simple now that they were all married and had a different set of problems. I was trying to avoid that altogether.

"I can't have her walking around my house, cooking and cleaning. She'll think she can stay."

"Are you planning to kick her out?" Alec asked.

"No, of course not. I'm not a total asshole."

"Then why do you care if she cooks and cleans for you?"

"Because, those things lead to a certain comfort level. Then, she's fighting with me about where things go and trying to change the way I do shit in my own fucking house. Just ask Ice. He went through it with Lindsey."

Ice looked around the training center and then leaned in, whispering quietly to all of us. "Look, between us, she *did* do that and now nothing in my life is the way it should be. My tools aren't where they should be. My kitchen cabinets are all rearranged. I can't even put my fucking toothbrush on the side of the sink that I want to. And every fucking time I piss her off, she has to bring up something about bed bugs. It's a fucking pain in the ass, but if you ask me in front of her, she's the best thing that's ever happened to me and I love everything she's done to rearrange my house and it makes everything so much better."

"And she's your wife. I barely know Morgan. I've only fucked her a few times."

"What you need is to have a few freak outs," Hunter said. "Yeah, it worked for me. I mean, I wasn't trying to do it, but she got the hint real quick and moved out." He frowned slightly, shaking his head like he was baffled. "I had to really work my ass off to get her back, but it's an option."

I just stared at him stupidly. It was the worst fucking idea I'd heard, but just in case no one else had any better ideas, I'd keep it in the back of my mind. "Okay, any other ideas?"

"Amnesia worked pretty well for Jules," Chris suggested.

"You could fake your death like Knight," Alec said.

"Does anyone have any other ideas besides freaking out on her, getting myself seriously fucked in the head, or faking my death for a year? Seriously? Are these the only good ideas we have anymore? We're just recycling what all you assholes have already tried?"

"Hey," Ice said defensively. "This shit worked for us. I mean, it wasn't intentional, but it worked. You just need to find a way to really piss her off accidentally on purpose."

"That's it!" Hunter exclaimed. "Bring another woman home and fuck her in your bed. Nothing says move on like having another woman around."

This was what I was left with. For as smart as these guys all looked, they were giving me some fucking horrible ideas. "How is it possible that all of you managed to find and hang onto a woman?" I turned to Alec, who was still single. He had to have something that could help me. "What would you do if this was you?"

Alec looked over my shoulder, staring off in the distance. I turned, looking in the same direction, but all I saw was Florrie working with Knight. "I think you should go for it."

"What? No, I said that I don't want her to take over my space."

"Look, life is short and there's only so much pussy you can go through before you realize that one day, that pussy will be younger and stupider than what you're willing to settle for. In another twenty years, you're gonna want a woman that will still want to be with you, despite your shriveled dick."

"Hey, I'll only be fifty-five. My dick will be just fine."

"My point is, you need to find someone that wants to be with you for you. If you're always chasing someone that will leave in the morning, you're going to be very lonely when all the guns and missions are gone."

"I'm working until someone puts me in the ground," I said.

"Fine, you'll be lonely when you're shuffling down the hallway of the nursing home with a gun strapped to your waist. Maybe there'll be a jello fight you can break up. Only, it's not gonna be hot women fighting in jello, it's gonna be toothless grandmas fighting for the last cup. And I doubt you would shoot someone over that shit," Alec said.

"So, what you're saying," Hunter interjected, "is that we need to have a retirement community on the property also. Kind of like the school and training center for the kids. That way, we can stay amongst our kind. I like that idea," Hunter grinned. "And since I'm the medic, I get to hand out the medications."

"Let's put a plug in this fantastical idea for now. Let's not put us in the grave prematurely," Chris growled. "I still have plenty of working days left in me."

"It's not a bad idea," Ice shrugged. "It doesn't hurt to be prepared."

"What's wrong, old man? Are you feeling that ache in your bones already?" I jeered.

"You're like five years younger than me. By the time you get married and have kids, you'll be forty, if you're lucky," Ice shot back. "That makes you sixty when they go off to school and seventy or eighty by the time you see your first grandkid. Let that sink in for a minute."

"Yeah, all those things you think you're going to teach your kid are suddenly just a little too hard to do," Chris pointed out.

"Wait." I shook my head, trying to figure out how this got so off topic. "I'm trying to get a woman *out* of my house, not invite her to stay longer. There was never any conversation about kids or grandkids. It's not happening, so just drop it!"

"That's what we all said. Just keep that in mind while you're making your escape plan," Ice said just before Cap called and told me to get my ass upstairs for the meeting.

---

"Where is everyone?" I asked when I entered Cap's office. Nobody was in the conference room, so I assumed that we were meeting somewhere else.

"I thought you were getting everyone and we were meeting in the conference room," Cap said in confusion.

"I took Morgan there, but she's gone."

Cap looked at me strangely and we both started searching the floor for Morgan. If she had wandered off, she might be having a hard time finding her way back. However, our suspicions faltered when we walked into the IT room and saw Becky holding Cap's second born, Clara, and Caitlin, his first daughter, running around and pressing buttons.

"Where's Maggie?" Cap asked as he caught Caitlin from pressing more buttons.

"She left with Morgan. Something about taking Morgan into the city to talk to a contact," Becky shrugged.

"Shit." Cap swore and Caitlin grabbed his face, looking at him sourly.

"Daddy, that's a bad word."

"Yes, but Mommy did something to make Daddy say it."

"Mommy always does stuff to make you say bad words," Caitlin said solemnly.

"Yes, she does. Now, you stay with Becky while Daddy finds out what Mommy's up to this time."

"I can go with you, Daddy. Knight taught me how to sudbue a man using just two fingers," Caitlin said excitedly.

"Subdue, and I'm really glad that you know that, but we don't need to subdue Mommy." He set Caitlin down and then turned to me, jerking his head for the door. "At least not yet," he grumbled as we headed for the elevator. He pulled out his phone and put it on speakerphone for me to hear.

"Hi, Sebastian!" Freckles was being too cheerful, which meant that she was doing something she shouldn't.

"Don't be all sweet with me. Where did you take Morgan?"

"Now, Sebastian-"

"No!" Cap barked. "She just barely escaped with her life and now you're dragging her back to the city."

"I didn't drag her. She came willingly. Besides, we didn't go alone."

"Who's with you, Freckles?"

"Sebastian, don't be mad."

"Who, Freckles?"

There was a sigh and then a shuffling sound.

"Yo, Cap. Your friendly, neighborhood Sinner here."

"What the fuck are you doing, Sinner?"

"Cap, she was gonna go anyway."

"You could have stopped her. You're twice the size she is!"

"Not really. She's pregnant. Her ass is already- ow!" There was a smack in the background, probably Maggie beating the shit out of Sinner. "Fuck, I was just saying that you could probably sit on me and- shit! Would you stop hitting me? I'm just trying to- Ow, ow, ow..."

There was more shuffling in the background, some squealing of tires, more moans of pain, and then finally Freckles came back on the line. "Sorry about that. As I was saying, we're just meeting an old contact. I promise, it's nothing dangerous."

"How do you know that this contact won't hurt Morgan?" I asked. "You don't even know all the details of the case!"

"When have I ever done anything to put anyone in danger?" she asked.

"On your wedding day," I said.

"When you ran off to New York City," Cap added. "When you went into the warehouse when I told you not to."

"And let's not forget about you offering yourself up in place of Kate," Sinner said. "That's how she got me, Cap. She pulled the whole missing finger routine and then started crying and telling me that she needed to feel alive."

"She's been pulling that for years now. You shouldn't have fallen for it," Cap hissed.

"I know, but...you know I can't help it with Freckles. She's good at manipulating me. But I'm telling you right now that if she goes into labor, I'm leaving her ass on the side of the road with Morgan. I can't do that again."

"I'm only six months pregnant!" Freckles shouted in the background.

"Could have fooled me," Sinner muttered. "Ow! Damn, woman. Stop hitting me!"

"Sebastian, you could stand up for me here!"

"I'm too pissed at you right now. Besides, your lists only work if I'm actually in the same room as you."

I heard her grunting in disapproval and some more shuffling around.

"Listen, Cap. I gotcha covered here. I'm not gonna let her go off and do anything crazy. She only has one gun on her."

"Do you know how much trouble she can get into with one gun? Besides, Freckles never just has one gun. Did you check her purse?"

"Of course, I did," Sinner said in exasperation.

"And her ankles?"

"No, but Cap, seriously? Have you seen her ankles lately? There's no way she could hide an ankle holster down there with the size of those things."

"Try to not talk about my wife like she's a whale."

"Ow!" Sinner's voice screeched through the phone. "I didn't say you looked like a whale. He did!"

This was going nowhere fast. If I had to keep listening to this shit, I would never find out where they were going or what they were doing.

"Freckles, tell me where Morgan is. I don't like her going off on her own into the city."

"She not alone," Freckles snapped. "She's got me and she's got Sinner."

"That doesn't make me feel any better. Give me the address where you're going now or I'm gonna tell Cap your secret."

"Ha! He knows all my secrets."

"Does he really? Think hard Freckles."

There was silence on the other end for a minute.

"We're headed to Frick Park."

Cap sighed, slamming his fist against the desk. "Freckles, that park is over six hundred acres. I need a specific location."

"Frick Environmental Center, and that's all I'm saying!"

The line went dead and Cap stared at me. "So, what's she hiding from me?"

I shrugged. "I don't know, but it's Freckles. I figured there was something. Come on, they have a good head start on us."

## Chapter Twenty

# MORGAN

I wasn't sure if this was technically considered kidnapping. I had come along willingly for the most part, but I had no control over where we went. In fact, I was starting to think that Maggie was nothing but a troublemaker. Everyone seemed to think that she was always hiding something and would run off at a moment's notice. Which she kind of proved the way she wrapped Sinner around her finger and got him to go along with her plan.

"So, you didn't say who we're meeting," I said for the third time, hoping this time Maggie would say something to clue me in.

"It's a contact of mine. I haven't actually spoken to him in years, probably since my days working at *The Pittsburgh Press*. But he had his own column and every once in a while, he would write a piece on things that were going on in the city that he felt people needed to know about. It usually had something to do with illegal activities. He always knew the best people to go to for a story, but he never really shared any information."

"Then why would he help us?"

"Well, I figure that if we tell him about your daughter, he might be able to shed some light on other things that are going on. He's kind of a conspiracy theorist, but there's usually some truth to what he says."

"Wait, if there's only some truth, won't that possibly lead us on a wild goose chase?"

Sinner looked at me in the rearview mirror. "Most conspiracy theorists have about fifty to seventy-five percent of the information correct. Plus, since they're usually pretty paranoid, they really dig until they have the last scrap of information."

He pulled into the parking lot and put the SUV in park. "Where is the Environmental Center?"

Maggie shrugged. "It's over there," she pointed to a stone structure. "But we're not meeting him there. We're headed for one of the trails."

"Of course we are," Sinner muttered.

"Hey, do you want to hear what this guy has to say or do you want him to run off? I'm gonna have a hard enough time getting him to talk with Morgan around."

"And me," Sinner added with a meaningful look.

"No," Maggie said firmly. "There's no way he'll meet me with a guy like you around. He'll just turn and run in the other direction."

"I'll be there. You tell me the trail and I'll hide in the trees, but there's no fucking way that I'm letting the two of you meet with this guy without any backup."

"Fine."

They got out of the SUV, so I followed suit and trailed behind them to the entrance. Maggie grabbed a map and pointed something out to Sinner.

"Right here."

Sinner gave a curt nod and took off in another direction. I followed behind Maggie, curious as to what I had actually gotten myself into. We walked for a good mile before we came to another side trail that was darker and seemed to be alive with demons down the darkened path.

"Are you sure we should be coming down here without Sinner? This doesn't look very safe."

"Don't worry. Sinner's in the trees. I just hope we can get what we need before Sebastian and Chance show up. I figure we had a fifteen minute head start, but I know Sinner was driving slower to allow them to catch up. We have ten minutes at best."

"Who is this guy we're meeting?"

"He's just what I said earlier, a conspiracy theorist. He's one of the most accurate conspiracy theorists I've ever come across though. If there's anyone that can help us, it's him. He blends in with everyone and finds ways to spy on the most careful, watchful people. He has so much dirt on the politicians of this state."

"Why doesn't he expose them?"

"Some of them he has. Others, he's digging for the bigger story. He knows he'll never get the big fish if he goes after the smaller ones first. See, with these guys, there are so many players involved and they all have their fingers in a separate piece of pie. If you go after one of the smaller fish and hope to extract information, all you end up with is a dead fish."

We walked for a few more minutes as I let that sink in. I felt way out of my league here, even more so than when I was working at the club. It might have been because Maggie seemed so on top of her game, so knowledgeable. It made me realize that I really didn't stand a chance on my own of finding out who was behind all this.

We stopped and sank back into the shadows of the trees, leaning up against the trunk of a rather large tree and waited. Ten minutes passed before we saw someone walking in the opposite direction that we came from. The man wore a trench coat and a fedora, looking like a spy out of the fifties.

Maggie took a step forward, motioning for me to stay back. The two of them spoke for a few seconds and then he followed her back to the tree I was resting against.

"This is Arnold. He's my contact."

"It's a pleasure to meet you, Arnold. I'm Morgan."

"Yes, I know who you are," he said shrewdly.

I looked at him in confusion, as did Maggie. "Um, how do you know who I am?"

"You're the one that tried to get in with The Broker. The news of your death was greatly exaggerated. I guess you weren't actually supposed to be killed. The Broker never leaves someone alive unless he means to."

"Well, I wasn't exactly-"

"Trust me, my dear. If he had wanted you dead, nobody would have even found your body. He doesn't waste time with torturing people or drawing out deaths for his own satisfaction. No, if he wants you dead, a bullet is put right between your eyes and then you disappear before anyone even knows you're missing."

"What does that mean exactly?" I was nervous now that he was making it sound like there was a reason I was alive. What did this mean for me? What did he want from me?

"It means that he still has plans for you."

The man stepped closer and I could now see that he had a greying beard, neatly trimmed, across his roughened face. But his eyes were what really caught my attention. He looked like he had all the knowledge in the world inside those eyes.

"Maggie, my dear, why don't you tell me exactly what you're looking for," Arnold said as if he hadn't just told me that The Broker was still after something from me.

"We're looking for information on a little girl that went missing about six months ago. The little girl was Morgan's daughter, Payton James. She was snatched by a white van from a playground and there were no leads on the case. It's like she just vanished."

Arnold's posture had stiffened as soon as he heard my daughter's name and he took a step back, looking around wildly as if someone would pop out of the trees at any moment. I started mimicking his movements, nervous now that I had made a mistake coming along and would be dead before the end of the day.

"You shouldn't have brought this to me. Let it go and accept that your daughter is gone. You'll never see her again."

"What?" I asked in shock. "What do you know? Tell me!" I said frantically. I started forward, but he stepped back. "Please, she was only four. I have to find her."

His gaze kept swiveling around, but whoever he thought was there hadn't made their presence known. "Look, there are things that you need to stay out of and this is one of them. You'll never get your daughter back because it's very likely she's already in the hands of very powerful people."

"What do they want with her?" My eyes were filling with tears as I thought about all the different things that could be happening to her. "Please," I begged. "Please, I need to know what's happened to her."

Arnold looked at me, his eyes filling with sympathy and his face hard. His eyes flicked to Maggie once again and then he sighed, finally relenting to my pleas. When he spoke, he was quiet and talked quickly.

"There have been children from different cities disappearing all over the country. With most abduction cases, there's some kind of evidence. You have fingerprints, even if they can't be matched. Or someone ends up dead while trying to take the child. There are suspects that the police investigate and that usually leads to more suspects or at least points them in another direction.

"The difference with the abductions of these children, like your daughter, is that there are no leads. Someone may witness the actual abduction, but no one ever sees faces or finds any evidence of the child actually being taken, like hair or fibers. The children are just gone. These people are professionals and they don't make any mistakes."

"Why are they being taken?" Maggie asked.

"No one knows. I have my suspicions, but nothing concrete. From what I've been able to piece together, they're flown out of the country."

"But someone would be able to track them. You have to be listed on a flight manifest."

"Not these people," he shook his head. "Whoever these people are have so much power that they can make anything happen, anyone disappear without a trace of evidence."

"But why my daughter? What's so special about her that someone would take her?"

"The children that are taken come from single parent households that don't have the resources to dig too deeply into the child's disappearance."

"They aren't worried about the other parent trying to figure out what's going on?" Maggie asked. Arnold looked at me questioningly.

"Payton's father never wanted to be part of her life. I contacted him several times over the years, but he always pretended like he wasn't the father and had no interest in taking a paternity test."

"But the police are still involved and usually the FBI at such a young age," Maggie insisted. "It's not like they could keep the FBI from digging into these abductions. Surely, they can connect the dots and figure out there's a pattern or a connection between these children at the very least."

"The FBI is well aware of the connection, but they also can't find anything to track this trafficking ring. Either that or they're being bought off."

"Wait, there's still one problem, a mother that's desperate enough will continue to search for her child," Maggie said. "Obviously, they know this considering that Morgan did just that. I'm sure she's not the only mother to take matters into her own hands. So, what are we missing?"

Arnold looked nervous, like he didn't want to reveal the last bit of information. "The mothers have disappeared also, along with a few fathers that were the single parent. Usually, the parent doesn't have any family around to raise any questions about his or her disappearance."

"The trafficking ring at the club," I surmised. "There were plenty of single mothers there, trying to put enough food on the table for their kids."

"But you were the exception," Arnold admitted. "You need to find out why he spared your life. The Broker has something else in store for you, and if I had to guess, I would assume that he wants you for himself. That you've caught his eye."

"But he had his chance," I argued. "He had me and drugged me. He could have taken me at any time."

"True, but his focus that night obviously wasn't you."

"He didn't want you taken into the trafficking ring," Maggie concluded. "But maybe he wasn't ready to take you yet. Maybe he needed more time."

"This is insane," I cut in. "This sounds like a bunch of guessing. You're not showing me any proof. You're just guessing here."

"Morgan, he's the best. I swear-"

"No! There's no proof, nothing suggesting that my child was taken into this elusive trafficking ring or that I would be taken by The Broker. He's not even the one running all this."

"He's trying to tell you-"

Her voice was cut off by the sound of something sharp hitting the tree just inches from us. We all dropped to the ground and Maggie shoved me deeper into the trees. I crawled on my belly, trying to find some cover. Every few seconds, bullets pinged off trees and hit the ground close by. My heart was beating out of control and I was shaking so bad that I could hardly crawl. I glanced back and noticed that I was the only one crawling away. Maggie was leaning behind a tree on her butt, loading a weapon. Arnold was nowhere to be seen.

Maggie looked up at me and waved me on, but she was pregnant and there was no way I was leaving her behind. She turned and shot several times before taking cover again. I realized then that she wasn't the only one firing from this side. I could hear shots coming from all around us, but I couldn't see anyone. Suddenly, I was hoisted up from the ground and flung over a shoulder. I wanted to scream, but Maggie motioned for me to be quiet. Whoever was carrying me was running deeper into the trees, so fast, it was as if I weighed nothing at all. I saw another man pick up Maggie, carrying her differently since she was pregnant and hauled ass in the same direction we were headed. I wanted to slap whoever had me and tell them to put me back down, but the man's shoulder was bulky and poking me hard in the stomach, making it difficult to speak. Before I knew it, we were at a dirt road and I was being thrown into the back of an SUV.

I scrambled to sit up and find out who had taken me and where we were going. I didn't recognize the person in the back seat with me and I pushed back further against the door. He didn't look at all worried that I would jump from the vehicle. I gripped onto the handle, but the door didn't budge. It must have been a childproof lock because the man just laughed when he saw me try the handle out of the corner of his eye.

"Who are you?" I asked with more courage than I felt. Inside I was shaking like a leaf. There were two people sitting in the front seat and one turned around and smiled at me. I breathed a sigh of relief when I saw that it was Gabe. The man in the driver's seat looked vaguely familiar. I dug through my memories and had a faint vision of his face above mine, but it almost felt like a dream.

"I'm Rocco. Not sure if you remember me, but I was the one that took care of you when your boy found you at the well and then again back at the safe house."

"My boy?" I asked. He couldn't possibly mean Chance. He wasn't mine in any way.

"Chance would be here, but he's out there trying to take out some of those assholes that were shooting at you."

"Why? Why would he be the one to stay behind?"

"Sniper, you've heard the nickname from Chief, his former superior. He was a sniper in the military," Gabe said.

That sounded familiar. Hadn't Chance already told me that? Everything seemed to be running together until nothing really fit together in my mind. I felt like I needed a mental recharge.

"Um...so, who were those people shooting at us?"

"I would assume someone who wants to kill you," the guy beside me said. "I'm Chris, by the way. I work with a different team, but since Freckles decided to go rogue, we had to scramble to get some guys together to come save your ass."

I flushed bright red, feeling terrible for causing so much trouble. "I'm sorry. I didn't-"

"Don't worry about it, darlin'. You're not the first or last woman that will be a pain in the ass. In fact, if you stick around, I'm sure you'll fit in quite nicely with the rest of the women."

"Don't mention that he said that to any of the ladies," Gabe said quickly. He glared at Chris. "I just got out of the doghouse with Isa. No need to send me back there so soon."

"So, where are we going? And why was I grabbed before Maggie? She's pregnant. Shouldn't she have been taken out first?"

Chris snorted beside me. "Good luck with that one. Freckles can take care of herself, for the most part. She'd never let one of us drag her out of a gun fight, except, maybe Sinner."

"What about Sebastian? He's her husband, right?"

"That's why he wouldn't try to get her out. Those two are like oil and water. Maggie would stay just to spite him."

"So, he'd just leave her there? In the middle of a gunfight?"

"It's not like he'd allow her to get hit. He made sure to start moving the fight away from her. That way she doesn't realize that he's protecting her."

This was the weirdest group of people I had ever met. A pregnant woman in a gunfight and men that were worried about getting in trouble with their wives, all looking out for each other so none of them got in too deep. I'd never met a group of people that were so close, yet so weird.

## Chapter Twenty-One

# SNIPER

I slammed the door to the SUV as I got out and stomped toward the elevator. I had my bag for my sniper rifle slung over my shoulder and if it weren't for the fact that I promised to help Morgan find her daughter, I might point the rifle at her and tell her to run. What the hell had she been thinking, running off with Maggie to get information about her daughter? It was reckless and stupid. She could have been killed.

I put my rifle away and was just about to head upstairs when I ran into Knight. He eyed me, always assessing and reading each of us like we were open books. The man had a talent for picking up on cues better than most. Anyone could tell when someone was angry or happy, but he seemed to see through all of that and know exactly what was wrong and how to help with whatever we needed. It was one of the reasons he was so good at his job.

"Follow me," he said as we stepped onto the elevator. I didn't argue with him because there really wasn't any point. If I tried to walk away, he would just beat the shit out of me until I chose to follow him.

We got out on the floor with the training center and made our way over to the ring. He tossed me a pair of boxing gloves and got out the tape. After he wrapped my hands, I slipped on my gloves and got in the ring with him. I loosened up, hopping from foot to foot as I felt the tension still humming through my body.

Knight nodded to me and seconds later he was coming at me, his fist flying through the air toward my face. I ducked and threw a jab of my own at his ribs, but he dropped his elbow. I pulled back just before I would have hit his elbow and broke my hand. I was swinging like I was in an actual boxing match because I was so angry, but that was a good way to get injured and I didn't want to be taken out of the work rotation because I was stupid enough to get injured.

We continued to spar, both of us taking hits from time to time. Mostly me though. Knight was one hell of a boxer and rarely lost a match with one of us. I was running out of steam after what felt like ten rounds and made the mistake of letting my guard down. One heavy swing had me falling to the ground, smacking my head on the ground with a swollen eye. Knight leaned over me, barely looking winded, his eyebrow raised as if he was asking me if I'd had enough.

He helped me to my feet and we bumped fists before I left the ring and went to take a shower. I was considerably less angry now that my energy reserves had been significantly depleted. When I was dressed, I went upstairs to see Morgan. She was sitting in the conference room with Maggie. Both of them looked pissed and I could only guess that Cap had already had a talk with them.

"Maggie, can you give me a few minutes with Morgan?" My eyes didn't leave Morgan as I spoke to Maggie. This wasn't her fault, well, not all her fault. Morgan was an adult and had chosen to follow Maggie without asking if it was safe to do so. Maggie slipped from the room, shutting the door behind her. I took a seat across from Morgan, not wanting to sit too close.

"Do you realize how dangerous it was to run off like that without telling anyone?"

"You can save it. I've already gotten yelled at from Sebastian," she said angrily.

"Well, now you're gonna hear it from me. I swore that I would help you find your daughter. Why the hell would you run off without telling me?"

"We had Sinner with us."

I slammed my fist on the table, my anger rising once again. "It doesn't fucking matter. If we hadn't shown up, you could have been killed. Sinner's a good shot and he's damn good at his job, but he can't defend two women against several men, especially when one of those women is pregnant."

"It was my choice to make. I told you that I would do anything to find my daughter and I meant it!"

"And it was Maggie's choice to take you, but Maggie has always acted without thinking. She's pregnant and Cap would be devastated if something happened to Maggie or his unborn child. You should have stopped her and told her it was a bad idea."

"Sinner didn't think it was a problem," she shot back.

"Hell yes he did! The problem is that when Maggie makes up her mind about something, she follows through because she's stubborn. Sinner knows that Maggie will do whatever the hell she wants, no matter what anyone else says."

"Then why the hell did it matter if I went along or not?"

"Because you could have been killed! I told you that you were a target. Maggie was put in danger because of you. You should have come to talk to me first. Hell, talk to anyone about it."

She stood, her fists going to her hips. "Listen, I didn't ask you to look out for me. You made me a promise that I didn't ask for. I have never let anyone else stop me from going after my daughter and I never will. She's my baby and she's all I have left. I can't give up and I won't sit by while someone else decides what we will or won't look into."

"I'm not saying you have to, but fuck, let me in on things. Let me help you!"

"You told me you would help this morning and then you disappeared. You were gone for like, an hour. How long was I supposed to sit around and wait for you to decide to discuss things with me?"

This was going nowhere. We were just going round and round with all this shit. If I continued to try and make her see things my way, it would only push her further away. She would make some stupid mistake and end up dead. Though, in the back of my mind, I was wondering why I cared. She was just someone I slept with. If she wanted to go off on her own, I should let her. But no matter how much I told myself that's what I should do, I just couldn't follow through on that. I needed to help her and I knew there was no way I could just walk away.

"Look, I get it and I promise that won't happen again. But I can't let you go off and do this on your own. It's dangerous and you're already a target. Please, let me and the rest of Reed Security help you. We're good at our jobs."

She looked like she wanted to argue some more, but pursed her lips and gave a swift nod. "Maggie was filling Becky in on what we found out. I guess we're waiting to hear what she finds."

"Good. How about we head home and get some takeout. You can tell me what you learned over dinner."

"Alright."

We left the building, but something I had said kept running through my mind. I had said we would go home. Not my home. Why I had said that could be as simple as a slip of the tongue, but somehow it didn't feel that way. I couldn't start thinking of us as being a pair, even if this was just as a partnership. I would start to feel attached and that was something I just didn't want to do again. I'd have to really watch how I handled things from here on out or I'd find myself slipping into old habits that I'd had with my ex, and nothing good came out of that relationship.

---

"So, this guy thinks that Payton was taken by some really powerful people, but he didn't say where she would be taken or for what reason?"

We were sitting in the living room eating Chinese food and she was telling me about her talk with Arnold.

"He didn't specify. He basically just told me that I should stop looking because there was no way I would ever see her again. I can't give up though. There has to be a way to find her."

"You don't know for sure that this guy's information is correct. We don't run off half-cocked without proven information. That's dangerous and will get people killed," I said, wanting her to understand that none of us would follow up on leads that weren't corroborated in some way.

"He...he also said that if The Broker left me alive, it was for a reason."

"What reason?"

She shrugged as she toyed with her food, but the slump of her shoulders said that she had a pretty good idea.

"He put you in a well. There was no way that we could know for sure that we would find you. I would guess that he did want you dead."

"Arnold said that The Broker makes sure a body is never found when he wants to get rid of someone. He said that he would have put a bullet in my head immediately." She looked up at me, biting her lip nervously. "If he just wanted me out of the way so I wasn't taken with the other strippers, that means that....that-"

"That he wants you for himself," I finished, understanding exactly what she was trying to get at. "You said that he said he would come back for you. And that night, he requested you to join him in one of the rooms." She nodded. "Has he ever given you any other impression that he wants you for himself?"

"He...uh...the first time I saw him, he touched me while I was on stage."

I tried to keep a rein on my anger, but I had already heard this from Storm and if anything, I was more pissed now than I was before. "Storm told me about that."

"It's not like I wanted it." Her face flushed bright red and she dropped her chopsticks, looking away from me.

"He put his fingers in you," I stated. "You let him violate you on the stage in front of all those other men. Why didn't you stop him? You could have called Storm over and he would have thrown his ass out."

"Because I wanted to find my daughter," she snapped, her face swiveling sharply to face me. I didn't see any shame or embarrassment on her face anymore. The only thing I saw now was resolve, but then tears started slipping down her cheeks as reality caught up with her. "He was obviously powerful and I thought...Don't judge me," she said as she swiped the tears from her face. "I know that I shouldn't have allowed it, but I was desperate. I'm still desperate and if he wanted me in exchange for my daughter being free, I would do it in a heartbeat."

"But you don't know that he even knows anything about your daughter. You're assuming that he's involved, but the truth is, we have no idea if he just would have had information or if he was part of her kidnapping."

I was trying to hold in my anger. I knew she was looking at this from a mother's perspective, but we needed to do this logically, not with our emotions.

"I can't keep doing this," she said quietly. "I need to get my daughter back. She's only four. I have no idea what's happening with her and that's killing me. Every day that she's gone, she's losing a little piece of herself and becoming someone that someone else wants her to be. It's been six months!"

She stood and walked over to the window, staring out into the darkness. I didn't even think twice as I walked over to her and wrapped my arms around her. "Just hold onto your hope. Without that, you have nothing."

She leaned her head back against my chest with a sigh, holding my arms tight to her. "I'm trying."

"Hey," I turned her around to face me and held her jaw, forcing her to look at me. "We're not giving up, but we have to be careful. I don't want you running off on your own. If The Broker is really wanting you for himself, we have to keep you safe and hidden. He can't know where you are and you can't go out looking for your daughter. If he takes you, what would your daughter come home to?"

She sighed, but nodded slightly. "I can try to stay hidden, but I can't promise that I won't look for my daughter. Please, don't ask me to."

The pleading look in her eyes was one that I understood all too well. It was the same look that a soldier gave when he was about to die and had one last request, something he needed to be at peace with before he died. We came to an understanding of sorts that night, one that involved a little give and take on both our parts. Nothing was set in stone, but at least there was some common ground between us now.

"Are you going to sleep on the floor again tonight?"

"I was planning to," I said hesitantly.

"Can I ask you a question?"

"Of course."

"Why did you flip out this morning?" I raised an eyebrow in question. She thought I was flipping out, but I was pretty sure she was the one that had lost her mind.

"Okay, don't take this the wrong way, but you've made yourself awfully at home in my house. It was just a little too much."

"In what way?"

"Well, with the whole grocery shopping thing and the laundry. This isn't your house and we're not in a relationship. I don't want you to start thinking that since you're staying here a few days that you can have run of my house. This is all temporary and the sex is just sex. I won't ever want more with you and I'm not going to change my mind on that."

Her lips were twitching and there was a twinkle in her eyes that was confusing me. It seemed like she was trying not to laugh at me.

"What? Why is that funny?"

She burst out laughing, doubling over and holding her stomach. "I'm sorry. I shouldn't be laughing, but you're just so serious and-"

"You're damn right I'm serious. I'm not joking around here, Morgan. This is my house and I'm not gonna tolerate any bullshit."

She laughed even harder, and the more she laughed, the more pissed I became. I hated women that couldn't take my lack of relationships seriously. Like they could change me or make me a man that would see the light and suddenly want it all.

"I'm sorry, it's just that...you think I want a relationship....with you," she said, laughing between her words. She calmed herself enough to speak and bit her lip to stop any residual giggles. I was actually a little offended how she stated that she didn't want a relationship *with me*, like the idea that I could make her happy was laughable. "I don't want a relationship, Chance. I like sex with you, but that's all I want. As for this morning, I just wanted to thank you for giving me a place to stay and for looking out for me. I wasn't trying to make something between us."

"But...you offered to fold my laundry. That's domestic bullshit."

"I only offered because you looked at me strangely. I figured you were thinking that I should fold it if I washed it."

"So...you really weren't trying to move in and..."

"Become a housewife? No, I have bigger ambitions in life than to wait on a man and make sure his socks are ironed."

"I don't actually iron my socks," I said in irritation.

"So, you're good with having sex while I'm here? Cuz, I liked the sex last night, but the floor was uncomfortable."

"Who are you kidding? You were laying on me all night like I was a pillow. I was the one with my back on the hard floor all night."

"Aw, would you like me to kiss it and make it better?"

I bent over and threw her over my shoulder. She squealed and I smacked her ass as I headed to the bedroom. "You bet your ass you're gonna kiss something, but it ain't gonna be my ass."

---

"I like fucking you," Morgan said as we laid in postcoital bliss.

She was laying on her side of the bed and I was on mine. It felt like there was an ocean between us, even though this was what we both wanted. Except, she looked like she was perfectly happy and for some reason, I was wishing she had laid on top of me like she had last night. I didn't want the whole package, but feeling her pressed against me was nice. But I had thrown down the gauntlet, making it perfectly clear that there never would be anything between us. I couldn't tell her I wanted her in my arms after the fight I put up.

"Same here, sweet cheeks."

What else was I supposed to say? I looked over at her, thinking maybe she was just hiding the need to be in my arms, but she had her eyes closed and a smile on her face. I rolled my eyes, crossing my arms over my chest with a manly pout. This shit wasn't right. She was supposed to want me to hold her. She was the one that was supposed to be tripping over herself to get just a small piece of me. Yet, here I was, sulking because she was content on her side of the bed. It didn't even make any fucking sense. I really didn't want a girlfriend. I didn't want a commitment or someone even thinking she had some say in my life. I never wanted to feel like I was being used again. And Morgan was making it perfectly clear that the only way she was using me was for her own pleasure. And that actually kind of hurt.

"So, what's the plan for tomorrow?"

She wanted to talk about tomorrow? We'd just gotten done screwing and she was already thinking about tomorrow. Talk about a kick to the nuts.

"We'll meet up with Becky and see if she can verify anything Arnold told you."

She turned to me, propped up on her elbow and rested her head in her hand. "And if what he said is true? Where do we go from there?"

"We have to figure out if we can link The Broker to the other cases. If so, we need to get our hands on him, which won't be easy. He's got tighter security than the President."

I stared at her breasts as they hung heavily to the side. They were perfect, full with large nipples that I wanted to suck into my mouth. I could very easily get attached to this woman's body. Everything from her creamy skin that was so smooth to her sexy curves that made her ass sway as she walked gave me a hard on.

"-just the guy with information."

I shook my head, trying to regain my focus. I hadn't heard most of what she said and she could tell by my lack of response. "Sorry, say that again."

"I said that even if he is connected, he's probably not the guy that we really want. He's rich and has too much to lose to actually be involved in anything that could get him in trouble with the law. He's just the guy with information."

"A guy with information can be very useful, but you're probably right. He probably just gathers information from around the city and turns it over to whoever's in charge. I would guess that he very rarely finds out who the targets are or how they're sold. That would make him an accomplice. Everything else would be hard to prove in a court of law."

"You know, if the sex trafficking ring is related at all to the ring that takes the children, we could send someone undercover to find out more information. I could-"

"No," I said forcefully, sitting up and turning away from her. The thought of her ever being in a sex trafficking ring made my stomach churn. "Don't even think of offering yourself up as bait. There's no way to communicate with us. Every woman would be searched first and after that, most of the women are drugged to keep them under control. We wouldn't even have a very good chance of getting a trained person out of a situation like that."

"Then how do we find out who's behind this?"

I didn't have an answer for her. I hadn't dealt with something like this before and I would have to rely on others to help guide me. I was a killer. I gained intel by watching and waiting. I didn't think that would work in this situation.

I sat back down on the bed and looked into her desperate eyes. "I don't know," I said quietly. "We wait until morning and see what Becky has. That's all we can do. There's no point in trying to figure it out until we have more information to go on."

Her face fell and she plopped down on her back, staring up at the ceiling. I laid down beside her and pulled her into my chest. I told myself it was to comfort her, but it was really to get what had been missing after we had sex. We laid in silence for the longest time, just staring at the ceiling, her resting her head against my chest and listening to my heart thump. It was the most at peace I had ever felt.

"Why did your wife leave you?"

I was taken aback by her question. I had been expecting more talk of getting her daughter back and my wife rarely entered my mind anymore. "She didn't like me being gone all the time. She said she couldn't handle it."

"Is that really the reason she left?" It was like she could read my mind, like she knew that it was just an excuse that I made up to get through the day. I found that for once, I didn't want to lie about it. I didn't want to give the whole, *my job is too dangerous* speech.

"She was using me," I admitted quietly. "She saw me as a meal ticket. One that she wouldn't have to actually deal with. Every penny that I earned, she took for keeping up the house. She said she couldn't work while I was away, that she was too depressed to hold down a job. And I believed her. I kept telling myself that I would get out and make something real with her. When I told her that I was coming home, she made me believe that she really was excited. But when I walked through the door, she was already packed. It wasn't more than six months later that we were divorced and she was living with another guy."

"How can you be sure that she was lying?"

"After she left, I found a letter from my commander. He was asking me to reconsider re-enlisting. See, you can't just get out of a contract. I served my full contract and then requested to be discharged, which is pretty damn difficult to achieve. With how much money is spent training a SEAL, they really don't approve that many people to be discharged unless it's for medical reasons or misconduct. I had to fight tooth and nail, and I hated every damn minute of it. I didn't want to leave The Teams and I sure as hell didn't want to leave the men I served with. But I fought for her, and in the end, she was already gone."

"If she wanted to leave, why didn't you just re-enlist?"

That was a good question, one I still wasn't quite sure I had the answer to. "Embarrassment maybe? I think I was so ashamed that I had pushed to leave The Teams and then she left me. I had given up on my brothers for nothing. I guess I didn't want to be seen as a fool."

"Is that really how you see it? That you were a fool for trying to make her happy?"

She looked at me skeptically, but she had hit the nail on the head. That was exactly how I felt.

"Have you ever given everything to someone and they just walked away like you never really meant anything?"

"Yeah," she said after a minute. "I spent years with Matt, Payton's father. When he found out I was pregnant, he was gone the very same night I told him. There was no thinking it over. He didn't stay in contact with me. He didn't even call to see if we had a boy or a girl. I sent him a letter saying that I had the baby and he could come visit if he wanted. I never heard from him. Yeah, I can say I felt like a fool for believing that what we had was strong enough to make it through anything."

"He was an asshole for walking away."

"She was a bitch for walking out after begging you to be with her."

We sat in silence, holding each other and comforting each other for what our loved ones did to us. It was strange to think that I could talk to a woman that I was fucking and feel more commiseration with her than the men I worked with that had fought for our country and understood the horrors we saw. Knowing that she not only lost the man she loved, but was raising her child on her own seemed like a low blow. Her child being kidnapped and losing the one thing that made her life whole was something I couldn't even begin to comprehend. I got over leaving the Navy. I didn't think she would ever get over it if she didn't find Payton.

## Chapter Twenty-Two

# MORGAN

For the first time in six months, I slept through the night and actually felt refreshed when I woke up. It was because of Chance. The way we talked last night made me feel like I wasn't completely alone, like what happened to us shaped us into untrusting shells of who we once were, and we both understood the feeling. I fell asleep on his chest with his arm wrapped around me. His body warmed me all night, making me feel like there was a safety net surrounding me. The steady beat of his heart lulled me to sleep and was the first thing I felt when I woke in the morning.

Chance's phone dinged a few minutes after I woke up and I felt him come awake beneath me. He pulled the phone off his nightstand and then set it back down.

"We're supposed to meet at Reed Security this afternoon. They're still looking into a few things."

I nodded against his chest, but didn't move. It was probably wrong of me, but I didn't want to leave the cocoon of his arms just yet. For a fuck buddy, he was doing a really good job of holding me together when I felt like I might lose it.

"Tell me something about Payton," he said quietly.

A million memories ran through my mind all at once. It was hard to think of which one to share. "She's got blonde hair that is really thick and wavy. It looks like I actually curl her hair every morning. And her eyes are the most beautiful, vibrant shade of blue with a dark ring on the outside of her irises. Everyone always said her eyes were captivating."

I fell quiet, wondering if he wanted to hear more or if he was just trying to be nice.

"What's she like?"

"She's very outgoing. She loves to make new friends and she would help anyone that needed it. She's the sweetest little girl you've ever met, but has an attitude that could rival a teenager's when she gets in a mood." I laughed, thinking about her sassier moments. "When she was three, she was all about being a little girl and playing dress up. Being a princess was the ultimate at playtime. But when she turned four, her attitude came out more and more. She would cock her hip and put a hand on her hip. She could pose like she was a model without having any lessons and her hair always had to be done in a cute hairdo that made her look and feel like a princess. She always wanted her nails painted so that she could look just like me."

He picked up my hand and studied my fingers. "You don't wear nail polish."

"Not anymore. I used to like to go for manicures when I got the chance, but I just didn't have the desire to do it once I lost her. On the day she turned four, I took her for a manicure and pedicure at my favorite salon to make her feel like a big girl. All the ladies in the shop were saying how beautiful she was. I even got a call a few months back asking when I would be bringing her in again. All the ladies wanted to see how big she had gotten. That was an awkward conversation. They hadn't heard about her disappearance."

"How did they not hear? Amber alerts go out for every missing child."

"I'm not sure. I guess not everyone pays attention." We both fell into silence for a moment, but now I had a burning question. "Do you think there was ever a possibility that someone would have been able to save her? Or do you think this was a well orchestrated kidnapping?"

He swiveled his head so he could see me better. "I think there's nothing you could have done. You can't keep someone in a box to keep them safe. You have to live life, and unfortunately, there are bad people in this world that prey on those that are weaker. It was a terrible twist of fate, but none of that is your fault."

It was kind of scary how well he could read my thoughts. Yes, I did blame myself for her disappearance. I had chosen to take her to a daycare provider that I didn't know, and because of that, she was put in danger she might not have been in otherwise.

"What do you think you'll do when you get her back?"

When, not if. It warmed my heart to hear the confidence in his voice. "I think I want to move someplace quiet. The city no longer holds the appeal that it once did. Now I just want to live a quiet life where nobody knows me."

"You can't shut yourself off from the world. Bad things happen all the time and it doesn't matter if you live in the city or in the middle of nowhere."

"I know, but look at where you live. It's so peaceful here. The town isn't too big and it seems like everyone is friends around here. I don't think I've ever known one of my neighbors while I lived in the city."

"You could always come live here when you find her." My head swiveled his way in disbelief. Was he asking me to move in with him? When he saw the questions on my face, he quickly amended his statement. "I mean, in this town. You've met so many people recently and we look after each other here."

"That might be nice, but I'm not sure. I don't know that I could live so close to Pittsburgh anymore. It would be a constant reminder of what happened."

"It's just something to think about."

And I definitely would. I did like the people I had met so far. The one issue that I had was that I was starting to feel the slightest bit of something for Chance and that was dangerous. He'd made it perfectly clear that he didn't want more, and I thought I didn't either. But I'd never met a man like him, one that so willingly put me first. What would I do when he moved on to another woman? Would I be able to watch him take other women home? What if he decided to get married one day? I wasn't sure that I would be able to stand watching him fall for another woman and promise her everything he could never promise me. Yes, Chance was definitely starting to mean more to me than I ever thought he would.

---

I sat at the conference room table with Chance and Sebastian. Becky was just coming through the door with a large stack of folders and started passing them out. I didn't know what they were, but it was obvious she had done a lot of work in the past few days.

"Okay, I did a lot of digging last night, like so much that sleep wasn't an option at all. I've had so much coffee that my coffee needs coffee to stay awake," she rambled.

"Becky," Sebastian said, stopping her rant. "Let's just get to what you found and then you can go to sleep."

"Righty-o, bossman. So, I started with the idea that other children had been taken by this ring and gathered every single piece of information I could. Some of my program is still sorting details of the police reports, but here's what I have so far. It looks like about twenty children have been taken over the past two years, all with the same kidnapping markers as Payton's case. I can't be sure yet that all the cases are connected, but all of these children are still missing."

"How does The Broker fit in with all of these cases?" Chance asked.

"Well, almost every single one of the cities that a child was taken from is a city where Weston Hughes has one of his businesses located. There are a few that didn't match up, but weren't far away either. However, other than that, there's no link that I'm seeing between him and the kids or the moms that went missing. It seems that Morgan is the first woman he's made contact with that is linked to either of these rings."

"So, we can't prove his involvement in any way," Chance said angrily.

"Not that I can see. I've gone through all his accounts and there are no deposits that aren't legitimate. Unless he's funneling through one of his companies, which I could technically hack the records for, he's doing this all in cash or offshore accounts. And honestly, I don't think he would cash a check that had *for trafficking children* in the memo line. Either way, there's no way to confirm that he's involved."

"What about acquaintances?" Sebastian asked.

"He has many, but none that pop out as anyone nefarious. He keeps all his social and business dealings on the up and up. Basically, the only way that he does anything even remotely illegal or has an association that would be seen as unsavory is as The Broker. And The Broker only deals in cash."

"Crap," Chance muttered.

"So, you found nothing," Sebastian said.

"Not necessarily," Becky grinned. "The agent that Jeremy Wick was in contact with, Agent Finley, has several interesting oddities in his accounts."

Becky took a remote and turned on one of the screens on the wall. In seconds, she was flipping through windows and clicking on links until she came to what she was looking for.

"What are we looking at?" Sebastian asked.

"This is Agent Finley's account that is supposedly hidden under a false name, Brett Michaels."

"Brett Michaels? Seriously?" I scoffed.

"Apparently he's as unoriginal as he is stupid. The account can be traced back to him by any decent hacker. Whoever was hiding his account was not a professional. There are deposits, dating back from the very first kidnapping, of $10,000 per child. Each deposit shows up in his account two days after the child is taken."

"$10,000 doesn't seem like a very large amount for the kidnapping of a child," Sebastian surmised. "When you consider the consequences if you're caught, why would Agent Finley put his career and his life on the line for $10,000?"

"I found old gambling debts that he's been slowly paying off over the years. The interest alone will assure that he will never pay it off in this lifetime."

"So, the $10,000 goes to that?" Chance asked.

"It hasn't gone anywhere," Becky said. "That's the insane thing. If you owed money and were doing this to pay off debts, you would be making those large payments to get rid of the interest that was accumulating."

"That means he's collected about $200,000." Chance looked over at Cap. "That's not enough to run away on. He would need more than that."

"He could be collecting enough to disappear in the future, but that would take a hell of a long time. $200,000 over the course of two years is the equivalent of what he would bring home in less than four years. I'm not seeing that as a big windfall," Cap said.

"How much are his debts?" Chance asked Becky.

"About $500,000. It was less, but the interest is killing him."

"He could have paid that down significantly over the past two years. Why is he holding on to it?" I asked.

"I don't have the answer to that. However, it also made me wonder what part Jeremy Wick had to play in all this. I didn't find a single thing connecting him to Agent Finley in any financial way. It appears that he truly thought he was trying to help take down a prostitution ring."

I glanced to Chance, wondering what he thought about all this. His former Master Chief being involved in this was a lot to take in and finding out that he had been fooled by an agent was even worse. They served this country in the Navy and then Jeremy was taken advantage of in the worst way.

"Alright, so our next step is to get our hands on Agent Finley and find out how deep this goes. If he was getting paid for his part, we need to know exactly what he was doing and who else he might have known that was involved," Cap said to Chance. "Get your team on surveillance. Becky, get a dossier on Agent Finley and have Rob get communications set up for the job."

"Will do, bossman."

Chance stood up and I followed, not sure what I was supposed to do now that he was going to do a job. I was pretty sure that I wouldn't be invited to tag along on this assignment. Where did that leave me?

"I'll leave the two of you alone," Sebastian said as he left the room.

"What do I do?" I asked.

"You go back to my house. Take my truck, but don't put any fucking dents in it. I'll get a ride from one of the guys."

"What am I supposed to do? Just sit on my ass while you're out getting information?"

"Morgan, this is a Reed Security job. I can't have you come with me."

"This is only a Reed Security job because you took over this investigation from me. I didn't ask for you to do it and I don't even have the money to pay you for it."

"It doesn't matter. It's an issue of liability for the company and you're not trained to do any of this."

"I've been investigating on my own for the last three months. You wouldn't even know about The Broker if it wasn't for me. *I* did that. I'm the one that's put myself on the line every day for my daughter, letting men touch me like they own me. I can't just stop now like it was all for nothing!"

He pulled me close, wrapping his arm around my waist. His other hand slipped to the nape of my neck. "I know all you've sacrificed and you shouldn't have had to do it in the first place. I know how personal this is for you and I want to help you. We all do, but this is what we do and we're damn good at it. When we take Agent Finley, it's not gonna be a nice, sit-down conversation. I don't want you involved in that, no matter how much you think you should be."

"This is my daughter we're talking about. I won't be left out."

"I won't leave you out of the loop, but I can't..." His jaw clenched and he took a slight step back, glancing away from me, like it was too painful to look at me. "You mean something to me," he finally said, looking intently into my eyes. "I'm not sure what exactly or...shit, I don't know much of anything. I do know that I don't want you in danger in any way. You're the first woman since my wife that I've allowed into my life. I just..."

He couldn't finish for whatever reason. Maybe he didn't know exactly what he wanted to say or maybe he didn't even know what he was feeling. Either way, I could see that he needed to protect me from whatever they were going to do. He had promised me that he would help find my daughter and at the moment, this was what he needed from me.

I slid my hand along the scruff of his jaw, forcing him to look back at me. "Okay. If that's what you need, I'll wait at your house until you tell me otherwise. Just promise me that you'll keep me updated on what's going on."

"Thank you." He rested his forehead against mine and I watched as his eyes slipped closed. His hands skimmed my arms and then wrapped around my waist, pulling me into him once again. He pressed a kiss to my forehead and then stepped back, clearing all emotion from his face. Gone was the man that had just struggled to express his emotions to me, and the man that I first met stood in front of me. I understood it. I wasn't myself when I was on the stage, dancing for men that wanted my body to satisfy their needs.

He pulled his keys from his pocket and placed them in my hands. "There's an envelope of cash in one of the kitchen drawers. Get whatever you need."

"I don't-"

"You don't have any fucking clothes. Please, just get what you need and get food for the house. There's nothing in there anyway."

"Okay."

"You have to disarm the alarm when you go in. I'm going to have at least two people at the house with you, just to be on the safe side. Just wait here and I'll find out who's available."

I nodded, not really sure what to say to him. I was just about to sit back down when he grabbed me by the back of the neck and pulled me into him, crushing his lips to mine. His tongue slipped through my lips, caressing my tongue and driving me crazy with his touch. I couldn't recall a single time that any man had made me feel just an ounce of what Chance made me feel. When he ended the kiss, he turned and walked away without a second glance, leaving me confused and turned on.

## Chapter Twenty-Three

# SNIPER

Confused didn't even begin to describe what I was feeling. I had just kissed Morgan like she was mine, and she never could be because I didn't want to ever be tied down again. It had to be because I had talked with her this morning about her life and Payton. It had reminded me of everything I could have had with my ex-wife. That had to be why I was feeling so much for her right now.

With Jackson and Gabe coming with me on our assignment, I had to find someone else to look out for Morgan while I was gone. Ideally, I would have one of my married coworkers look after her, but that wasn't fair to have someone leave his family to look out for someone that wasn't even mine. Hunter didn't have any kids yet, but he was obsessed with Lucy and was more along the lines of Knight now, taking protection to the extreme.

Which meant that I would have to ask Alec, Florrie, Craig, or Rocco. Really, my only option was Florrie. I couldn't trust the rest of those assholes to keep their hands off Morgan. Not that they would in my house, but I didn't even want to take a chance with them. Unfortunately, Lola wasn't working on this side of the business anymore, so I would have to have one of the guys go with her.

"Florrie," I shouted as I walked into the parking garage, just barely catching her before she left for the day. She slammed her door and walked back toward me.

"What's up?"

"Can you do me a huge favor?"

She groaned, rolling her eyes in irritation. When it was time to go home, no one wanted an extra job at the last minute. "What is it? I have plans."

"Hot date?"

"Sort of." One eyebrow rose, like she was urging me to laugh at her. Florrie's idea of a date wasn't what the average woman wanted. She liked gun ranges and motorcycles. Anything that was fast and made her feel alive was exactly what she wanted to be part of. I'd never heard her turn down anything an adrenaline junkie would want to do, but ask her to go to dinner and she asked what they were shooting. The woman was not normal.

"Morgan is staying at my house while I go do surveillance. Could you and one of the guys take her back to the house and show her the alarm system and then stay with her until I get back?"

"You haven't showed her how to use the alarm system yet?"

"She's only been there two days and it was never meant to be for that long."

"If you weren't interested in having her stay longer, why is she? Take her to a hotel."

"She doesn't have any money on her. Everything she owns is back in her shitty apartment in Pittsburgh and if we went back there, we might as well put a bullseye on her back. Besides, after her little stunt with Maggie, I'm not sure it's safe for her to stay at my place alone."

"Put her in a safe house," Florrie argued.

"My house is safe."

She narrowed her eyes at me. "How long are you gonna keep fucking her? Because you never want any woman longer than a night, but here you are, practically moving the woman into your house."

"Florence," I said, stressing the name she hated. She glared at me, her fingers digging into her arms as she tried to keep her cool. "What happens with Morgan and me is irrelevant right now. I have to go out on this assignment and I need someone to show her my security system and stay the night. It's as simple as that."

"Fine," she sighed, "but don't expect me to sit and have girl talk with her."

"I would never expect that."

"You owe me big time."

Shit, this wasn't good. I knew she was going to ask for something big. There was never an easy favor with Florrie. "What do you want?"

"You bought that rifle from Cazzo. I want to take it out to the gun range. For an entire day."

"That's going too far. I haven't even gotten to shoot that yet."

"Then I can test it out for you and tell you how it shoots."

"Pick something else," I snapped.

"Have fun getting home in time to show Morgan how to use the system."

She turned and walked back to her truck, leaving me no choice but to allow her to use my gun. "Fine! I'll let you take it out on Saturday, but if you break that rifle, you owe me $166,000."

"Please, I've been shooting since I was four. I think I can handle your one hundred and seventy year old rifle."

I gave her the keys to my house and walked away. I felt sorry for the man that bagged Florrie. She was any man's worst nightmare. Not because she was uptight or too girly. She didn't nag or want a commitment. She was just too badass and she could take any one of us or manipulate any man into doing what she wanted. Not only that, she was a better shot than most men and everyone knew it. Now I was going to have to listen to her brag about *my* rifle before I even got a chance to use it. Sometimes I really hated strong women.

*Chapter Twenty-Four*

# MORGAN

"I don't see why I had to have a babysitter take me home. I can find a door by myself and I'm pretty sure I can press buttons on my own," I grumbled. "I worked at a bank for years where I was trusted with money and accounts and occasionally, giving little kids suckers."

Florrie snorted next to me, obviously finding my predicament hilarious. She had insisted that she drive me home and have Alec drive Chance's truck. Apparently, Chance's truck was sacred and wasn't to be touched by anyone, even though Chance had given me the keys himself.

"And why does it take two of you to bring me home? I'm guessing one of you will show me how to press the buttons and the other will show me how to turn the handle on the door."

"Actually, we're here to make sure Chance's pillows and bed are still safe."

"Haha. That's so funny," I said dryly.

"I'm not joking. A few years back, Chance's house was shot up and someone broke into his house and slashed his pillows and bed. He was fucking pissed."

"I could understand the house, but the pillows and bed?"

"You must not know Chance too well. He's insanely possessive of his hypoallergenic pillows and his bed. He paid big money for them and that's the one thing he really wants as far as creature comforts."

"So, I could steal anything in his home but his pillows and bed?"

"Pretty much," she grinned.

We pulled into Chance's driveway and she parked to the side of the garage, while Alec hit the button to open the garage door and parked inside. I got out and followed Florrie to the door and watched as she showed me the very simple instructions for securing the house, and getting back in. It wasn't rocket science, but apparently, I was not able to do something like this on my own.

Alec walked around the property while Florrie and I walked inside. She helped herself to the fridge, grimacing when she found it lacking. "We should order some pizza. This is seriously the worst selection of food I've ever seen."

"You should have seen it when I first got here."

"Well, we aren't always home a lot, so it doesn't make sense to stock a lot of food. It'll go bad before we can eat what we buy."

"So, you just eat take out all the time?"

I sat at the island and kicked my shoes off. My foot was still sore from the cut I got in the well. As long as I didn't stand too much, it was okay, but I had walked around a lot today.

"Mostly. It sucks. I would give my left arm for a home cooked meal, but I don't have the time to cook."

"Do you have a boyfriend?"

She glanced away, blushing as she stared out the window. "Sort of."

"You sort of have a boyfriend. Okay, so why doesn't he cook?"

"Uh, he's got a pretty busy schedule like me."

"Does he travel like you?"

"Pretty much."

"Well, I'm sure you're not always gone at the same time. Why doesn't he just cook for you when he knows you'll be home?"

"We're pretty much always gone at the same time," she mumbled, still staring out the window. I got up and looked out the window from behind her. Alec was out in the yard doing something with the shed. I looked at Florrie from the side and saw it written all over her face. She was in love with the guy. The question was, was he in love with her?

"So, does anyone else know?"

"Know what?"

"About you and Alec?"

She whipped around, her face morphing into embarrassment and anger. "I never said that there was anything going on with Alec."

"You didn't need to. You've been staring at him the whole time."

"Shit." She glanced back out the window and sighed. "I'm usually better at hiding it."

"Why would you hide it?"

She slumped over on a bar stool and dropped her chin to her hand. "I'm sure it would be fine, but Cap might take us off the same team. It's not really a good idea for people to be involved and work together. Especially in our profession. There are too many risks, too many times that a relationship could make a mission complicated."

"Like, if something was dangerous and one of you freaked out about it?"

"Right, though it would be Alec freaking out, just to be clear. I'm the level-headed one between the two of us. Well, except the one time."

"What happened?" I asked, fully engrossed in this story. It wasn't very often that I heard about someone else's life, and at the moment, I could use the distraction.

"A few years ago, we were trying to rescue a little girl that had been taken as a ransom. It was dangerous because of the location she was being held and what we had to do to get inside. When we were in the room, at some point, they figured out we weren't who we said we were. Alec was shot at point blank range. I was protecting the little girl, but all I could see was Alec laying on the ground and bleeding out. When I finally got the chance, I went to him, but my head was all over the place. I was....well, I definitely wasn't acting like myself."

"You know that's normal, right? You're not supposed to be stoic when someone you love gets shot."

"We weren't an item back then. I mean, we flirted a lot and I knew he was attracted to me, but we didn't do anything about it for a while after that. He had rehab and then had to get cleared to go back to work. I would go over almost every night and check on him. A lot of times, I would stay the night just to reassure myself that he was okay."

"So, what changed?"

"I don't know, really. One day, we were combustible. We both knew that we had to have each other and then we were in bed, fucking like rabbits. We've been together ever since, but we've kept it quiet. We don't want anyone to know about it. Right now, Craig, Alec, and I work well as a team, but that could all be taken away and then everything would change. We would be gone at different times, and we would probably worry more because we weren't there to have each others backs. And then the bubble would burst."

"The bubble?"

She gave me a half-hearted smile. "Right now, we're in a bubble where no one knows about us. Everything is perfect for us, but if people knew about us, there would be this pressure that isn't there right now. There would be expectations that we're not worried about at the moment. We know each other so well that we don't need to talk to anyone but each other about our issues. But men at Reed Security seem to think that they all have to solve each others' problems."

"That really sucks. If you love someone, you shouldn't have to hide it."

"Like you?"

I looked at her strangely. "What do you mean?"

"Oh, come on. You and Chance are practically on fire when you're together."

"Um, sexually, yes. I don't think we really have anything else in common. Not that I would really know. We haven't talked a whole lot about anything. Well, that's not true. We talked about his wife this morning."

"Shut. Up. He actually talked to someone about her?"

"Well, I mean, I'm not sure how much he's said that's actually considered relevant. We talked about why she left and what that did to him, but-"

"The only person he's ever talked to about that bitch is Cap and that was just a little bit while Chance was driving him back from Pittsburgh years ago. He doesn't say anything but minor things about her.

Like, *I'm never getting married again* or *I was married once and it failed that time. I won't be trying again.*"

"Yeah, that pretty much sounds like him. He's very clear at all times that what we have is temporary. It's like he thinks I'm going to decide we're more and make him bend to my will."

"Well, if you're good enough, you could."

"But I don't want to do that. Actually, I'm using him just as much. He's a distraction for me while I try to find my daughter. We're basically using each other."

"Right," she smiled. "So, the way he was holding you in the conference room and the scorching kiss he gave you was just for sex, for later tonight. And the way he put his forehead against yours wasn't him trying to find comfort in you or him trying to feel better about what was going on between the two of you. It was strictly sexual."

"Yes," I insisted.

"Well, I do know a lot of couples that are fuck buddies and they strictly fuck with their foreheads."

"Shut up!" I laughed. "That wasn't what I meant."

"Sure. *Come here, sugar. My forehead needs to feel yours gliding against mine,*" she said in a deep voice.

"Whatever. You're such a bitch."

We laughed about it for a few minutes and then she snagged my hand and pulled me off the stool.

"Where are we going?"

"I want to show you something, but if you tell anyone I showed you, you'll be on my hit list."

"Sure," I said, rolling my eyes. She stared at me and the blood slowly drained from my face. The woman could be quite frightening when she wanted to be. She dragged me down a hall to a door I had assumed was a closet, but when she opened it, a steel door was on the other side. She started entering a sequence of buttons and did some scans before she was finally able to get the door open. It made a hissing sound, like it had been pressurized, when it opened. There were stairs in front of me and I hesitantly walked down and stepped through the doorway at the base of the stairs. I gasped when I saw the scene before me. There were about a dozen beds, all queen or king sized with pillows on them. The beds weren't made, but were still wrapped in the plastic covers they came in.

I walked around, feeling the beds and the firmness of the pillows. There was an armoire in the corner of the room and inside were dozens of sheets and pillowcases. There were also blankets and comforters stacked, though not as many as the sheets. This was freaking crazy. Who had a room like this?

"Okay," I said, slowly turning around. "This is like some crazy serial killer room, except instead of killing people, they go to sleep on the world's best mattresses and pillows and never wake up."

"It's pretty creepy, isn't it?"

"Creepy? How about psychotic? Who has a room like this? I mean, there are some scary people in the world, but I've never seen the equivalent of a torture chamber in the form of a Mattress Firm. *Please, sir! Don't lock me in the room with the comfy beds! I swear I'll be good!*"

"Laugh all you want, but Chance takes his sleep very seriously."

"But...if he had all this, why did he sleep on the floor when I was over here that first night?"

She shrugged with a slight grin. "Maybe he just wanted to be close to you."

"But he could have just slept in the same bed if that was the case."

"He could have..." she nodded. "I guess you'll just have to ask him about it."

"And tell him what? I saw your beds that you have hidden behind a steel door and I want to know what you plan to do with them and why you didn't sleep on one?"

"I would start with the second question. The beds behind the steel door might be a sore subject for him."

"Yeah, because it's not weird enough that he slept on the floor when he had other beds. Let's throw in a whole dungeon filled with them." I glanced around and noticed there weren't any windows and the room seemed to be made entirely of steel. "Wait, is this an actual panic room?"

"Sort of. None of these guys ever play it safe. Everyone has their own panic room with their own necessities. This is Chance's."

"What about food and water? What good does sleep do if you're dead from starvation?"

"I'm guessing he has food and water here, but sleep is also very important. It's hard to plan out an attack on someone when you're tired and worn out. This was actually a pretty smart idea. If we were ever attacked again, I bet everyone would want to come here just to get a good night's sleep."

"What's in your panic room?" I asked curiously.

"That is something you'll never find out," she said as she sauntered out of the room. I hustled out behind her, not wanting to be caught in the dungeon of beds. I didn't care what anyone else said, that was quite possibly scarier than if it had been filled with machetes and hacksaws.

---

"Damn, that was some good pizza," Florrie said as she leaned back in her seat. "Fuck, I'm full. Alright," she slapped the table as she stood, shoving away from the stool. "We've got watch for the night."

"Wait, you're staying?"

"You didn't really think Chance was going to leave you alone here after that stunt in Pittsburgh, did you?"

I flushed bright red, ducking my head in embarrassment. I hadn't realized how much trouble I would be causing when I went along with Maggie. If I had, I would never have agreed to go without Chance.

"Yeah, I guess he wouldn't."

"Anyway, we'll be keeping watch outside. Lock the door behind us and enable the alarm. If we need you, we'll knock."

Alec and Florrie walked out, leaving me alone in a house that wasn't mine and never would be. It was sad to walk around this place. Chance didn't really have anything homey around. It was all hard lines and man furniture. It was nothing like the home I used to have with Payton. I walked into his bedroom again and looked at the few pictures he had with men from The Teams, which I only knew because of the shirts they wore.

He looked happy back then and it made me sad that he had left when he really didn't want to. Although, I never would have met him if he had stayed in the military. He might have died over in some other war torn country and had a funeral where he would have joined thousands of other soldiers in the ground. It was a depressing thought, but probably the way he would have preferred to leave the military.

A thunk coming from the front of the house had me leaving the bedroom. As I got closer to the kitchen, I realized someone was knocking. I rolled my eyes as I thought of Alec and Florrie running some kind of security drill with me. They were really taking this whole thing to the extreme. I swung the door open, ready to give her shit, and immediately froze as I saw Wes's face. It took all of two seconds for instincts to kick in and I ran, sprinting toward the bedroom where I knew Chance kept a weapon in his nightstand.

My hair was yanked back and I crashed into the wall in the hallway, but then the pressure was gone and I was back up on my feet and racing down the hallway. I just made it to the bedroom when I was tackled into the doorframe and collapsed into the bedroom. I clawed at the carpet to get out from underneath the weight of his body. His hands gripped onto my pants, keeping me from getting very far. My heart was thundering and my hands were shaking, but I couldn't lose it if I wanted to make it out of here alive.

I swung my leg up as much as I could, barely making contact with his leg. I didn't give up. I just kept kicking out, swinging and punching, doing anything to get the asshole off me. I finally got a little wiggle room and pulled my leg out just enough to slam my foot back into his face. Blood spurted from his nose, allowing me just seconds to crawl out from under him.

Adrenaline shot through me, forcing my body forward and propelling me onto the bed. I rolled across it and landed next to the nightstand, flinging the drawer open and yanking the gun out. When I looked up, Wes was standing up and charging toward me. I didn't hesitate. I flicked off the safety and fired several times until he finally stopped and fell to the ground. I sank back against the wall, shaking in terror and unable to do anything more than stare at the man lying in front of me.

To my horror, the man stood up, his grin sending shivers down my spine. He ripped open his shirt, revealing a bullet-proof vest that had caught every single shot I put in him. I raised my gun again and fired, but there were no bullets left. I hadn't bothered to check how many shots were in the magazine since I started staying here. I never thought I would need it. Now I wished I had. I would have made better use of them.

He stalked toward my cowering frame, each step measured and calculating. There was nowhere for me to run. Two men stepped into the room behind him and blocked any route of escape. He towered over me, pulled a gun from his holster, and pointed it right at my head. As he motioned for me to stand, I had to hold the wall to actually make it up. Leaning against the wall was the only way to stay upright at this point.

"I told you I would be back for you. Did you doubt me, Shyla?"

"You sent me to die," was all I could say.

"Please, if I wanted you dead, I would have put a bullet in your head." He spun around and shot one of his men right in the middle of the forehead. His body slumped to the ground in a bloody heap and the other man kicked him over and out of the way. "See?" Wes grinned as he turned around to face me. "I knew those men wouldn't give up until they found you. It would have been a shame if they weren't smart enough to find you. Such a waste of a good body."

"I'm not going anywhere with you, so you might as well put a bullet in my head now," I said with as much confidence as I could muster.

"Do you really think you have a choice?" He laughed and then shrugged. "Well, how about this. I'll make you a deal. You can choose one of two fates. One, you come with me and be mine, in every way that I demand, or two, you stay here, with your brains splattered on the ground."

"I'll take number two."

"Let me tell you the provisions that go along with both. The first, you will tell me everything you can about getting into the Reed Security building." I was shaking my head before he even finished speaking. There was no way I could give up information on the men that had already done so much to help me. "Don't say no yet. There's something that you want more than anything. Would you like to know?"

I didn't want to say yes. A man like this couldn't be trusted. But even when my head was telling me not to trust him, my heart was thundering out of control, telling me that he might be able to give me the one thing that I desperately wanted to find. My daughter. I gave a tight nod.

"See? I knew you'd want to hear me out. If you come with me, I will help you get your daughter back. I know where she is and I can infiltrate them and have her back to you in no time. But my dear, you will never leave my side after that, at least, not until I choose to get rid of you."

"What's the second option," I asked in a shaky voice.

"Ah, the second option. I will either shoot you and let you die instantly, or tie you up in here and barricade the doors and windows while I set the house on fire and give you a chance to get out on your own. It's not much of a chance, but it would still give you the slightest opportunity to get your daughter back. However, after I eliminate Reed Security, there'll be no one left to help you."

"So, my options are to go with you and become your prisoner for the rest of my life, however long you choose it to be, but I will have my daughter back. But I also have to betray the men that have been helping me in order for you to gain access to their building. Or, I can stay here and die by a bullet to the head or try and fight my way out of here while a fire rages on."

"Yes, that's correct. But make no mistake, if you choose to come with me, I will never let you or your daughter go. You will stay with me until a time that I get tired of having you around. And if you don't come with me, you'll most likely die, but at least you have a shot of getting out of here and getting your daughter back. You could live your life on your own terms and I won't ever come for you again. So, Shyla, which will it be?"

## Chapter Twenty-Five

# SNIPER

Watching Agent Finley all afternoon just pissed me off. Knowing that he had worked with this sex trafficking ring and I couldn't just go beat the shit out of him really pissed me off. I was tired of waiting. Now was the time for action.

"Cap," I barked into my phone. "Let's just grab this asshole. We need information and we're not getting it by watching him go get coffee and flirt with women."

"Chance, we need to watch and-"

"Yeah, I fucking know. We watch and learn, but we already know this asshole is involved. Let's take him and get what we need. We have an innocent girl out there waiting to come home."

I heard him sigh into the phone. I knew this wasn't what he wanted, but dammit, I was tired of waiting.

"If we snatch him, you know that whoever's behind this is gonna follow and they'll take him out as soon as they get the chance. You're gonna have to be quick and get what you can before they attack."

"I know, Cap."

"And they'll probably try to take you out." He sighed into the phone again and spoke to someone in the room. "Let's meet up. Before we do this, we need a plan in place. I'll send Knight and Lola to take over watch for you. As soon as they relieve you, get your asses back here and we'll come up with something solid."

"10-4, Cap."

"What's the plan?" Gabe asked.

"We're meeting back at Reed Security. Knight and Lola are taking over watch while we put together a plan."

"Shit," Jackson swore. "This is gonna be a fucking mess."

"I'm guessing everyone will be called in for safety measures," Gabe said.

"I'm sure. We'll see what Cap says."

Twenty minutes later, we were back at Reed Security in the conference room. Everyone had gathered around and the tension in the room was so tight that it wouldn't take long for any one of us to snap.

"Alright, let's get down to it," Cap said, his expression stern as he stood at the head of the table. "I think we all know that we're about to head into another shit storm. If we take on this trafficking ring, we'll be putting our families at risk. So, our first order of business is protecting our families. I want everyone in the panic room before we put our plan in motion. I'm guessing once The Broker gets wind of what we're doing, he's going to pass that information along to the right people. That means Reed Security will no longer be safe. I've already contacted Cash Owens about getting some guys out here. The panic room will be enough to keep everyone safe and then Cash will have his men take everyone to Knight's property in Colorado. You all have ten minutes to get ahold of your families and make the necessary arrangements to bring them all in. I want everyone here within the hour. Pack only what's necessary. They'll need to move fast once Cash gets here."

"Cap, what about extended family?" Sinner asked. "I know we don't have all the resources in the world, but I can't just leave Cara's brother and his wife behind. They have kids and then there's Kate's family, Cole and Alex-"

"I know what you're saying, Sinner. No one gets left behind. If the men choose to stay behind, that's their decision. I'll get on the horn with Sean and make sure he's aware of what's about to go down so the police department can prepare for what's coming."

"You're not worried about blowback from the department?" Hunter asked.

"We'll cross that bridge when we come to it. Right now, our only focus is getting these kids back to their families and saving any of the women we can before they're sold off."

"Does Cash still have his contacts at the bureau from the ring we took down in California?" Ice asked.

"I don't want to make any calls until we interrogate Agent Finley. We need to know how deep this goes so we don't alert any more people than we have to. Any questions?"

"Yeah," Irish said. "Am I gonna have to build another house after this? Cuz I just built that deck off the back porch and I'm not really looking forward to having to redo that."

Cap smirked in amusement. "We'll try to keep it away from our homes, but to be on the safe side, if there's anything you don't want destroyed, have your wives hide it in your panic rooms. Chance."

I glanced over to Cap with a chin lift.

"Make sure those hypoallergenic pillows are stashed. I don't want to hear any bitching this time about your creature comforts."

"Already taken care of," I shot back.

"Alright, you have ten minutes to call your families and then get your asses back here. Oh, and Sinner, you're responsible for making sure Maggie doesn't try to slip out of the panic room once she gets here."

"Dammit! She's not my fucking wife."

"No, but for some fucked up reason, she'll listen to you more than she will me."

"This fucking sucks," Sinner muttered.

The guys started dispersing and I pulled out my phone to call Florrie. It rang, but she didn't pick up. I didn't always have good reception at my house, so I was going to have to go get them all and bring them back.

"Shit. Cap, I've gotta go get Morgan. Florrie's not picking up."

"Be quick. I'll give you twenty minutes."

I gave a quick nod and headed down to my truck. As long as

Morgan was safe, I could take on these assholes and focus on getting her daughter back.

"Hey, Chance!" I was just about to get into my truck when Craig called me. He was jogging toward me, his body more rigid than I would have expected from him. "I'm coming with you."

"You need to stop by your place?"

He shook his head as he climbed in the passenger side. "Nah, I'm just tagging along."

"Any particular reason?"

He shrugged again and stared out the window. Something about the way he was acting was sending my head into survival mode. I kept glancing at him out of the corner of my eye. He was acting all nervous, scratching at his beard and his knee was bouncing out of control.

"What is it, man?"

"I just have a bad feeling about this," he mumbled as he continued to stare out the window. I slapped his arm, getting him to finally look at me.

"What's going on?"

"You ever get these really bad feelings, like shit's about to blow up and your whole world is gonna implode?"

"I've had bad feelings before, but I wouldn't say it's ever been that bad. Why? Is that what you're feeling about this?"

He nodded, biting his lip. "There was only one other time I felt like this."

"Okay," I said slowly. "When was that?"

"I was a kid, just barely in high school." His voice drifted off, like he was getting caught up in memories. I waited, knowing that sometimes, you had to allow yourself a minute to pull your shit together before you could deal with the demons in your head. "There were so many people that died that day. A lot of people were burned alive. Others were severely injured....I can still smell the burning flesh."

He drifted off again and it was killing me not to push and find out what the hell was going on. Police sirens sounded in the distance and my stomach churned. I glanced over at Craig to see him looking out the windshield, looking for where the sirens we're going.

"It's just like that night," he whispered. "I'm telling you. I felt it that night. I just knew that something was wrong."

He was starting to freak me the fuck out, but when another police car went flying past me, I knew whatever he was feeling was legitimate.

"Craig, what the fuck is going on?"

"Put your fucking foot down. We have to get to your house."

He pulled out his phone and I slammed my foot down on the gas. I didn't know how the hell he knew there was a problem, but the urgency in his voice convinced me.

"Cap, we need guys out at Chance's house.....I don't fucking know. Just trust me. Something's going down.....Fuck, Cap. I'm asking you to trust me right now. There are sirens headed out of town, right toward his house. I'm fucking telling you- oh fuck!"

And in that moment, I saw what he did. A huge plume of smoke was filling the darkened sky in the distance, so thick that it could only be something big. If I could have driven faster, I would have. I tore down my driveway just minutes later and practically crashed into a tree at the scene before me. My house was engulfed in flames. The first police car was here and I could hear more sirens on their way, but none of that mattered. Morgan was inside there.

I jumped out of my truck and ran forward, ignoring the officer's instructions to stay back. Alec and Florrie were lying on the ground by the officer and neither of them looked alive, but I couldn't stop and check. The officer was looking them over and that would have to do while Morgan was inside. The heat was scorching and small explosions rocked the integrity of what was left of the house. I got close enough to the front door for my heart to sink into my stomach when I saw the boards nailed over the door. Glancing at the windows, I could see the same was done there. Someone had fucking trapped her inside there and left her to burn to death. I ran around to the back side of the house to see if the back door was the same.

"No!" I shouted at the top of my lungs as I saw there was no escape from the house. "Morgan!" I ran for the door, convinced that I could break down the door and get to her. She could still be alive inside. Steel bands of arms wrapped around me, dragging me back from the fire.

"What the fuck? Morgan's in there!" I struggled to break from his grasp, kicking and punching until I finally broke free from his arms. I stumbled to the ground as I jerked away from him, but was back on my feet, dirt flying from under my feet and I pushed forward again. The heat was terrifyingly hot, but I pushed on anyway, needing to get to Morgan.

I was tackled to the ground, slamming harshly into the leaves and sticks around the yard. Now I was being dragged backward by multiple men, but I still struggled. I could see the window to my bedroom, the room that I had just shared with her this morning. The room where I had finally admitted to my biggest fear of being used again by another woman. Something happened between us this morning, something that was the start of what I knew would be the best thing in my life if I just allowed it to happen.

"Morgan!" I shouted until my throat was raw. My skin was slick with sweat and it made it hard for the men to hold me back. I broke their hold again, but this time, someone wrapped an arm around my chest, whispering in my ear.

"There's nothing you can do, man. She couldn't have survived that."

"I can't-"

"I know, but you can't go in there. There's no one to save."

My knees buckled and I collapsed to the ground, the man behind me still holding on, keeping me tight to his body. I didn't know who it was and I didn't care. All I could do was stare at my house and watch it burn to the ground as tears slipped down my cheeks. I had let her down and I never let anyone down. I hadn't protected her. I should have done more to help her. I should have taken her with me, knowing The Broker was after her.

I dropped my head into my hands, falling forward to the ground as agony tore through me. I had failed her. I had failed everyone. The pain of losing my wife was nothing compared to this. I felt like I had just lost the one woman that I had ever really connected with, had ever really... I could feel it inside now. While I was struggling to keep her at a distance, I had been slowly falling for her; falling for her strength and her tenacity, and the woman that made me finally admit my fears. I didn't know if it was love, but it was something that could have been amazing. I hadn't fucking seen it and now she was gone. She had died a horrible death, never knowing if her daughter was alive or dead. But I wouldn't let it go at that. I would find her daughter and make sure she had the life Morgan should have had.

Gathering all my anger, pain, and loss, I pushed up off the ground, swiping at the tears that stained my cheeks and shoved the arms off me that tried to calm me down. There was no calming down now. There was only revenge and the need to kill.

## Chapter Twenty-Six

# SNIPER

"Chance!"

I didn't stop when my name was called and I didn't back down when Ice and Chris stood in my way. I shoved past them, yanked the SUV door open and jumped inside. Now was the time for action. I cranked the engine and kicked up gravel as I backed up out of my driveway. My tires squealed as I tore down the road, heading for Pittsburgh to get my hands on Agent Finley and find out everything he knew.

Headlights shone behind me, probably two or three different vehicles. Whether or not they followed me to Pittsburgh was up to them, but I had a plan in place and nothing would stop me right now. All that mattered was getting Payton back.

The vehicles kept up with me the whole way to Pittsburgh and when I reached his apartment, I didn't bother knocking.

"Think about this, Chance." Chris was right behind me, trying to grab at me to stop me, but I couldn't. I planted my boot against the door and slammed the fucking thing against the wall. Storming into the apartment, I walked right up to Agent Finley and threw my fist into his face until he was bloodied and barely conscious.

Hauling him up by the neck of his shirt, I threw him into a chair and took tv cables to strap him down. Chris, Ice, Craig, Hunter, and Cazzo all stood watching me, waiting for me to completely flip out or tell them what I needed. But what I needed right now was to get information and I could accomplish that on my own.

When Finley didn't come around right away, I slapped him hard on the cheek. He roused slightly, but still wasn't awake enough for me. I grabbed a jug of milk from the refrigerator and held his head back as I poured the milk over his face. The thick liquid clogged his nose quickly, snapping him back to the present. He looked around the room in confusion, not knowing what the hell was going on.

"Tell me who's running the trafficking ring."

"What?"

I slugged him in the face. "Tell me who the fuck you're working for," I shouted.

"I don't know what-"

I shoved my boot against his chest, kicking his chair over and slamming him into the ground. I stood on top of his chest, pushing all my weight into him until he was gasping for air. I probably cracked a few ribs too.

"You were working with Wick. You wanted him to think he was helping gather information and save those women, but that's not what you were fucking doing! You trafficked those women and used him to fill your own pockets to pay off some fucking debts!"

"No," he gasped. "I swear! I didn't. I don't work trafficking. I mean, not in that way."

"Then in what way do you?"

"I'm a case manager, but I only oversee how the operations are going as far as resources, finances, assets-"

"Yeah, and Wick was a fucking asset!"

"No! I've never even heard that name before."

"Don't fuck with me, asshole. I know about the money that you've been putting away in your so-called hidden accounts. You've been getting ready to run."

"No, I don't-"

I picked up his head by the hair and slammed it back to the floor.

Walking to the kitchen, I grabbed the largest knife I could find and headed back to the living room.

"Hey, Chance," Cazzo stepped in front of me. "Think about this. There are ways we can get information out of him that won't leave all this evidence behind."

"All I want right now is Payton back and he's going to tell me how to get to her."

"I don't know!" Finley shouted from the floor.

"Shut your fucking mouth!" I started toward him, but Chris cut me off, taking the knife from my hand.

"Let us take care of this. We know you need answers right now, but you're gonna kill him before you get what you need."

I was breathing so hard that my nostrils were flaring with every breath. My chest was heaving with every shake of my body. I was losing control. I could feel it slipping away with every minute that passed. I took a step back and nodded to Chris.

"Just take a seat over there," Chris pointed to the chair in the corner. I did as he said and watched as Ice walked over to Finley and righted the chair he was in. He motioned for Chris to hand over the knife and then held it up to Finley.

"Now, we're going to ask you some questions and you're going to answer them truthfully. If you don't, I can make your death very painful."

"I swear, I don't know what you're talking about."

"So, you don't know the club *Stripped To Nothing?*"

"Yeah, I know that club. Everyone in Pittsburgh knows it. It just opened a few years back. It's more of a gentleman's club."

"And you know the owner?"

"Sure. I've talked to him quite a few times. He's ex-military."

Ice looked over at me, raising an eyebrow. This was all coming a little too easy, like he was just handing over what we wanted to hear. Either that or he was telling the fucking truth.

"What can you tell me about the women that are being trafficked in the city?"

"Not much."

Ice slammed the knife into Finley's leg, just above the knee. Finley screamed in pain, his leg jerking around the knife, which only made the cut worse.

"That's not the answer I want," Ice growled. "There are missing women and children and I want to know who is in charge of everything!"

"The men running the investigation haven't figured it out yet," he sobbed. "Nobody can find this guy. He's too good at hiding."

"And you just sat on your ass while women were getting kidnapped and sold like cattle!" Ice yelled, his spit flying into the man's face. "You didn't think you should push the investigation harder or try to find out what the fuck your agents were actually accomplishing?"

"I have so many cases–"

Ice withdrew the knife and slammed it into the man's shoulder. More screams filled the apartment and Cazzo casually walked to the front door and closed it as best he could with it being broken.

"We might want to wrap this up soon. I'm guessing The Broker will be here soon. He doesn't like loose ends," Cazzo said calmly.

"The Broker?" Finley stuttered.

"So, you *do* know who I'm talking about," Ice said. "Tell me what I want to know! Who's running the ring?"

The glass shattered in the window and Finley's eyes went dead as a bullet pierced his skull. His head slumped to the side and then we were all taking cover, our guns out and at the ready. A clean exit would be difficult at this point, but on the upside, we had drawn out more men, even if we hadn't gotten much out of Finley.

Cazzo was on the phone with Becky, asking for satellite imaging to help us out. A second shattering of glass sounded and then the distinct sound of something rolling across the floor filled the silence.

"Grenade!" I shouted as I leapt out of my spot and shoved Ice out of the way just as the grenade exploded. I was thrown from the force of the explosion into the chair holding Finley and then fell to the ground. The room was hazy and the ringing in my ears was so intense that I couldn't hear Hunter as he stood over me. I could see his mouth moving, but no sound met my ears.

I let my eyes slide shut and then looked over at Ice, who was also laying on the floor, unmoving. Shit. I had done this. I choked on something, plaster or some other kind of garbage I had inhaled. I looked around the room, not wanting to move my head until the spinning stopped, and took in the destruction. There was a hole in the side of the building, and as I stared out into the night, I could swear that I saw men moving on the roof across the street. But when I blinked to get a better look, they were gone.

Hunter was smacking Ice in the face and he slowly came around and then stood. I breathed a sigh of relief that I hadn't gotten one of my teammates killed. Finally feeling like I could get my bearings, I rolled to my side and pushed myself up off the floor.

"Holy fuck!" The sound was muted to me, but I understood the urgency in Hunter's voice. I started to turn to him, but he stopped me and I felt sharp pricks in my back as he pulled shrapnel out.

"We don't have time for this, Hunter. We've gotta get the fuck out of here. Becky said they're moving in!" Cazzo yelled. I didn't wait to see what Hunter wanted to do. I took off for the door, following Ice, Chris, and Cazzo out the door with my weapon raised. I was still a little disoriented from the ringing in my ears, but I pushed on. Craig was already clearing the hallway ahead of us and Hunter was pulling up the rear.

We stepped out into the alley on the side of the building, our weapons at the ready. The darkness made shadows play across the buildings and the streets, but the images of men running toward us were easily discernible. Cazzo signaled for us to spread out along the alley, taking cover behind a dumpster, some garbage bags along the other building, and a doorway that was slightly inset for the building we just came out of. Hunter had the best view from behind the dumpster and was signaling that there were ten men, five on each side of the alley. That wasn't the best odds for us, but we had the advantage of cover.

We waited as they approached until they were right up on the dumpster. Hunter gave the signal and we all popped up, taking out as many of them as we could. Four of them had time to run for cover before they were taken out, which left us in a bit of a standoff at the moment. We took turns firing at each other, but we were getting nowhere, and the longer we stayed in this position, the more time they had for reinforcements to come.

"I'll draw their fire," I said to Craig, who was hiding behind the garbage bags with me. "Cover me over to that fire escape. We should be able to knock a few down."

"Are you fucking crazy? You'll get shot."

"If we stay here, we're sitting ducks while they call for backup. Besides, I can't be that unlucky, right?"

He was about to protest again, but I was already jumping over the bags of garbage. I heard him swear at me, but he started firing, covering my ass as I ran for the fire escape. I was just about to the wall and jumped, pushing off the wall with my foot and then twisted to grab the ladder that was hanging about ten feet off the ground. My hands found purchase just seconds before I swung myself up, using my upper body strength to pull my body up rung by rung.

Bullets pinged off the metal around me, but the only ones I felt were the ones that hit my vest. I ignored the restricting feeling in my chest, knowing that if I didn't push through, I would be dead in seconds. Luckily, I had caused enough of a distraction to allow Hunter and Cazzo to take out two more of the men.

I pulled myself up to the first landing and spun, taking out the two remaining men. Craig and Ice were the first to move forward, checking for any survivors, and then Chris followed up. When they gave the all clear, I made my way back down the ladder and let go, landing on my feet. Cazzo walked up to me with a grin on his face. I was just about to fist bump him when his fist caught me in the chin, sending me sprawling to my ass.

"What the fuck was that for?"

"That was for racing over here without a plan and almost getting us all killed, and then running out in the open like an idiot and almost getting yourself killed."

"It worked."

"It could have fucking failed and then you would be dead too. Who would get Payton back then?"

"You," I said confidently, knowing that none of the guys would give up if I was gone. I ignored the stab of pain in my chest at the reminder that Morgan was gone now too. Cazzo reared back and punched me again. I didn't try and block it. He obviously needed to get his anger out.

"What the hell was that one for?"

"That was for showing off with that fancy wall jumping move, trying to make us all look like slackers. You want to do that shit, go join the circus."

*Chapter Twenty-Seven*

# CAP

"Change of plans!" I shouted after I got off the phone with Craig. "Something's going down at Chance's place. I don't have details, but I need a few guys to head over there. Everyone else, get your families here. If you can't get ahold of them, go get them and haul ass back here. Irish, call Knight and Lola and tell them to get their asses back here. Make sure their families get here and if they don't have transport, go get them."

The room erupted in chaos as several of the guys stormed off toward the elevator to go over to Chance's house. Everyone else was on the phone, calling anyone that needed to be brought in. I dialed Maggie but there was no answer. I hung up and called again, still no answer.

"Sinner!" He spun around, still on the phone with Cara. He finished up with Cara and gave me his full attention. "Freckles isn't answering. I have to go get her and the kids. Make sure everyone gets into the panic room."

I took off, not even waiting for confirmation from Sinner. I didn't need it. None of the guys would leave anyone behind. It took more than ten minutes to beat the traffic and get back to the house. I kept dialing Maggie's number, but she still didn't pick up. The last time that something like this happened, Maggie had been taken and my child was left alone. But this time, we had two kids and Maggie was pregnant.

The lights from the house shone bright as I pulled into the driveway. I ran inside, happy to see Maggie on the couch with Clara and Caitlin playing a game on the floor. Everything was fine.

"Hey," Maggie said with a smile that faltered when she saw the panic on my face. "What's going on?"

"We have to leave. Grab whatever we need. We need to be gone in five."

She nodded curtly, knowing that now wasn't the time to ask questions. I grabbed Caitlin and ran out to the truck, buckling her into her car seat and then went back for Clara. After getting her buckled in, I ran back to help Maggie get the essentials. She was just coming down the stairs with a small duffel when I saw someone creeping through the kitchen. I pulled my gun from the small of my back and crept toward the kitchen, signaling for Maggie to get back upstairs. With a quick glance around the corner, I saw the man mirroring my motions. I fired, not waiting to see what he wanted. No one walked into my house uninvited.

But he wasn't alone. As soon as I fired, three more men came in through the back. I just had time to dive for cover before bullets peppered the walls. I only had one weapon on me and I was running out of bullets fast. Pinned down here, I wouldn't be able to get a decent shot off and get us out of here. Calling for help wouldn't do jack shit right now. I needed some fucking backup.

And then it came. One at a time, the three men fell as bullets pierced their skulls. Burg stepped through the back door, kicking the man on the floor that was closest to him. When the man didn't move, Burg walked over to me, holding out his hand for me. I took it and jumped to my feet.

"Were you waiting to see if I could take them on my own?"

"I think it was pretty obvious that you couldn't. Hell, the owner of a security company shouldn't be cowering behind a counter."

"I wasn't cowering. I was waiting to make my move."

"Yeah? What was that? Were you going to jump out and yell *boo*?"

"I was just gonna tell them to turn around. The sight of your face would have killed them in less time than it took you to shoot them."

"You're real fucking funny, Cap," Burg snarled.

"I hate to interrupt you, but maybe one of you could help me?"

I spun around, gun raised, to see Maggie with a gun pressed against her head and her hand cradling her belly. My first thought was that something was wrong with the baby, but she didn't appear to be in pain. The man was behind and slightly to the left of Maggie, maybe enough for a shot, but it wouldn't be a sure thing.

"Put the gun down," the man said calmly.

His head moved just an inch to the left and I took the shot, putting a bullet right through his eye. Blood spurted all over Maggie's face and she leaned against the wall when it looked like she might pass out. I hurried over to her and grabbed her hand, dragging her with me to the door. Burg was on my six as we headed out the door. At the sound of gunshots, I ran faster, letting go of Maggie's hand so I could get to my kids. When I rounded the house to the garage, I saw Sinner fire at one man just as another man snuck up behind him, about to slash his throat.

"Sin-"

I didn't get a chance to finish. Sinner spun, grabbing the man's hand and bent it back, shoving the knife right into his chest. The man stilled and then fell to his knees. Sinner yanked the knife out of the guy's chest and shoved it right into his throat. The man fell over sideways, sprawled out on my driveway.

Sinner spun his gun around like in some old western movie and dropped it into his holster. "Just like John Wayne," he said with a grin.

"I'm pretty sure John Wayne never had those moves," Maggie said from behind me. I grabbed her hand and hauled ass to the truck, shouting over my shoulder to Sinner.

"No, he had better ones," I countered. "Hell, no one would have gotten the drop on John Wayne."

Sinner jumped in the passenger side of the truck with Maggie and Burg got in the back with the kids.

"No one got the drop on me. Do you see any knife wounds on me? Not a single fucking scratch."

"You were about to have your throat slit," I shot back as I tore out of the driveway.

"John Wayne fought cowboys that couldn't shoot worth a damn."

"Obviously these guys couldn't shoot worth a damn either if you took out four in my front yard."

"How did you know I would need backup?" I asked, confused as to why they had followed in the first place.

"Come on, Cap. It's Maggie. If she's not causing the trouble, it's following her," Sinner said.

"Hey, I have nothing to do with this!" Maggie said defiantly. "I was just sitting at home with my kids and then you three showed up and shot up my house!"

"Technically, the bad guys shot up your house," Burg clarified. "My shots were all kill shots."

"So were mine," Sinner said. "What about you, Cap?"

"I got one."

"One?" Sinner snorted. "Just the one?"

"He was hiding behind the counter," Burg laughed.

"I wasn't fucking hiding. I was taking cover so I didn't get killed."

"Like I said, he was hiding."

Maggie was sitting closer to Sinner and Burg was leaning over the seat. I quickly threw back my elbow, hitting Burg in the face to shut him up.

"What the fuck! I save your ass and you fucking elbow me in the face?"

"Sorry, didn't see you there, man."

"Wait, why are you driving with us?" Maggie interrupted.

"Burg decided to crash his truck into their SUV. He wanted to take out the driver, except no one was actually in the vehicle."

"Hey, the headrest looked like a person in the dark," Burg said defensively.

"You crashed your truck to kill a headrest?" I laughed.

"Let's laugh about this later," Burg gritted out. "We've got company."

Behind us were several pairs of headlights coming up fast. I slammed down on the gas and turned down the road to Reed Security.

"Get Becky on the phone and tell her to open the fucking gate!"

Sinner was on the phone just seconds later. "We're coming in hot. Open the gates now!"

In the distance, I could see the lights on the gate flashing, I just hoped they would be open wide enough by the time we got there.

"They're gaining on us, Cap." Burg lifted the seat and pulled out my weapons I had stored.

"Sinner, set the charges." I tossed the remote that I kept in the truck back to him. "973476. Set it for two minutes."

The tires squealed as I broke through the gates. They hadn't fully opened yet and the front end of my truck took a beating, but we wouldn't be able to use it after this anyway. After we cleared the gates, Burg leaned out the window and fired at the sensors placed around the gate, triggering an explosion that took out the first vehicle behind us.

The garage was open already and instead of heading toward the elevator, I drove to the back of the parking garage and hit the button for the hidden door. The truck just barely fit in the single lane tunnel and just moments after we entered, the entry exploded, crumbling to the ground and blocking the way.

"I really don't think we use enough explosives," Sinner said as he handed back the remote I had given him.

"Two in one night isn't enough?"

"Maggie hasn't even gotten to throw a grenade," Sinner pouted.

"She's pregnant." I emphasized the pregnant part, hoping he would get it that now wasn't the time for her to play with explosives.

"She got to play with them on her wedding day. I don't see why a baby should make any difference."

I parked in the garage at the end of the tunnel and flung open my door. I really didn't want to get into a debate over what weapons were good to use while pregnant. And the fact that Sinner was encouraging it was pissing me off. Oddly enough, Maggie was quiet about it the whole time. I stopped at the truck bed and headed back to the truck, standing by the passenger door. Maggie sat in the front seat with her purse pulled tightly to her stomach.

"Hand it over," I said, holding out my hand to her.

"What?"

"You know what." When she looked at me strangely, I narrowed my eyes and gave her my *don't fuck with me* face. She rolled her eyes and pulled open her purse, snatching a grenade out from inside.

"Here," she said, slamming the grenade into my palm.

"You want to be a little more careful with that?"

"Whatever."

"Now, the other one."

"What other one?"

I motioned for her to hand it over, but she still pretended like she didn't know what I was talking about.

"Maggie, I know you have another one. Hand it over so we can get the fuck out of here."

Her lips tightened, but she pulled out the second grenade and handed it over. I turned to walk away, but then remembered this was Maggie we were talking about. I appeared one last time in the doorway of the truck and held my hand out once again.

"And the gun."

She pulled the gun out of her purse and handed it over.

"And the one at the small of your back."

"Right, like I could have one there while I'm pregnant," she snorted.

"Give it to me."

Sighing, she pulled out the gun at the small of her back and handed that one over as well.

"Now the ankle holster."

"What am I supposed to use for protection?" she asked in exasperation.

"That's what we're here for," I chided.

She bent over slightly and pulled up her pant leg, pulling the gun out of her ankle holster.

"And the one at the back of the car seat."

"Sebastian, I-"

"Maggie, we talked about storing guns near our babies."

"It's at the back," she grumbled. "It's not like the kid can reach around and unstrap the gun, slam a magazine into the gun, flick off the safety, and still have enough strength to pull the trigger."

"Now, the knives."

She looked at me in shock, but I knew her too well. This woman would pack any weapon she could into any space available, which was kind of a scary thought.

"I can do this all night, Maggie."

Slowly, she unstrapped five knives from various parts of her body and threw them down on the ground. Scowling, she hopped down out of the truck.

"You can get the kids."

She stormed off, her ass shaking as she made her way to the secondary entrance for the panic room where everyone else was waiting. Burg and I grabbed the kids and bags while Sinner grabbed the car seats. At least she was heading off to Colorado and she would be Cash's problem. I hadn't told him yet, but when I did, I didn't want to be within a hundred feet of him.

---

"Rocco, how are Alec and Florrie?"

We were all gathered in the conference room, making our plans for The Broker. Chance was sitting in the corner of the room, slumped in his chair. He had seemed okay when they first got back, but as time went on, I could see the reality of everything hitting him.

"Concussions, but they're both okay. Just resting for now."

"Good. Becky, what have you found out from the police department?"

"They have no idea who set the fire, but it's been determined it was arson."

"I think we all figured that out by the boards over my fucking windows," Chance muttered from the corner.

"Um...there is one other thing that the fire investigator has said about the fire," Becky said hesitantly.

"What's that?"

"As of right now, there are no signs of a body."

Chance stood up in the corner, stalking over to the table. "What the fuck do you mean there's no sign of a body? And why are you just telling us this now?"

"He still has a lot of his investigation left, but as of right now, he's not seeing a body. I didn't want to say anything until I had something more concrete."

Chance's gaze whipped to mine, a tiny bit of hope sparking in his eyes.

"Did they look in the panic room?" Florrie asked, stepping into the room with a sling around her arm.

"I never showed her the panic room," Chance said.

"I did. It's possible she saw me enter the code."

"You mean that she could still be in that fucking room?" Chance exploded, running out of the room and down the hall. I chased after him, snagging him by the arm before he got a chance to get to a vehicle and storm out of here.

"You have to wait. You can't just show your face out there. If Wes is still watching, he'll see you out there and take his shot at you."

"I need to see. She could be alive!"

"I know, but let me have Sean look into it. He decided to stay behind and he's been at the scene. I'll see what he knows."

Chance nodded reluctantly and followed me back to the conference room. I pulled out the sat phone and put it on speakerphone, dialing Sean's number.

"You guys okay over there?"

"Everyone is here and safe. We have a favor to ask of you."

"Shoot."

"We need you to check the panic room at Chance's house." I glanced up at Chance, his face anxious and his body strung tight. "There's a chance Morgan is in there."

"I'm at the house now. Do you have a code for me?"

Chance stepped over to the phone. "Sean, it's Chance. You have to bypass the system. Let me know when you're ready."

A few minutes later, Sean was there, ready to get into the panic room.

"Okay, you have to press and hold zero and one at the same time for five seconds. Then release and press 8637."

"Doing that now." We waited for what felt like an eternity while he entered the code. "Okay, I've got a blinking green light."

"Good. The code is 7835490 and then the pound sign."

"Got it. Opening now." I heard him walking and then a switch. "What the fuck?"

"What? What is it?"

"Why are there so many fucking beds in here?"

All of us looked to Chance, but he just glared at me. "You really want to talk about this right now?" I shook my head. I didn't want to talk about it at all. "Sean, in the back of the room is a short hallway and a few small rooms. Check to see if she's there."

Doors opened and closed and Chance's face fell with every door that shut. "She's not here."

"Thanks, Sean."

I looked up at Chance, trying to read what he was thinking.

"If she's not there, that means she's alive. We have to find her. She's out there with that maniac."

"We will," I said confidently.

Becky was already searching on her computer, different pages appearing on the screen on the wall as she checked different sites, and reports on Weston Hughes were flying across the screen.

"He has a flight scheduled for takeoff in two hours. It's his private jet. His flight plan is for London."

"We need to go now," Chance said, heading for the door.

"Chance, wait! We need a plan."

But he wasn't listening. He was already headed for the elevator. I ran toward him, but just as the elevator doors opened, men in black tactical gear stepped off, weapons raised. They definitely weren't ours. There were only two people that weren't accounted for and they were on their way here now.

Chance didn't have even a second to draw his weapon. The butt of the gun came down like a sledgehammer on his head and he slumped to the ground, unmoving.

"Code Black!" I shouted as I drew my gun out of the small of my back. I fired several shots, hitting a few men, but suddenly, men were converging from all different areas of the floor. The cold steel of a gun was pressed against my head just a second later. The conference room was packed with men, leaving us nowhere to go. We didn't have enough weapons and we would all be dead by the time one of us was able to get to the reserves.

"Listen up!" one of them shouted. "If you don't want to die, you'll do as we say!" I gritted my teeth, not wanting to yield to this asshole, but not really having any other choice. We weren't going down though. None of us would ever give in to assholes like this. It might kill me, but I would find a way to get us in the position we needed to fight back.

I glanced back at the guys in the conference room giving a slight nod to them to stand down. They all placed their weapons on the table, at least the ones in their hands. I saw Becky set down her computer and press two buttons, the buttons that would save our lives right now. We had all come up with several hand signals after the last attack on Reed Security so that we would always have a way to communicate with each other in the event that our building was under siege.

I pulled on my right earlobe for just a second as I turned back, giving the signal that they all needed to take cover. The man in front of me grinned and I grinned back just before I lifted my boot and slammed it into the side of his knee, breaking it and making him fall to the floor. I grabbed the weapon in his hand just as a bullet tore through my shoulder. I gritted my teeth and ignored the fire burning through me. I chose my shots carefully, taking aim at those that wouldn't be affected by the blast as much.

Spinning around, I saw that everyone was fighting, some using hand to hand combat and others using their guns. It was tight quarters and anyone could get killed in a situation like this. We had to spread this out and move the fight out of here, but not until our diversion went off. Just a few more seconds.

I was tackled to the floor, falling on my side, my gun jammed between my side and the floor. I threw my elbow back, nailing the guy in the face and then rolling to pull my gun up.

Before I could fire, the IT room blew up, the explosion blowing the walls into little bits of plaster and sending a thick cloud of white throughout the room. The rest of the building burned, the flames thick and fast moving, just as planned. We had to get out of here.

*Chapter Twenty-Eight*

# LOLA

"Shit!" I yelled as the wall of Reed Security exploded outward, flames licking at the sky and the rest of the building.

"Back entrance," Knight yelled beside me. I drove around to the back of the building and squealed to a stop by the underground entrance. Knight and I raced up the stairs, stalled by every door we had to enter codes through and do the facial scans. Every minute that we were stalled, more of our teammates were being killed. I thought about Derek and Hunter, wishing I had never left the team and I was there fighting right alongside them right now.

"Follow me," Knight commanded. I wanted to yell at him for telling me what to do, but I bit my tongue and followed him. He led me up some stairs, one floor above the level the conference room was on. I had never been here before, didn't even know it existed. Knight opened a hatch and hopped inside, flicking on a light and illuminating a small room and then doors that led out into other hallways.

"What the hell is this place?"

"This is my backup plan. I had Cap do some updates after hours over the past two years. It was just completed a few months ago," he said as we loaded weapons that he had just pulled out of a gun closet. He had a fucking arsenal in here. "There's a hallway that leads around to the other side of the building, near Derek's office. You head that way and I'll head through this other door. Keep moving. Don't give them the opportunity to get a shot off at you."

He took off before I could ask anything else, so I grabbed my weapons and started running down the hallway, checking for the best position. When I had it, I laid my guns against the wall and got into position, looking through my scope for my target.

There were too many of them to count, so I just started firing, taking out whoever I could, but then I saw Ice lying on the ground, blood pooling under his body and Chris fighting to get over to him. I repositioned and took out the man that Chris was fighting. He was over to Ice seconds later, pressing against the wound in Ice's stomach, but Ice didn't even flinch.

I kept moving, just like Knight told me to and found another position. There was so much blood all over the room. It wasn't confined to the conference room where it appeared to have started. Men were fighting all over and I now understood why Knight told me to keep moving. I picked up and ran, finding anyone else that I could, taking shot after shot, only hearing the steady beat of my heart as I found a rhythm and fired, taking out the assholes that were here to kill us.

"Fuck!"

My head snapped to the side. I moved quickly to a new position. Burg was fighting two men, one that had his arm wrapped around his throat and another that was slamming a new magazine into his gun. Following my sights, I fired, taking out the man that was about to shoot Burg, but as I swung my gun to take out the second man, I realized that I was just seconds late. Burg had a knife embedded in his leg. The second man was just about to snap Burg's neck and I didn't have a shot. With Burg still struggling, there was only one thing I could do. I lined up the shot and fired, hitting Burg in the same leg, making his leg collapse from under him. I swiftly shifted positions and shot the other man in the head, making him drop to the ground dead.

"No!" That was Knight. I looked up, trying to find out where his shout was coming from, but there was too much going on. I stood and raced through the hallways, trying to find Knight. He would only yell out like that for one person. The one person that had stood by me through years of nightmares and torment. My pulse skyrocketed as I skidded to a stop around the corner of the hallway and saw Knight racing across the room below. I followed the path he was running and saw Hunter on his knees, his hand pressed to the side of his neck as blood dripped between his fingers. His hand fell from his neck just seconds later as his eyes rolled back in his head and he fell to the ground. I ran until I found a door that would allow me to jump down to the floor below and jumped through.

Racing to Hunter's side, he was pale and his eyes were closed. Knight was pressing hard against his neck and swearing at him, telling him to hold on. There was so much blood and when I felt for his pulse, it was thready and slow.

"Rocco!" I started running through the chaos looking for Rocco and when I found him, he was patching up Gabe, who had a wound on his head, but he was still conscious and Hunter wouldn't be alive in a minute. "You have to come with me. Hunter's been hit in the neck. He's bleeding out."

"Go," Gabe yelled.

Rocco and I ran back to Hunter, where Knight was still trying to patch him up. Rocco shoved his way in and yanked open his bag, pulling out a shit load of medical supplies. I couldn't do anything but grip Hunter's hand and stare at him, praying that he didn't die. I couldn't lose him. I couldn't lose any of them. I looked around vaguely at the chaos. Blood was everywhere. Men were lying all over the floor, some enemies and some of ours. I didn't know if anyone was dead, but I knew that things would never be the same after this.

Out of the corner of my eye, I caught movement over by the elevators. It was Chance, he was being dragged off by two men that were struggling to stay on their feet. I dropped Hunter's hand and pulled out my gun, firing until I emptied my clip, but I was too late. They were already on the elevator and there was no way to get to him before they dragged him out of here. Still I had to try.

I took off for the back stairs, being stalled at every door to enter codes and complete scans. The blood on my hands had me redoing the scans over and over again. I didn't have my keys for my truck on me. I had dropped them somewhere and now had to run around the building. By the time I got to the front of the building, their vehicle was peeling through the gates. I pulled a second gun from my ankle and fired, hoping to hit them and at least slow them down, but every bullet pinged off the vehicle and soon I was out of range. They were gone, and our guys were too hurt to go after Chance right now. I didn't even know who was still standing at this point. Hopefully Becky was still alive and could track down the vehicle. If not, Chance would be lost to us and could be dead by the time we found him.

## Chapter Twenty-Nine

# MORGAN

I watched the live feed outside the house as Chance struggled past his friends to get into his house. He thought I was in there and would probably blame himself for my death for the rest of his life. I couldn't decide which was worse, him thinking that he got me killed, or him looking for me for the rest of his life. Either one wasn't worth his time.

I had made my choice and it would always be my daughter. I didn't want to betray Chance and all his friends, but Wes was offering me my daughter. Yes, it had a time limit on it, but maybe in that time I could figure out a way to escape. It wasn't very likely, but I would rather take a few years with her over a lifetime without her. And living with him had to be better than wherever she was right now. With him, she would have luxuries that would never be offered to her otherwise. Not that it mattered, but at least it wasn't a cell. At least, I hoped not.

Still, watching Chance fall to his knees and his friends trying to console him was heartbreaking. We had grown to have something between us. I wanted to say love, but I wasn't sure he felt that way. But when he begged me to do what he needed, I could have sworn that his feelings were more than both of us ever thought possible. Now, I had betrayed him, the one man that swore to search for my daughter until he found her. The man that would have done anything to protect both of us. I knew I had to do what was best for Payton, but I couldn't help wishing this had turned out differently.

I shivered as a strong hand landed on my shoulder. "This is just the beginning. I'm going to tear them down. Every single one of those men is going to know what happens when they fuck with me."

"You didn't have to do that," I whispered. "I already told you what I know."

"Yes, and it's been very helpful. I have my best people working on the facial scans. It's not the easiest thing to do, but I'm pretty sure we'll have everything we need in a few hours."

I wished I had burned the house down before he had gotten any of Chance's fingerprints or DNA. If I had done that, maybe I could have prevented Wes from getting as far as he had. I hadn't given them everything though. There were the codes and I had noticed Chance entered several codes for different locations. As far as the facial scans, I just didn't think that was possible.

"What now?" I asked painfully.

"Now, we get on our plane and go home," he smiled. "Your new home."

I choked on my sobs, forcing them to stay hidden from him. He didn't deserve my tears. "And my daughter?"

"She'll be with you soon enough."

He took my hand, wrapping it through his arm, and walked out of his hotel room and down to a waiting car. Every step felt like a death sentence, which I already knew it was. But since I didn't have my daughter yet, I couldn't help but feel that I had made the wrong choice.

We boarded the plane and were seated in what could only be described as a luxury hotel in the sky. The champagne that was brought out and the fruits that were set on the table in front of me weren't something I squealed in delight over. Instead, I looked at them with disdain and immediately regretted it when Wes's disapproval showed. I forced myself to eat the fruit and hated that it was probably the best fruit I had ever tasted.

A few hours into the flight, Wes started fiddling with a tablet, but I ignored him, not caring what he was doing. I didn't want to be involved in his life in any way. I wanted my daughter and everything else was irrelevant.

"Ah, here it is. We're just in time for the show."

"What show?"

He handed the tablet over to me and I gasped when I saw what he was talking about. I recognized the room as the conference room in the Reed Security building. Men were lying all over the place, blood pooling around them. I watched in horror as men were shot, including some of Chance's friends. I didn't understand. How had they gotten in there so fast? I hadn't given them codes and they still needed DNA and facial recognition, among several other things that I hadn't told them.

The screen zeroed in on one man in particular that was lying by the elevator. Someone wanted me to see exactly what was happening. I watched as two men grabbed his arms and started dragging him. I recognized him once they lifted him off the ground. It was Chance, and either he was unconscious or he was dead.

A new ache filled my chest, one that I thought I would never feel. As he disappeared into the elevator, it finally sank in that I had made the worst choice possible. I swiped at the tears that fell from my eyes and looked at Wes. "Is he dead?"

"Does it matter?"

"Yes."

He smiled and stood, holding out his hand to me. I took it hesitantly, wondering what he had planned for me now. He led me to the rear of the plane and opened the door to a bedroom. I swallowed down my revulsion, knowing what he wanted, and stepped inside. To my surprise, he didn't follow.

"Get some sleep. We have a long flight ahead of us."

I laid down on the bed and stared at the ceiling, wondering how I was going to live with myself after everything that had happened. All those men in Reed Security were in danger or possibly hurt and it was my fault. I chose to go with this monster, and even though I hadn't given him everything he needed, he still managed to get in. I tossed and turned, trying to get some sleep, but all I could think about was that I had traded one life for another. Yes, my daughter was everything to me, but all those men had families too, and I had just sacrificed every single one of them.

Hours later, when we landed, I was ushered to another car and was taken to my new home. I shuddered when the tall gates opened to the long driveway that wound through thick trees. I couldn't see the house yet, but if the gates were any indication, Wes had spared no expense on security. I would be lucky if I could even find my way off the property, for how long it took us to get down the driveway.

When we finally broke through into a clearing, I bit my lip to keep from crying. The house was beautiful, but all I could see was a luxurious jail. I would rather take my shitty apartment any day over staying here with Wes. He helped me out of the car and showed me around downstairs. I didn't really see anything. I couldn't have made my way to the kitchen, let alone described the color of the furniture in the living room.

When we got upstairs, he opened the double doors to what I assumed was the master suite. I walked in numbly and looked around. The room was huge and the bed was the focal point of the room. I could see a door that opened to the bathroom and two walk-in closets on either side of the room. Probably his and hers closets.

"This will be your new home. While you stay with me, I expect you to sleep in my bed. You will not leave the grounds and you will not make any phone calls or use the internet. I'll have men with you at all times, except when you are in here with me. However, because you lied to me, you get to stay somewhere else until I feel you've served your punishment."

"Lied?" I asked. My body trembled when he looked at me with so much anger that I wondered if I would even be alive tomorrow.

"Did you think I wouldn't know that you left out some very important details about how to get into Reed Security?" He smirked and trailed a finger down my cheek and then gripped my chin harshly. "I already knew how to get in, my dear. It was a test and you failed. Now you're going to pay for that."

He grabbed me by the arm and roughly dragged me back down the stairs. I was tripping and falling against the wall as I tried to keep up with him, but he didn't slow down. He pulled me through the rest of the house until we came to another door, this one old with multiple locks. My heart pounded in my chest as he swung the door open and led me down the cold steps, into the darkness.

There was a small window up high that barely let in any light, but that wasn't what sent chills down my spine. There was a small cell in the corner of the room. There was no bed, only a small bucket in the corner. Wes opened the door and flung me inside. I fell to the ground, smelling urine that must have been covered up by dirt. I wasn't his first prisoner.

The metal door slammed behind me and I quickly rolled over to my butt, watching as Wes locked me inside with an evil grin.

"When will my daughter be here?" I asked shakily. I could handle this, as long as I knew my daughter would be safe.

"Payton. Yes, she'll be here soon. You just have to be patient."

"And until then?"

A slow, evil grin curled his lips as he shoved the key in his pocket. "You're mine now. No one is coming to save you."

He turned and stomped up the stairs, slamming the door behind him. I heard the locks sliding into place and then it was quiet. I looked around the dark room and scooted into the corner of the cell, pulling my knees to my chest. This was my home now. All I had was the darkness and my thoughts.

This is book 1 of a 3 part arc. The next book in this arc is Jackson, which will be released in May. The third book, Chance, will be released in June. Thank you for reading.

# ALSO BY GIULIA LAGOMARSINO

*Thank you for reading the first part of Chance and Morgan's story. There's still more to come further down the line, so keep reading. The Reed Security gang will be back in Jackson's story!*

Join my newsletter to get the most up-to-date information, along with new content in the Reed Security series.

https://giulialagomarsinoauthor.com/connect/

Join my Facebook reader group to find out more about my obsession with Dwayne Johnson!

https://www.facebook.com/groups/GiuliaLagomarsinobooks

Reading Order:

https://giulialagomarsinoauthor.com/reading-order/

To find the individual series, follow the links below:

*For The Love Of A Good Woman series*

*Reed Security series*

*The Cortell Brothers*

*A Good Run Of Bad Luck*

Made in United States
Orlando, FL
10 April 2024